THE OPREE LEGACY

BOOK ONE: THE PROMISE

WRITTEN BY:
L. ANNA LENZ

Edited by Meghan Kass & Kelly Lurve
Copyright © 2013 Shadow Fox Publishing, LLC
All rights reserved.

ISBN-13: 9780615861562
ISBN-10: 0615861563

Library of Congress Control Number: 2013948852
Shadow Fox Publishing LLC, Smithtown, NY

For My husband who puts up with me and to my ever supportive family, especially Grandma & Grandpa whose confidence in me never wavered, and whose house I wrote this in. Thank you Grandma for every pep talk and for the ice cream sundaes that kept me going when things got rough!

PROLOGUE

"And the first father gave each of the children of the sky, the harvest and the sea a drop of his blood and he spoke ,'as you, my children worship me as your god, I give to you my blood to create your own children who shall worship you,' and humanity was born."

The Itara, Creations 13:23

PROLOGUE

The sounds of the battle raging on the outskirts of New Empire City were getting closer, but Rebecca and Alexi Harker had made a point to act like it was just a normal day for the sake of their four small children. Alexi, a retired general in the imperial army had been briefed of the situation and was confident the skilled and technically advanced military could handle the invading forces.

Rebecca was not as sure as her husband. According to the papers, these mysterious invaders calling themselves the Navat came over from the desolate Fire Plains, destroying the entire colony of Kyrant in a matter of weeks. Now this force was on their doorstep. The servants left at the first news of the invasion. Alexi had given them permission to go. Her husband's compassion left a bitter taste in Rebecca's mouth. All transports and routes out of the city were blocked with the chaos of people fleeing New Empire in droves. There would be no way out of the city tonight.

A loud explosion, the loudest yet, caused the fine china in the cabinets to rattle. The proximity of the blast was unsettling and Alexi reassured himself that everything was going to be just fine. Throughout its thousand-year history, the Empire of Opree had never once been defeated. They were the most unified and unstoppable force in the world.

Alexi helplessly paced his study reviewing the latest news from the city gates and then reviewed them again. It was fortunate that he still had contacts in the military that were keeping him informed of the situation. The first line blocking the narrow pass in the mountains fell less than an hour before and the enemy had their guns within the city limits. He was unaccustomed to just sitting around his house like a broken tool. It had only been six weeks since the Senate forced him into retirement. There was a bitter dispute about how to address the situation in Kyrant. It ended in harsh words about the General's Iranti heritage and a physical altercation between himself and a prominent Senator. The incident could have landed him a Court Martial, undoing a remarkable twenty-year career, but he left quietly with his name untarnished so that his sons wouldn't have to bear the brunt of his failure.

In the growing darkness, the glow of mortar fire and explosions lit up the eastern horizon. Every half hour or so, a loud boom or blast would shake the house a bit. After awhile, the family would hardly notice. Rebecca rocked her ten-month-old daughter, Grace, while Alexi led the boys in their evening prayer ritual. Despite keeping the language and social customs of Opree, it was always important for Alexi to have his family keep the harvest gods of their ancestral homeland of Lo Irant.

The power had gone out shortly after dinner and the great room was bathed in candlelight. The sounds of the blasts were getting louder. All transports out of the city have been disabled and exits sealed, leaving millions still trapped including the Harker family. He quietly cursed himself for his stubbornness.

He kissed his wife's hand as her arms wrapped around his shoulders and he lost himself in his wife's beauty. Fifteen years and she was still just as stunning as the day they met. His moment was interrupted by another loud bang, triggering the cries of Grace, who now demanded her mother's full attention.

Ten-year-old Devon was all too aware of what was happening, although he wasn't particularly worried about his own safety. His father was a soldier; the biggest and strongest there had ever lived. The boy's thoughts wandered to his friends, who didn't have strong, giant soldier fathers to protect them. To keep his mind off of his friends, Devon took on the duty of keeping his younger brothers, eight-year-old Gregory and four-year-old Nathanial distracted with toys and games.

When the commotion outside became more interesting than the games and toys inside, Devon and his brothers snuck over to the window to see what was happening. All they could make out in the darkness was an empty street and flashes of light off in the distance. Bored by the underwhelming amount of nothing happening, Nathanial wandered over to his mother and kissed a crying baby Grace on the cheek.

"The Navat are trying to get in but the army is going to stop them!" Devon proclaimed, his binoculars pressed against the window hoping to catch a glimpse of the action. With his father's much too large combat helmet strapped around his neck hanging on his shoulders, the curious boy resembled a turtle, a turtle eager and ready to take on the enemy.

Nathanial looked out the window again and to his disappointment there wasn't any army or Navat. Hopefully, whatever was going on would be over by tomorrow because that was the day they were supposed to go to the zoo, something young Nate had talked nonstop about for weeks.

It was almost midnight and the boys were sprawled out on the floor. Alexi had received yet another call and was locked away in the study. He would be furious that the boys were still awake. Rebecca wasn't used to dealing with the children without the servants. Letting them stay up was easier than fighting to get her anxious sons into bed.

A bright white flash and a loud bang blew out the windows interrupted the family's peace.

The room was dark and empty, Nathanial saw no sign of his mother anywhere. Panicked, he climbed over the debris caused by the explosion, protecting his ears from the noise of the sirens.

"Mama! Papa!" Nathanial screamed, but his voice was drowned out by the battle raging outside. Cold rain pelted him through the shattered windows as he ran back to the great room looking for his family. He heard her call out for him, but he couldn't find his way through the maze-like hallways.

Sharp cracks of gunshots peppered the chaos and another explosion shook the pictures off the walls. He could hear the cries of baby Grace get louder and his mother's voice calling for her sons. Large hands wrapped around his torso, lifting him off the ground. The room spun around with him.

"I found him! He looks okay." His father wiped a small bit of blood from under the child's nose, checked him over and carried him to the front door where the rest of the family were waiting.

He reached for his mother, who shoved a hat onto his head. Even amidst the danger, she couldn't shake the habit of licking her thumb and wiping dirt off her son's face. Her nose crinkled as she frowned with concern.

"Is this blood?" she asked her husband. "I thought you said he was fine."

"He is fine," his father snapped. "The transport is outside, ready to take you and the boys out of the city. I need to stay here." His expression softened and he gently stroked his wife's face.

Her eyes protested his decision, but she dared not speak against her husband.

"Mama, I'm scared." Nathanial cried for his mother's attention. Another explosion rocked the house. This time he felt it shake in his chest.

She smiled at him and kissed him on the forehead. "Hush now, little bird. It's going to be okay."

The lights were out, but the fires throughout the city bathed the streets in a flickering red glow. An armored transport idled outside of the family's home.

"Sir," the soldiers addressed his father. "We need to go now." Standing in the doorway, the family said their goodbyes.

"I want to stay and fight with you father," Devon said.

"I need you to protect your mother, Grace and your brothers. Understood soldier?"

"Yes, sir."

A screaming hiss barreled down the street, the man grabbed his eldest son's arm and dragged his family back into the safety of the house. In a hummingbird's heartbeat the transport was reduced to a ball of flaming wreckage. Nathanial caught a glimpse of the destruction just before his father shut the front door.

"Everyone get to the basement!" Alexi yelled.

While bolting down the hall in his father's arms, Nathanial heard the same hiss and scream as before. The blast sent the child flying. He hit the floor hard and debris tumbled on top of him, plummeting his world into darkness.

He was only unconscious for a half a minute, but when he awoke couldn't see anything, hear anything or feel anything except the pain that made his head spin and his stomach want to throw up. The light came back first. He focused on it until he could recognize the shapes he was seeing from under the ruble. If he tried he could hear beyond the loud ringing and if he focused on his other two senses hard enough, the pain faded.

The first face he saw was baby Grace's. She was on the floor right in front of him on her belly, red-faced and crying, her yellow blanket soaked with blood. The ten-month-old's lip quivered between heavy sobs. Their eyes met, and he stretched his arm out to reach his baby sister, wiggling out from under the rubble.

He was only a few inches away when the bit of rubble he was still under came down on him, sucking the air out of his lungs and crushing his little body. If the large boots hadn't let up when they did, he would have popped under the enormous weight of the creature. More boots followed, but they stepped around the hidden child.

Grace howled. He saw several pairs of the black boots amass in the hallway around the crying baby. There wasn't enough visibility through the cracks to get a good look at who was in the boots. The second attempt to reach for his sister failed, the pile crushing down on him once more.

They spoke in grunts, low hisses and clicks. Their boots tromped through the house as the ringing in his ears subsided. His mother was screaming somewhere. He struggled to pull himself out from the pile on top of him to no avail. The sound of the boots faded off to where the screams were. There were two shots, then no more screams. He focused his attention back to baby Grace, still sobbing on the floor. She saw him, and he tried to coax her to crawl to the safety of his hiding place.

"C'mon Gracie, come to me." He beckoned with a forced smile.

The baby girl rocked back and forth on her hands and knees unable to coordinate her amidst her cries. Out of frustration she rolled to a sitting position, stretched her arms out and wailed. The boots came closer, until they almost completely blocked his view. He could smell the mud and leather.

One of the creatures clicked and gently kicked baby Grace over. Nathanial's view was still blocked and only part of Grace's head was visible. He could see the black leather boot pressed softly against her cheek, toying with the infant, like a child would a rubber ball.

Grace's shrill screams made him wish for the ringing noise again. He watched, hopelessly trapped, while the monster's boot came down hard on his sister's skull, crushing it, embedding her soft peach skin in between the treads of his soles. Grace was silent. A glob of blood-soaked flesh and a tuft of blonde hair was left stuck to the floor after the monster passed.

The boots were somewhere else in the house now, leaving the boy in terrified silence. When his brothers found him, his hands were still clasped tightly over his face.

"He vomited," Gregory pointed out as his younger sibling was pulled out from the wreckage.

"Shh, it's okay." Devon dismissed as he brushed off their trembling little brother. "We need to find Grace and get to the basement. Do you know where she is?"

With a small shaking finger, Nathanial pointed to a pile of battered flesh wrapped in a once-yellow blanket. Tears rolled down his face.

The boys made their way down the hallways of the servants quarters undetected.

"I forgot Juno, Devon!" Nathanial stopped and franticly searched his person. Juno was Nathanial's stuffed dog and best friend.

Devon tugged on his arm. "Forget it, we got to go!"

"I'll get her! I saw her by where we found you." Gregory was already halfway down the corridor.

"Wait here," Devon said, putting his younger brother in the small service elevator. It was designed for laundry or dry goods, but the boy was small enough to fit inside.

Alone in the dark, the child waited. Sounds of the house being ransacked and the fighting outside were muffled in the tin box where he was hiding. He poked his head out to see if his brothers were coming and to look at something else other than a silver wall. The hallway was barely recognizable, glass and debris everywhere. Amazingly, the stained glass window in the door of his mother's painting room was still intact. The flames from the burning city danced in the distance behind the colorful glass.

Devon came back to the elevator, out of breath and white as a sheet. "When you get to the basement, I want you to stay there okay? Don't get out until someone comes for you." He got out in between heavy breaths and tossed Juno inside. "She will keep you safe."

"Where is Gregory?"

Devon didn't answer, just looked down at the red bits on his shirt.

The moment was broken by the loud thuds of boot steps and the snarls of an angry creature. Devon slammed the door of the elevator shut and hit the button.

Devon never looked away from his brother, even when blood spattered the glass and the life faded from the ten-year-old's eyes. Two glowing orange eyes of the creature that killed Devon peered down at him. They were last thing the boy saw before the elevator descended into the darkness.

It had been six months since the attacks on New Empire and several other Oprian cities. The cost was the lives of over twelve million people in New Empire alone. Six months of fighting a war and still so little was known about this new enemy. Despite forces being able to push them beyond the borders of Opree, the whole Empire was at war with the Navat in Kyrant. Theories about their origins ranged from a race of people who had adapted to life on the Fire Plains, demons spawned from the fiery pits of hell, to the King's own men in using the war as a power play against the Senate. Whatever these creatures were, they managed to alter the face of the entire Empire in less than a year.

The rebuild effort was already underway; damaged buildings were rapidly climbing back into the sky. The need for labor skyrocketed and the economy just began to stabilize. Petty feuds between houses and castes were forgotten almost overnight. The tragedy was a commonality that, at the time, strengthened the connection they had to the one bloodline they all shared as humans.

A well-dressed member of the High Born caste walked into the home for Vistany caste children orphaned by the attacks. He had received a message that he had a family member, a son of his wife's niece (twice removed), who needed to be retrieved.

According to the Senate, orphanages and refuge homes were becoming a painful reminder, hurting the recovery of the Empire not only emotionally but financially as well. They ordered all children placed into the care of their next of kin, no matter how far removed.

The line of people waiting to pick up their new charges at the orphanage wrapped around the building. Some were upset at the fact they now had to take care of the children of veritable strangers, but most were just elated to have kin who survived. As a High Born, the man got preference in line and walked right up to the front desk.

The sounds of children playing and laughing were disturbingly absent. For a moment he became lost in the sad silence, children still bandaged from wounds. A little girl in the corner no older than eight was just rocking back and forth in the corner hugging her knees to her chest. Trapped in some terrible memory, her eyes focused on the invisible horrors that replayed in her mind over and over again.

For the first time the man worried that the child he was supposed to get was broken like these kids were. After going through such an ordeal, how could he not be? His wife had died in the attacks and they were childless, he knew nothing of being a parent.

"Mr. Demetri Montclair, here is Nathanial's case file. He is just collecting his things and will be out in a minute. I am Kendra Allister, the social worker assigned to him." Kendra was a middle-caste woman in her mid-thirties. Demetri thought she'd be pretty if she didn't look so tired.

"Thank you," he said, flipping through the file. "How is the child?"

"He is still unable to fully understand what happened, which is a good thing. Younger children tend to be more resilient in traumatic situations. He didn't sustain any physical injuries in the attacks. He lost his mother, father and three siblings when the Navat attacked their house. They found him hiding in a utility elevator, three days later." Kendra was numb to the gory details and every ounce of sentiment in her voice was disingenuous. If she allowed it, she'd drown in the sadness that these children brought with them. "Normally placing a child is a process that takes months of preparation and counseling. Now we're lucky to have twenty minutes before we hand these delicate and traumatized children over to veritable strangers." She realized she was beginning to rant and composed herself. "Do you have plans for the child? We have parenting classes available. It says in your file that you are a widower with no children, might want to look into that, just so the transition goes smoothly."

"I've made arrangements for him to attend Penderghast. I recognized his father's name in the paperwork you sent me. He was a very well-respected General and I figured it would be a good fit." Demetri said uncomfortably.

Penderghast Military Academy was an elite and prestigious school. It was rare for anyone who was not a member of the High Born aristocracy to gain admission. Nathanial's military pedigree, in addition to the hefty grant Demetri made to the school was enough to gain him acceptance.

Nathanial was in the room that he had been sharing with dozens of other boys, his few belongings already packed ready to go. He was excited. Miss Fairview, the lady at the front desk, told him his family was finally coming to get him. He missed them so much. Those were the best words he had ever heard in his whole entire life. Miss Kendra said his family had died and was up in the great fields of the Harvest Gods, but they weren't dead. They were here. Miss Fairview said it herself. He couldn't wait to show his mother how he learned how to read and do math but first, above everything they were going to the zoo. He could hardly contain his excitement as he fidgeted on the bed waiting for Miss Kendra.

"We're finally going home, Juno." He whispered into the ear of the tattered stuffed dog. Juno said nothing.

The door opened and there was Miss Kendra and an older man Nathanial did not know.

"Is my family here yet Miss Kendra? Can I see them now? Miss Fairview said my family was here, but I can act surprised when they come if you want me to." Nathanial asked eagerly.

Kendra's heart sank as she cursed the dimwitted Fairview for being so careless with her words.

"No, sweetheart, I'm sorry, but we talked about this remember? Your Mother, Father, Devon, Gregory and Grace died. They are all up in the Great Fields with their gods; they are not coming back." The hardest part of Kendra's job was explaining what death was to the little ones. For months children like Nathanial would constantly ask about parents, siblings and friends, as if she were able to control the answer and somehow make it better.

"But, Miss Fairview said they were here, we were going to go to the zoo."

Nathanial looked up confused and lost, with his big blue eyes welling up with tears.

Kendra wasn't withholding this child's family like they were a piece of candy hidden in her pocket, but Nathanial couldn't understand that. Guilt crushed the little strength she was holding on to and the tears she thought had dried up months ago flowed again.

The boy stopped himself from crying by biting his lower lip. Kendra comforted him and explained how Demetri was his uncle and was going to bring Nathanial to a new school. After the explanation, the boy was calm and composed. He understood now. Nathanial took a moment in the silence to let it sink in that his family was never coming back. The painful reality started to rise up in his throat like a large hot rock and he swallowed it, pushing it back down deep into his belly.

"Miss Kendra says I'm going to be a soldier. Is that true?" The boy asked his uncle, looking up with big hopeful eyes.

Demetri just nodded. After such a terrible introduction, the man was at a loss for words. As they walked out Nathanial didn't hesitate or look back. None of the children ever looked back.

NATHANIAL

"Serve the Father with love in your heart and be in his favor, serve with hearts full of pride and vanity and he will smite thee down as an enemy."

- *The Verinat, Lithica II 11:19*

CHAPTER 1

Penderghast Military Academy for High Borns stood in sharp contrast to the city around it. The large stone castle loomed over the glass and steel buildings nestled in the shadows of the Shaurin Mountains. The ancient institution served as a reminder of the past: a time of kingdoms and castles, before the twelve nations came together to form The Empire of Opree.

It was well after midnight, but the north lawn was clear in the light of the full moon. Twenty-one year old Nathanial Harker stood in the black shadow of the Arbinger challenge, an ancient monster of a contraption constructed out of wood and iron.

It was a tradition at Penderghast. Nine obstacles, increasing in difficulty and danger made up the challenge created by General Arbinger in the first year of the Academy's existence. Only a couple dozen cadets have beaten it in five hundred years, more perished attempting it.

Although Nathanial had made it farther than any other cadets in his class, his failure to conquer the Arbinger earlier that day ate away at the cadet's mind. It filled his stomach during dinner, killing his appetite and it howled in his ear after lights out, keeping him awake. It was last year at Penderghast. There would not be another chance to attempt the challenge again.

The heavy metal padlock was well secured on the equipment shed and would not relent to Nathanial's attempts to pry it open. Frustrated, he kicked at the rusted metal doors. The padlock rattled loudly against it, but the defiant doors still refused him entry. The sound of his attack on the equipment shed penetrated the quiet stillness of the cool early fall night, loud enough to wake the dead, as Captain Normandy would say. Luckily, for Nathanial the dead weren't in earshot and more importantly neither were Captain Normandy nor Headmaster Warrens.

At some point between shouting obscenities at his inanimate foe and cursing his gods for daring to deny him the strength to punch through metal, an angry fist met the side of the stubborn shed and a jolt of pain reverberated through his arm. His storm-blue eyes focused on the thin but durable bar of the lock. A quarter inch thick piece of nickel-plated steel had rendered the cadet helpless. It sat there mocking him, as he tugged on it some more and he remembered there was a bolt cutter in the utility room at the far end of the campus. They once had been used to free him from the footlocker Xander Marland locked him in years before, in primary grades, when he was much, much smaller. It would only take a few minutes to run and grab them, but Nathanial didn't have much time to spare and was uncomfortable destroying academy property.

He pulled on the lock hard just one more time, hoping it would magically come apart, it didn't. In the wake of his disappointment, a small weak voice inside of him pleaded him to turn back, telling him the risk was too great. It was a few months until graduation and he could still be in a world of trouble if they caught him out here alone. What he was about to do warranted expulsion. What he was about to do could get him killed. In recent years, the academy had upped safety measures with the Arbinger, pads, helmets, and harnesses rendering the carnage the beast could inflict down to a broken bone at the most. Without the safety equipment that was locked inside the shed, attempting the Arbinger alone, in the dark, would be suicide.

The demands of his wounded pride drowned out all reasonable concern for his own safety.

"We honor our gods and our families only through excellence. Never shame them with anything less."

Nathanial heard his late father's words inside his head. Not able to remember exactly what his father's voice sounded like, the speech repeated itself in ghostlike whispers as he envisioned the disapproval of his gods burning through him.

It didn't matter that the gods were his only witness. In their name, he was going to finish this, tonight, safety equipment or not. Cadets five hundred years ago did the challenge without pads, helmets and harnesses and so could he.

Despite the advances in technology, the Arbinger Challenge had been left untouched for centuries. It was a mechanical triumph in its day. These days it looked more terrifying than magnificent. Nathanial wrapped his fingers around wooden lever that started the machine, taking time to look at the barbed bars and large wooden gears that triggered the deadly barrage of swords, hammers and a slew of other nasty surprises.

With a straining grunt, Nathanial used all of his weight to pull the large wooden lever down. The massive contraption started with a grinding roar. It was moving much faster than it was earlier in the day. Captain Normandy, their combat instructor, had a way of controlling its speed, but that knowledge was lost on Nathanial. His brain tried to reason with him. The machine was moving way too fast. There was no way he was going to be able to get through that without lopping off a limb or worse.

He looked up at the first challenge, 'The Eagles Nest.' It was a long wooden pole, stretching nearly forty feet in the air. The goal was to climb to the top, balance on the pole and jump to the next challenge. Nathanial lunged at the first obstacle between the waves of fear and sanity.

The wood splintered in his already sore hands. It would be impossible to climb all the way up bare handed and he had left his gloves back in his room. Gripping the pole tightly with his legs, he took off his jacket, wrapped the edge of one of his sleeves around his left hand, wrapped the jacket around the pole and took the other sleeve and wrapped it around his right hand. He pushed his legs out, testing the strength of the fabric and stitching. His uniform was quality and Empire made. It could probably hold him and another man without ripping. Nathanial could've kicked himself for not thinking about doing that before. As he climbed higher, the pole began to sway. Nathanial shifted his weight to maintain balance. His jacket trick made it simple. Nearly no effort was required and he soon found himself lost in the thoughts of his cleverness.

Two spikes jutted out of the wooden pole, catching him off guard. They gored the fleshy part of Nate's thigh. The ground was hard when he hit it and a nauseating pain radiated down his leg. The Arbinger was first and foremost a teaching tool and its last lesson was painful enough that he only needed to learn it once. He tore off a piece of his shirt and tied it around the gash in his thigh before he attacked the challenge again.

Clayton Wood had heard Nathanial Harker leave the dormitory and followed him onto the field, keeping out of sight. A couple of years behind Harker, Clayton looked up to him. The older cadet was fearless, and had become sort of a legend at the academy, not just because of who his father was, but the story surrounding how he came to be at Penderghast in the first place.

Penderghast Military Academy for High Borns was created as just that, a place for High Borns to get educated. Over the centuries, however, the ranks of the dying aristocracy were dwindling and the upper echelons of the civilian caste, the Vistany, had more wealth and power than ever. The academy had been accepting Vistany with blood or marriage ties to the aristocracy for over a century, even more since the attacks. Until Nathanial, the academy never had an Iranti-born, the name given to those born in the Empire whose ancestors came from the colony of Lo Irant.

Clayton had heard rumors, just whispers really, that Harker was accepted because at just four years old he defeated a whole squad of Navat soldiers during the invasion. Others claimed that he was the bastard son of his father the General and a Kyre witch. The witch, devastated when her son was taken away, raised the Navat from the ninth hell to punish Opree. Harker's witch blood protected him from the Navat and the Empire wanted to use him as a weapon. The stories always varied and seem to get more outrageous every passing year.

Clayton didn't believe any of those stories, not fully anyway. He just knew about the things Harker had accomplished at Penderghast. The whispers of his future greatness echoed in the halls by instructors at the academy.

The sound of the Arbinger being turned on sent Clayton into a panic. Nate was going to get himself killed. He didn't want to stop the machine himself. Harker would beat him purple. He couldn't tell Captain Normandy, he would beat Harker purple, and in turn Harker would beat Clayton to death. There was only one option left, wake Garitel.

Prince Arryn Garitel could sleep through a full on aerial assault. He wouldn't have noticed Nathanial leaving the room if he'd done so with a parade. It took almost six whole minutes of a near deafening mix of banging and Clayton Wood's nasally squeals to pull him from his sleep.

He knocked. "Garitel! Garitel! It's Wood! Wake up!"

Although he could command it, Arryn never had any of his classmates refer to him by his title. It was a preference he shared with his father.

Arryn was the third-born son of Jonathan Garitel II King of Opree, not that it mattered much to him or anyone at Penderghast and not just because nearly everyone there was the son of a Duke or a Baron or something. The aristocracy held no real power since the revolution and title held little merit against coin and empty titles were fast becoming a novelty of the Vistany, who would buy their way into the royal families. The political elite were in charge and Arryn accepted it. He didn't want to rule anyway. If it wasn't for the tradition for the nobility to send their third-born sons into military service, Arryn would have been happy to live out his life like the other wealthy young High Borns and children of the Vistany elite, partying in Pier City or living a life of leisure on the sandy shores of Gailenai.

Being woken up at this hour in the night however, Arryn wished he had the power his ancestors had. Someone needed to lose their head over this.

"What in the ninth hell do you want, Wood?" Arryn answered the door with a sleepy and annoyed scowl.

"Garitel, it's Harker, he's on the fields." Clayton was trying to catch his breath.

"Wood, that still doesn't explain to me why you are knocking at my door at this hour," Arryn hissed. He didn't care much for Clayton Wood. He was the son of a Vistany Senator, an outspoken opponent against Arryn's father.

"He's on the Arbinger in just his field clothes..." Wood struggled to talk between breaths, "no protection or harness."

Arryn wasn't surprised. Nate had been quiet all evening since coming in from the challenge. He knew a plot was brewing in that fat blonde head of his. They had been best friends and roommates since their first year at the academy and though he greatly adored his friend, he had learned a long time ago controlling him was a lost cause. Still, this little stunt could get him killed, or expelled. It was yet another mess Arryn was going to get his friend out of.

By the time Arryn, Clayton and about ten fellow cadets gathered by the Arbinger, Nathanial was standing on the pole getting ready to jump onto the next obstacle, a series of bars. The first one was about ten feet away and six feet higher than the pole. It was covered in barbs except for two points near the middle. Most of the cadets who managed to balance themselves on the wobbly pole failed at the first jump.

"Nathanial, you're going to get yourself killed, you idiot!" Arryn screamed, his voice drowned out by the roar of the machine.

Several of the other cadets had amassed by the lever, blocking Arryn's attempts to turn it off. One of them being a grotesquely large, mouth-breathing behemoth, who stood feet firmly planted in the ground. His arms practically the size of the Prince's torso were crossed as he spit at Arryn's feet.

"Marland I swear to our gods that I will rip those freakish tree trunks out from their sockets, if you don't move right now." Arryn demanded. Despite Marland's size, Arryn was a skilled fighter and more than capable of carrying out the threat.

"Aw, let the little mud rat try, your highness." Marland goaded. "If it kills him, I'll pay for a new Iranti footman myself." He pulled out a ten-Coin note out of his pocket. "I hope you brought change." The rest of the crowd laughed at the insult. Everyone gave Nathanial shit about his Iranti heritage, but Xander Marland took particular offense that an Iranti-born, was allowed to attend Penderghast.

Arryn clenched his fist ready to plow through Marland and anyone else who got in his way. The sound of Nathanial's painful cry distracted him.

As Nate made the first jump, his left hand missed its mark and landed on the steel barbs wrapped around it. He was still holding on and determined to continue. In the moonlight Arryn could see the determination in Nathanial's face and knew that if he stopped this now, his friend would never forgive him.

Despite being quiet and a bit reserved, Nathanial had always been fearless. It was more than just a competitive streak, from what Arryn could understand. The two were always in constant competition with each other, but

Nathanial was always out to prove something. He was the first in the class to jump off of Pinnacle Bridge (breaking his leg in the process), the only one to ride the giant plains bull at the Kyre Festival (breaking several bones and a wall). He even allowed himself to be tortured for their interrogations class (no broken bones, but he lost three permanent teeth and the ability to taste salt for six months). Nathanial had this almost inhuman ability to heal quickly after he broke himself and Arryn wondered if that ability was Nate's curse because it made him twice as reckless. He would be happy if Nathanial would just make it through the night with nothing more than some broken bones.

The blood pouring out of Nathanial's left palm made it difficult to get a good grip of the ascending bars, yet he managed to get across them anyway. He was already halfway through the fifth obstacle, which required him to navigate a field of continually retracting spikes while dodging a barrage of arrows and rocks. He hadn't seen anyone pass this obstacle in his entire career at Penderghast. While distracted for a brief moment by one of Marland's taunts, a spike pierced through the fabric of his pants and narrowly missed splitting him down the middle.

"Ten coin says Harker loses a limb or worse," Marland hollered. "Harker! I GOT TEN COIN ON YOU DROPPING A LEG, LOSE YOUR HEAD AND I'LL DROP FIVE COIN IN YOUR CASKET. I'D LEAVE IT TO YOUR WIDOW, BUT IT SEEMS ARRYN HAS PLENTY OF

COIN HIMSELF!" He laughed. Nobody thought Marland was as funny as he thought himself.

"Seriously, Harker could get killed. Give it a rest," Lucius Halloway scolded.

The taunts soon lead to cheers and faded into silence as Nathanial made it to the second to last part of the challenge. He had to wedge himself between two walls of solid obsidian and maneuver past a floor that resembled an industrial meat grinder. Nathanial had never thought about how sadistic Arbinger must have been to create such a terrible machine, but now it was at the forefront of his mind. Taking a deep breath, he jumped up, ensuring his hands and feet were at the exact angle to hold up his body on the slick walls. The pain radiated up his injured leg and he felt his muscle shake. The blood on his hands caused his hands to slip as he shifted his weight. Quick reflexes and the grace of his gods kept him from plummeting to his death. He only had to go about eight or ten feet but it might have well been miles.

The rest of his class watched in silence as they saw their fellow cadet falter. It was the hardest and most dangerous obstacle. If Nathanial got past this, he was in the clear but if he failed, without the safety equipment there was a good chance he'd be crushed to death. Arryn inched closer to the lever that turned off the machine and calculated how quickly he could turn it off if Nathanial happened to fall.

The grinding sound of the spiked cylinders rolling underneath him called to Nathanial. He could already hear what his bones would sound like being crushed like brittle sticks. He wiped the blood from his hands on his pants, in an attempt to gain better traction. The blood from his thigh was already seeping into the tourniquet, his leg quivering under the strain as it struggled to support his frame. The grinding sound of the blades was the only thing keeping him from collapsing. He allowed himself three breaths for the pain and on the fourth, forced his aching body further. Once his feet were planted on the wood plank, he said a small, silent prayer of thanks to his gods and an additional one to the sky gods for good measure.

Compared to the previous obstacle the final one was easy. All he had to do was climb across the wire connecting to the final platform and shut off the machine. Nathanial barely remembered any of that until he climbed back down to the ground where everyone cheered, all except for Marland, Arryn and Captain Normandy, who had made it out to the field just in time to see Nathanial finish the challenge.

"Harker!" The dark, raspy voice of Captain Normandy sobered the euphoric Nathanial up immediately. Just his tone told Nathanial he was in for a world of trouble.

It was sunrise, and Nathanial and the other cadets were sore, covered in mud and had been at Captain Normandy's mercy all night for Nathanial's little stunt. Unfortunately for them, mercy was a term alien to Captain Normandy.

"Harker," Captain Normandy drew his service pistol from its holster and inspected it.

"Yes, sir." Nathanial limped out front. He had been hiding the extent of his injuries during Normandy's 'mercy', but after four hours of 'replanting' the headmaster's boulder garden two hundred yards to the left, his normally soft golden complexion looked more like of a glass of cold, sour milk.

"Why did you attempt the Arbinger again?" Normandy sighed, taking notice of the pitiful state Nate was in.

"I knew I could do it, sir." Nathanial stated confidently, leaning on his good leg to keep from slouching.

"Knew, or thought?" His eyes zeroed in on Nathanial like a hawk on its prey.

He hesitated a moment. Captain Normandy had a way of turning a cadet's words against them. Nathanial had to choose his words carefully."I Knew, sir."

"Just like if I asked if you knew if you could fetch me that water pail over there, you would say yes."

This was a trap. "I'm not sure, sir?"

"Not sure, Harker? If you could get that water pail? Fuck, my grandmother could walk over there and get that water pail. Are you telling me you don't know if you could grab that water pail?" Normandy fiddled with the clip, before sliding it back into his gun.

"I know I could, sir." Nathanial gulped.

"Really?" Captain Normandy looked at the bucket a hundred yards away. "It's pretty far. I don't think you can. In fact I'm willing to bet on it."

Nathanial cringed. Captain Normandy never lost a bet. Whenever he offered to make at bet, it meant he was about to take away a privilege.

"If you bring back the bucket you and your accomplices can have the day off. If not, you are all going on a special trip with me for the next three days."

Marland shook with rage, staring down Nathanial with murderous intentions. Two weeks in the pits of the seventh hell was preferable to a three-day trip with Captain Normandy. The cadets looked to Nathanial to save them.

"Well, go ahead Harker."

Nathanial knew it wasn't going to be easy. The Captain was grinning with the patient contentment of a cat playing with its prey. Hesitantly, he walked up to the bucket, Captain Normandy close behind. Each step raised his blood pressure higher, until he could hear his blood in his ears. The tension hung heavier than the thick morning air and it choked the nervous cadet.

"See, wasn't that easy, Harker?" Normandy whispered right before Nathanial reached the end point with the bucket. "But you knew you could do it."

"Yes, sir," He answered with caution. "I did, sir."

Captain Normandy pressed his service pistol against Nathanial's head. "Would you bet your life on it?"

Nathanial felt the cold metal pressed against his temple.

"Um, no sir," The young cadet squeaked as his body tensed up. "No?" Captain Normandy asked, "Why not, Harker? I thought you knew you could do it."

Nathanial got the point, but was fairly certain Captain Normandy was not going to stop there.

"Not if you're going to blow my head off if I do, sir." His eyes were wide as he kept the barrel of Normandy's gun in his peripheral vision.

"But you got your whole team counting on you. What kind of leader sells his men up the river to save himself?" Normandy cocked the hammer back, the click made Nathanial quiver. The Captain's smile was more unnerving than the gun, however.

The bucket was heavy in his hand; the thin metal handle was digging into his fingers. For a moment he pondered whether getting shot by Normandy right there would be preferable to dealing with his fellow cadets. He was fairly certain Normandy wouldn't shoot him, not in the head at least. If he moved fast enough, he could place the bucket on the grass. It would undermine Normandy's lesson and put Nathanial in a whole new league of trouble but it would save the class. He was already so sore and unsure if he could handle anymore special attention from Normandy.

"It's not worth it, sir," Nathanial said, defeated.

"What isn't worth it? You're going to be viewed as a coward by your men. They will despise you. Just die as a hero. Valiantly win them their day off. We'll even put your name on a little plaque to sit in the great hall for all time. Isn't that what every soldier wants?"

"It would be a trivial victory, sir." Those words felt like nails coming out from the back of his throat.

"Trivial," Captain Normandy repeated as he lowered his weapon. "Well, risking your life for a trivial victory would just be fool's pride, right?"

"Yes, sir."

"Fool's pride isn't very becoming of an officer, is it, Harker?"

"No sir, it's not."

"The Empire invests a lot of time and resources training you and they don't appreciate you wasting their coin like that." The captain looked down at Nathanial's leg. The blood and mud soaked fabric hid the true damage. The way Nathanial nursed the injury, Normandy could tell it was more than a little scratch and probably hurt something awful.

"There is a fine line between honor and pride Harker. It would suit you to learn the difference. Get yourself to sick bay and get that mess cleaned up." He turned to the rest of the cadets kneeling in a tense silence. "All of you get to your rooms! You're useless to me like this. Get some sleep. Dismissed."

The cadets waited a minute in shock before dispersing. Nathanial stood, brow wet with sweat and body trembling with pain and fatigue.

Normandy understood what Nathanial was going through. He had to scrape and save to buy his family into the Vistany to earn his commission and there wasn't a day that went by that he wasn't reminded of that reality in one way or another. The military was full of brilliant outsiders who carried chips on their shoulder and it only served to their detriment.

"You have potential, Harker." His voice was gentle. "You will make an excellent officer. History doesn't always know the best officers but their men will. You aren't a god and you have limits. Respect your mortality or it will end up defining you. You get that? Dismissed, cadet."

Nathanial hobbled back to sickbay in pain, refusing help from Arryn. The pain was the only reminder that his victory over the Arbinger had happened not ages ago but just a few hours before.

CYRUS

"Beware my children the one who speaks with the tongue of a sheep through the teeth of the wolf."

Nes Porez, Book of Nir 9-93 (translation)

CHAPTER 2

The hall of the imperial Senate of Opree was grand. Lavishly carved from marble, the walls and ceiling were decorated with images that told the story of the Empire's rich two- thousand year history. Colonel Cyrus Mason looked up at the magnificent stained glass dome ceiling towering four stories above him. It depicted the sky gods, the ancients and the old ones looking down from the City in the Stars at Aranut, the mythic hero and first king of the Empire. Written right below the feet of Aranut was *"Power is the poison of virtue"*, words of warning given to the young king right before they abandoned the mortal world for the heavens, leaving the world to be shaped by humanity. It was the motto of the Vistany, who took direct power from the monarchy and gave democracy to the people. He always enjoyed the stories of the gods and felt it a shame that it was a history each generation tried harder and harder to escape.

Cyrus stood stiff and uncomfortable in his black dress uniform, just outside the Senate floor doors. He didn't understand why the Senate was suddenly interested with Kyrant. The message he received while in the field gave no information other than he was required to appear before the Senate at this date and this time. A military man, Cyrus was not accustomed to dealing with civilian government and had little patience for politics, or surprises for that matter.

The sharp cracking echo of approaching footsteps crescendoed in the cavernous atrium. Cyrus turned around to see which of the five hallways the sound was coming from, instinctively reaching for where his sidearm was usually holstered. The sound was coming from a small, wiry looking fellow in an ill fitting but expensive suit. The man's hand trembled as he adjusted his glasses, before extending it out to the Colonel.

"C-Colonel Mason, s-sir, I am Hobert Waller. The Senate sent me to be your legal advisor f-f- for this hearing."

Cyrus gave the small man a cold stare, his steel blue eyes contrasting against the shadow of his furrowed brow as he thought. *Legal advisor? What exactly is this hearing about?* With no intentions of returning the friendly gesture, he waited for Hobert to retract his hand.

"And why does the Senate believe I will require a legal advisor?" Cyrus's eyes narrowed.

Hobert gave off an uncomfortable laugh that thinly disguised his terror. "N-no tricks sir, I was told that this was just a preliminary hearing, just questions. I am here to advise you of your rights."

"I believe I am already aware of my rights." Cyrus sneered.

"The law is a complicated thing, Colonel Mason. This is the Empire of the people. It's the age of reason." Hobert gave off another nervous chuckle. "One day people like me will be viewed as the defenders of the Empire. Protecting the laws that grant us our freedom. We are not so different, you and I. Only you use your rifle and I use my mind."

Cyrus cringed at the thought of an army of Hobert Wallers defending the Empire, although, the thought of Hobert Waller pissing himself when faced with the Navat raised his spirits a bit before he entered the Senate floor.

The Senate floor had stadium seating that allowed for spectators during important votes and hearings. It resembled more of a sporting event, than government. Originally, the building housed meetings of the Ivory Counsel, High Born lords and aristocrats from the twelve families who advised and developed policies to be approved by the King in neighboring Ivory Castle. After the revolution, it was hastily remade into the Imperial Senate Hall. It was over three hundred years later and the royal blue color of the original council chambers could be seen in the chipping white paint .

Cyrus felt lucky there weren't many people in attendance, save for a few members of the media snapping away on their cameras, recording images for the news reports. The normally imposing man felt small in the largeness of the room, one hundred sixty pairs of eyes looking down on him in god like judgment from their elevated seating.

The soft murmurs of multiple private conversations ended when the seven members of the newly developed Defense Relations Committee entered the room and sat at a stage lined with podiums directly in front of Colonel Mason.

Senator Richard Dunn headed the hearings. He was one of the few High Borns in the Senate, a prominent member of the twelve families, he was also a Duke. Cyrus noticed that the majority of the Vistany controlled Senate belonged to or were connected with the twelve families in some way. The Senator looked over his papers then eyed Cyrus with an air of contempt.

"Colonel Mason, I assume you are a busy man and so am I, so I plan to make this short and quick. This is the first hearing of the defense relations committee...", Senator Dunn read off his papers, "...aimed at finding solutions to budgetary concerns. First matter of concern being the operations in the disputed area of Kyrant and the black canyons. These operations have cost billions in imperial coin and yet in the last three years attacks have been at an all time low." He looked up from his paper. "In your opinion, what do you feel is the necessity of such operations now that the threat level seems to have gone down?"

Cyrus was in disbelief. "If there has been little violence against the colonists in Kyrant, I would say the operations at the border are a success. Don't you think so Senator?" His cocky smile let everyone know that he thought this hearing was a joke.

"I am not doubting their effectiveness, but their need. Do you feel the threat against the Empire is great enough to keep the border operations going in Kyrant?" The Senator droned.

"Let me ask you a question, Senator. Did you fight at any point during the wars?"

"No."

"Were you in New Empire, Ivory Castle or Skylands when they were invaded?"

"No, Colonel, but if you are insinuating that I wasn't affected by-"

"Senator, the invasion cost the lives of almost twenty million citizens. It would be impossible for you to not be affected." Cyrus interrupted.

"Colonel Mason, please answer the question." Dunn's voice cracked trying to hold back his frustration.

"This enemy, an enemy we have all witnessed crawl out of the pits of the ninth hell and nearly destroy our empire, they know nothing of honor, compassion and humanity. The only thing they understand is that if they cross that line, my men, my Ni'Razeem Shadows will cut them down where they stand. Take away that defense, the re-building effort of Kyrant will have been for nothing and it will be just a matter of time before they attempt to invade Opree again. Yes, these operations are necessary. You have nine million settlers and the last few million Kyre people left in existence in this colony. To gamble their lives with several billion in coin, coin, I might add that your committees can piss away in minutes, is not only foolish but incredibly reckless."

There was a brief silence following Cyrus's response, followed by quiet murmurs.

"That is rather convenient for you Colonel? Nobody else is posted at the border besides you and your Ni'Razeem Shadows. Do you expect us to keep paying you to keep the bogey men away on just your word that they are still a threat?" Senator Kraig Raid chimed in.

"I'm sorry, Senator Raid, but I come from a time when a man's word is his honor and his honor cannot be bought at any price. How easily have you all forgotten what the Navat had wrought on our cities and our people? These are not the monsters in your child's storybooks. The threat is real"

"The threat of what? Monsters, Colonel Mason?" A few of the Senators laughed. "From the ninth hell? These are your words Colonel, and you expect us to take you seriously? I don't mock your service to this

Empire. You are skilled warrior and if it wasn't for the Ni'Razeem, the Navat Wars would have cost many more lives, but it worries me that you still keep to this superstition and causes me to doubt your objectiveness on the situation."

Cyrus took a deep breath to avoid losing his calm. The rumor about the Navat being men who have adapted to life on the fire plains, was ridiculous. Cyrus knew who they really were, an army of abominations created by an angry, dark god, bent on destroying humanity. It was unlikely the mostly secular Oprians would ever accept that truth because it was easier to sleep at night when they were dealing with a rational, mortal enemy.

"Senator Raid, it is impossible to maintain objectivity about the enemy in war. Visit the Kyre Memorial see what these creatures did. Better yet, come visit me and I'll show you Im Balti, a small village raided by just a small unit of Navat a year back. After we can discuss objectivity. The border cannot go unprotected."

"And that is a point I whole heartedly agree with you on," said Senator Dunn.

"The issue is not if the borders should be protected, it is by whom. If the threat ceases to be dire enough to use valuable military resources, it is our responsibility to find cost effective solutions."

Cyrus was furious. "You mean private contractors? Will these contractors also be siphoning money from the Empire to fund their slave trade in Lo Irant? Senator Crystol I am looking at you."

Senator Crystol nearly knocked his chair over while jumping up, ready to answer the Colonel's accusations with his fists. Hobert attempted to settle Cyrus down before he said anything truly damaging, but the diminutive man stood no chance.

"Colonel Mason, that is enough. Senator Crystol was cleared of all charges with the Apex Malacom scandal. All contractors are under strict governmental scrutiny. We are also not making any decisions just yet. This is just a hearing." Dunn smiled at his ability to rattle the notorious Colonel Cyrus Mason.

The blood boiled under Cyrus's skin his nerves ached for a confrontation. "I spent the better part of twenty years fighting the Navat and I can tell you, not a contractor in the world has the technology, skill and tactics able to keep them at bay for very long. Take the Shadows out of Kyrant and you are signing the death sentences of tens of millions of people!"

Having had enough of this circus, Cyrus abruptly stormed out of the room to gasps of shock. Hobert quickly scurried after him.

CHAPTER 3

After almost two decades of war in the forsaken colony of Kyrant, the lingering smell of death hung heavy in air. It was the kind of smell that hovered on the back of his tongue; the kind of smell that never went away, and for Colonel Cyrus Mason, it was the smell of home. He approached the base located across the dusty desert plains riding in the light armored transport. The air was hot and thick, but a breeze sent a wisp of fresh coolness as the night consumed the horizon, its darkness chasing the sun from the sky.

Officially, the Navat Wars had been over for nearly fifteen years. A treaty signed by the Senate gave the Navat all lands to the south and east of the Black Plains in exchange for peace. The Empire declared victory and sent the troops back home to a hero's welcome of parties and parades. Colonel Mason and his men, stayed behind to keep the peace.

The thought of how the war had been forgotten back in Opree pissed him off. They had rebuilt while he and his Shadows languished in this shit. There was hardly a place one could step in Kyrant and not see the scars of what happened once the Navat crawled out from the Black Canyons.

According to all three holy books, the history of humanity, everyone in the Empire who carried the one bloodline began in Kyrant when the great creator, the first father, gave a drop of his blood to the children of each of his three wives so they could create man and have children of their own to worship them. The one blood line connected all of humanity together. Before the wars, the colony was home to a wealth of vibrant cultures. Now, charred skeletons of buildings and stone monuments slowly being reclaimed by Mother Nature were the only reminders that people once existed and Cyrus knew even that too would decay.

The scar just over his heart throbbed. Over his uniform, his fingers traced around the curved symbol that had been branded into him when he first arrived here. *"We thank you for your sacrifice, but..."* The words of the sniveling twat Senator played in his head. They were bastards, the lot of them. What did they know about sacrifice? There was once a time when those in the Empire respected him as a hero. Each visit back to Opree made him feel like their respect was less about gratitude and more about fear.

He knew about the rumors, the whispers of how his Shadows defeated the Navat when no one else could. Most of them were fishwives tales that included witchcraft and dark Kyre magic. *I did what I had to do to save the Empire, no matter what the cost,* he thought. There was a time when repeating that mantra justified everything he had done, but each time he said those words, they became harder and harder to believe. The soft sting of guilt burned its way into the back of his mind as a lifetime of regrets leaked out from his subconscious. A flask full of fine whiskey he kept in his pocket, helped chase the regrets away.

Their camp for the last several months had been the abandoned village of Ire Gardil, just along the disputed borderlands. The streets littered with the remnants of the people who once called this place home. Dark windows in hollowed out buildings looked like the mournful eyes of a witness to incomprehensible tragedy. Although it was a scene he was used to, whenever Cyrus returned from a visit from Opree, he was always more aware of the massive devastation the wars caused when it stood in stark contrast to the Empire's vibrant cities.

He walked into the temple admiring its large stone columns. The ornate artwork that decorated the walls had begun to fade, its treasures that were offered in sacrifice, pilfered and sold. Once sacred artifacts became kitschy decor for wealthy homes in Opree. He pictured the Kyre gods ashen and atrophied without their children to worship them. It had been converted to their operations headquarters for the time being.

His second in command, Sgt. Channing, kept things running during the Colonel's absence. In the rest of the Empire it would be unheard of for an under caste enlisted to be second in command of anything, but Shadows held their own rank structure. Blood and breeding had nothing to do with it. They didn't need stripes, buttons or stars to distinguish hierarchy. It was ingrained from the moment they became a Shadow.

Channing had been there since the beginning. They had formed the Shadows together and fought beside one another countless times. Although technically Channing was second in command, Cyrus always considered him an equal and friend above all else.

Cyrus thought that if had Channing been born or bought into a higher caste, with his battle record, he could have been a general. A genius on the field, he was a shrewd and cunning strategist. Years before Cyrus had offered to pay Channing's way into a higher status. Out of pride, Channing refused. Now, the spoils of war had made Channing wealthy enough to buy his way in three times over, yet Cyrus knew it was more likely that the sun would fall into the sea before Channing would sell his name and his banners for the title of a gentleman.

In a small chamber in the cavernous marble temple, Cyrus observed as Channing stood over a map of the border, trying to ascertain where the Navat would make their next move. A red pin dangerously close to the border represented a new colonial outpost, a settlement from one of the corporations wanting to take advantage of the cheap land and seemingly endless resources of the ravaged colony.

In western, more secure areas of the colony, the ranchers, farmers and businessmen were gaining small fortunes working the land. At first it was mostly members of the under castes seeking a chance to secure a future for their families. Now, everyone wanted a piece of Kyrant as settlements pushed further and further east, closer to the borders and into disputed lands.

Channing was confident that the Navat were planning an attack on this new settlement.

Channing twisted the pin on the map between his thumb and forefinger, too lost in thought to notice his commander entering the room.

"You should be more vigilant my dear friend. I could be trying to kill you right now." Cyrus whispered into Channing's ear so low it made the click of the Colonel's pistol pressed against his temple sound deafening.

Channing's stocky frame sat stalwart in the chair, unmoved in the massive shadow cast by his commanding officer. Cyrus pulled back the hammer, a little more attempting to break his concentration and still nothing from Channing. He tapped the side of the Sergeant's temple with the barrel of his impatient weapon, which failed again to illicit a response.

Icy steel penetrated the back of his uniform and Cyrus's grin faded into a grimace. The sharp point of a field knife danced menacingly over his kidney, pressed just hard enough to hurt but not hard enough to break the skin.

"You shouldn't underestimate me, Colonel," Channing said, not looking up from his maps. His voice, although soft and a bit gravely, always carried a menacing tone.

Cyrus stiffened and took shallow breaths in fear that the knife would slide right into him with the slightest bit of pressure. The heat radiating off his assailant and the humidity from his sweat gave Cyrus chills. He smelled of sour milk and a whore's crotch and though he was breathing loudly through his mouth, he didn't utter a word. Cyrus's heart was keeping pace with every wretched breath as he shifted his weight in preparation for his next move.

"Valmer, for the love of your gods take a fucking bath." Cyrus turned around on the enormous Shadow and the room erupted with his deep laugh.

Sergeant Calvin Valmer grinned. The ex-con was a vicious bastard whose skills were unparalleled in the field. Nobody enjoyed the kill quite like Valmer. He embodied the stereotype of the legendary Ni'Razeem Shadow: a large, bloodthirsty warrior who bordered on the criminally insane.

Cyrus had recruited Valmer nine years ago at a Kyre outpost bar filled with exiles. The man had killed three men over a spilt beer and an insult against the Queen. It was a choice between the gallows or the Shadows for Valmer, but Cyrus had yet to see a Shadow more devoted to his duty of killing the Navat.

"Very good Shadow, dismissed." Channing broke his stoic expression with his distinctive hoarse chuckle.

Valmer saluted the two senior Shadows and left, but his smell lingered a few moments after his departure.

"How'd it go?" Channing asked, more interested in his map than with Cyrus's answer.

"Honestly, not well. The Senate wants to take Kyrant out of the hands of the military and put contractors in charge of border security. Vultures."

"Well good luck with that." Channing huffed. "The Senate can't decide on what paper they should wipe their asses with. They're completely useless, if you ask me. Honestly sir, it doesn't fucking matter."

"Doesn't matter? What happens when we're disbanded and replaced with contractors?"

"Go into business and make a fortune selling my services instead of getting a stipend as a humble servant to the Empire." Channing smirked. "We are warriors. We fight the Navat under our own colors. We take our authority directly from the gods themselves. Our sole purpose is to kill. We are the exterminators, forever sworn to our sacred oaths." He recited part of the creed he and Cyrus wrote together.

Cyrus didn't take much comfort in those words. For the last fifteen years they'd been left to their own devices, thank the gods for that, yet he knew it could all go away and the legacy of the Ni'Razeem would decay like the Kyre temple.

"Has there been any activity?" Cyrus asked, changing the subject from politics.

"Not yet. It's been six months since any news of raids, not even a scout. Somethin's coming though, soon." Channing placed a black pin on the map, close to the red one marking the new settlement.

"I hope so." Cyrus studied the map, stroking his beard. He saw no raids, not even a sighting. It was cause for concern. "How are the men holding up?"

"Restless." Channing paused and glanced down at the red stain on his pant leg."We had an incident with Wayland…"

"What happened?" Cyrus sighed deeply, not really wanting to hear the answer.

"He was at Haven, a small town and trading outpost, mostly ranchers and furs, someone tried to rob him-and it didn't go to well."

"How many dead?" Cyrus asked.

"Seventeen."It was difficult to find the right words to make it sound more pleasant. "Nailed the preacher's wife to the temple doors…before raping her. She lived, last I heard." he added.

"When?"

"About a week ago. Took us a few days to find him and by then..."Channing faltered."By then it was too late," he muttered.

"Where is he?"

"He didn't come down. We waited three days, but he started to go into the change. We tried to turn him, get him to come back, but fuck, I hadn't seen anyone go off that fast."

Cyrus felt his stomach knot. Wayland was recruited less than a year ago, from an Oprian monastery. Channing had always had his doubts about the young man's promise as a Shadow and thought Cyrus was a fool to believe that the boys faith would save him.

"You did what you had to. It would have been worse for him if he came down and had to answer for his crimes." The words were supposed to bring more comfort than they did. It was his fault. He was wrong. Wayland's devotion to his gods was his weakness, not his strength. He was a holy man, not a warrior. His experiment failed.

"Why wasn't anyone with him?" Cyrus growled before catching his temper.

"I don't know. He was with Hill and Bosch, but they lost track of him. Honestly, with those two it was better they weren't there for that. Both are pretty broken up about it. Most the men are."

"Alright." Cyrus took another drink from his flask. "Prepare Wayland for burial, we can't send him home after what he did. We will do Shadow Rites on him, alert the men."

A storm of orange flames swallowed the body of Timothy Wayland as the Shadows looked on. A few of the men stayed after the rites to sit around the fire, drinking to his honor. When a Shadow died in battle, his funeral was a celebration. Drums, dancing, whores and a feast marked the occasion. Wayland's had been a much more solemn affair. In everybody's mind, his body couldn't burn fast enough. He was stark reminder about where all of the Shadow's futures would end. Timothy Wayland was better left forgotten and in the morning he would be, but for now they paid their respects to their fallen brother.

Although it was the same, standard issue beige canvas tent as everyone else, Wayland's sat lopsided, leaning against the crumbling stone wall of what used to be a house. A menagerie of seven pointed stars, the symbol for the sky gods of Opree, was fashioned from bits of wood, metal and other found objects and hung from string in front of the tent. One was painted right at the entrance. Inside, pieces of the Verinat, the holy book of the sky gods, littered the canvas walls. Prayers and pleas painted all over begged for redemption and forgiveness for his sins. The dying light of the lantern cast sinister looking shadows that seemed to threaten Cyrus as he cautiously entered the tent. He could feel the boy's madness and unrest lingering as he rifled through the Shadow's belongings, looking for answers to a question he didn't yet know. Good sense told him it was better to not dwell, plenty of Shadows didn't make it through their first rage, Wayland was different though. The two recruits, Wayland and Hill, went through the ceremony like everyone else, but he didn't mark them, like he did the others. It was supposed to protect them from the full force of the curse, but his little experiment failed. Wayland succumbed in the end, the same as all of them would when the war was over.

With his hopes for redemption in their death throws, he wished he could just accept his fate, even embrace it the way Channing and most of his men did. He admired the artwork just over Wayland's rack. The defaced painting depicting the gods was a famous one. The children of the first father were leading the old ones and the ancients in battle against the abominations created by the dark gods, Ismarlen and Malrus. The gods were nowhere to be found in Kyrant. *Their absence was too painful for him*, Cyrus though the others were often too lost to notice the changes at first. They hungered for the power so much they welcomed it. His guilt haunted him with echoes of the past ringing in his ears.

The night Timothy Wayland became a Shadow was brutally hot. The ritual was the same as always. The giant bonfire burned hotter than all nine hells. Every Shadow gathered, adorned with Kyre tribal war paint. The jagged symbols, marking his body invoked a darkness and fear in Wayland, but he stood strong knowing that whatever was about to happen, his gods would protect him.

"In a time before time, in the era of the old ones and the ancients," Cyrus began, his voice carried surprisingly clearly over the roar of the fire in the dense heat. "The story of the Navat belongs to everyone who carries within him the one bloodline of the first father."

"We are one in his name." In unison, the men gave an unenthusiastic reply.

"We remember these stories told to us as children. We have dismissed them as fables, legends and tales to keep us in line. The Navat have returned from the fire plains from which they were banished, from the ninth hell, but the gods are long gone from this world. The Ni'Razeem, the men who walk in the shadows are charged with protecting humanity by destroying the Navat, at all costs. Shadows don't defend, Shadows attack. Our job is to kill, no retreat, no mercy."

"No retreat, no mercy." The men shouted back at their leader with much more gusto than before.

"Tonight we welcome Timothy Wayland and Evan Hill as Shadows and brothers. They will, for the first time, take part in this rite and when they wake in the morning will have earned a title that cannot be bought, or sold or given by any king or priest, it can never be inherited and elevates them to a status beyond blood or banners."

"Do you, Timothy Wayland pledge yourself to the defense of this Empire against the unholy plague?"

"I do." Hill eagerly blurted out.

"I do." Wayland's response was softer but said with just as much conviction.

"What are you willing to sacrifice for your Empire?"

"All that I have." They replied in unison.

"What are you willing to sacrifice for this rite?"

"All that I am." They answered.

"We take this power from the gods themselves, proving ourselves worthy of this rite and title.

Tonight these men become Shadows, tonight these men dance with the gods!" The Shadows cheered as Cyrus handed Wayland a leather bowl to drink out of, after, he handed it to Hill who did the same.

"Shadows what?" Sgt. Channing shouted to the frenzied warriors.

"Shadows kill!" screamed the men, their savagery bathed in the flickering.

"What?"

"Kill!"

"What?"

"Kill. Kill. Kill!"...

The memory played in the back of his mind, eroding away his righteousness. He asked them and they agreed. That justification had always allowed him to sleep at night in the past. Tonight, it sat like a stone in his throat that he could not swallow. He flipped through the journal Wayland kept hidden under his pillow, its tattered pages covered in the erratic ramblings and drawings that depicted a man slowly losing his mind.

"Sir?" Private Evan Hill poked his head into the tent.

Cyrus took a moment before turning around.

"Yes Shadow. What is it?" He grumbled.

"Um...sir, I wanted to say..." Hill fumbled outside of the tent, unsure whether to step in or wait for permission.

"Shit Hill, just come in." Cyrus waved.

Hill had intensity about him, a strength that Wayland lacked. The quiet seventeen year old looked like he could barely pick up a weapon, let alone fire it, but Cyrus had seen him single handedly take out over a dozen Kyre pirates during a raid on the ports of the Dermont Settlements. His father was an exporter. The two were cornered in an alley, his father was gunned down and the boy's fury was unleashed.

The young Shadow stood there anxiously twisting his cover in his hands. The guilt seemed to pour from his eyes. He stood at attention staring off and took a few breaths to settle his nerves.

"Sir, what happened to Wayland...it was my fault." He confessed. "We were all out in Haven together, I wasn't paying attention and we got separated. I knew he wasn't doing good. He told me he was possessed-that, that he was losing control and I ignored it." He lowered his head. "I am just as responsible for what happened at Haven and I am prepared to accept the consequences."

Cyrus paused. Hill had the makings of a great Shadow and an equally great man. In his experience, the two rarely existed in tandem.

"Wayland wasn't cut out to be a Shadow. There was nothing you could've done to prevent what happened."

"But if I only—"

"Regret isn't good for a Shadow," Cyrus interrupted sternly. "Wayland made the same vow you did. He pledged himself to fight the Navat at any cost, but he couldn't handle it."

Hill looked down at his boots and scratched his head. "Wayland said we was damned, possessed by demons. I just thought he hit the root water too hard, but then some of the others told me stories that we was all cursed. I knew Wayland, sir, he was smart, had lots of books. He wasn't the kind to go over with no reason-I guess I was just wondering...you know-if those stories are true, like if we is cursed?" He felt stupid for asking such a dumb question.

"Do you remember when the Navat raided the cities in Opree?" Cyrus inquired, still thumbing through Wayland's journal.

"Um, no sir. My mother was still pregnant with me."

The realization that a whole generation grew up knowing nothing about the world before the Navat Wars took Cyrus a second to process. He felt old.

"Well, when the war started, the Empire managed to push the Navat back into Kyrant, but we were still losing. If Opree fell, humanity would have fallen with it. The Navat are stronger, faster than us and crave death and destruction above all else. We needed a weapon that would give us a fighting chance." He looked up to see Hill hanging on every word, like a child listening to a fairy tale. "To be a Shadow is to sacrifice. You are a part of something much larger than yourself, understand? Sixteen years ago, I made a choice, the same choice you and Wayland made just six months ago."

Cyrus stopped on a page with an illustration of the Shadow initiation ceremony and opposite that, a black charcoal stick figure being swallowed by a dark abyss. He studied it, the sharp lines, the clumps of broken charcoal. Wayland was practically carving these images into the journal. Peeling back the folded corner of the page revealed that it was dated the day before Cyrus left for the Senate hearing.

"I was offered an opportunity to save the Empire. I would gain the strength, speed and cunning to keep the Navat at bay. I took it and the Ni'Razeem Shadows are now an unstoppable force protecting the Empire the way the gods once did." He flipped through the several pages of black, the charcoal darkening the tips of his fingers as if Wayland's madness was trying to pull him in.

"But?" Hill asked, not satisfied with Cyrus's explanation.

"But what?"

"Is that the story then? It doesn't make any sense. There is something you aren't telling me." He was tired of feeling left out of this big secret everyone else seemed to know. They would ignore his questions, telling him that in time, he would know.

"This isn't a story, boy." He snapped and continued turning the journal pages. A hollowed out figure screamed in agony as a snarling razor wolf curled up inside of him, its orange eyes was staring out at the page. "Ismarlen, the deal I made was with Ismarlen."

Hill took a step back. This had to be a joke, but Cyrus's stern look that led Hill to believe that it wasn't. "Ismarlen? The fire god, Ismarlen?" He remembered the stories in the Verinat. Brothers Ismarlen and Malrus were the illegitimate sons of the creator, the first father, who were denied the ability to create man to worship them. Out of jealousy, the brothers killed their father and tried to wipe out humanity with an army of abominations they created themselves. They were forever cursed to the fiery pits deep below the ground in the belly of Nellis, the harvest god of iron, along with their unholy children. It was a story so old and told so often that whether it was true or not was irrelevant. "So what happened to Wayland, it was a demon?" Although the notion sounded even more ridiculous as the words came out of his mouth, for some reason, it felt like he was speaking the truth. "Is what happened to Wayland, going to happen to me?"

"All of us have and at some point yes, you will too, but most likely you'll come down from it like the rest. You and

Wayland had yet to see battle. It's easier to go through your first rage there. You will feel invincible, like a god. You'll learn to manage the change, control it with time and the times you can't, you'll have your brothers to protect you."

"Why didn't you tell us?" Hill was more curious than angry. He was hearing all of this for the first time and none of it shocked him. It was like somehow he'd known deep down the whole time. He didn't feel any different, at least he didn't think he felt any different. He poked at his stomach a couple of times, half expecting the demon to growl but nothing happened. *Maybe the Colonel is just losing it after so many years in the desert?* Hill pondered.

"I don't remember either of you asking. Besides, had you known would it have made a difference?" He shut the journal as the images became too disturbing even for the seasoned warrior and he put it in his pocket.

"I guess not. "He shrugged. Cyrus was right. He had nowhere to go after his father was killed. He'd be barely scraping by, working on the docks had it not been for Cyrus. Cursed or not, being a Shadow was the best thing to happen to him.

"So we're all cursed, just like in the stories? Is that what drove Wayland mad?" Hill asked with such an innocent matter -of-factness, it threw Cyrus off guard.

"Wayland couldn't hold on to himself in the wake of the change. All of the holy books, the Verinat, the Itara, even the Nes Porez, consider personal sacrifice for the greater good as the holiest of actions. It assures the righteous a place among their ancestors and their gods. It's what attracts so many faithful to attempt to be Shadows. To them we are on a holy mission to fight evil, and that is true, but there is no glory or honor in it. When you change you will think things, sometimes even do things that will disgust your conscience. You will be in constant battle with yourself to retain even your basic humanity. Regret, dwelling on the past will drive you mad. Always remember that we do this to protect the Empire and humanity itself. Without us, the Navat would have destroyed everything. We are a part of something larger than ourselves. Our mission alone is usually justification enough."

"And the times it isn't enough?" Hill choked, swallowing back his tears. He prayed he could save himself from the humiliation of shedding them in front of the Colonel.

Cyrus pulled the pouch out of his breast pocket. The soft brown leather was worn. With great care, he laid out its contents on Wayland's rack. The syringe glistened in the glow of the lanterns. Lined up along side of it were three glass vials filled with a hazy green fluid.

"For those times, we forget," he said, making room for Hill to join him. Although hesitant, Hill complied and allowed his commander to take his arm and roll up his sleeve. Cyrus tied the tourniquet around his arm, holding the syringe between his teeth while he searched for a decent vein in the private's skinny arm.

"The itsy dust helps keep you in control. I'm not sure why, but if you feel like you are about to go over, let someone know." Cyrus pulled the cap off the syringe using his teeth.

Hill felt a sharp sting and then shortly after that the wave took him hard. To fight the nausea he fell back onto the soft canvas, melting into it as it cradled him. He relaxed and let the drug carry him off. The broad smile painted on Hill's face caused Cyrus to chuckle while he prepared a dose for himself.

Cyrus made it outside to sit by the dying flames of the pyre as the powerful narcotics took their effect. All of the others had left. He tossed Wayland's journal into the pit watching the flames jump up to swallow the madness before it smoldered back to bits of glowing orange among blackened wood and bone. The stars started to spin and the ground became unstable so he focused on the charred skull of Timothy Wayland, staring as the smoke fill black vacant cavities where his muddy brown eyes once were.

"So Colonel, when the fighting stops are we going to all turn into monsters like Ismarlen's children did? Is what's written in the Verinat going to happen to us?" a dazed Hill repeated as he stumbled to the ground next to his commander. Keeping his head up was proving difficult, so he simply laid himself down on the grass sprawled out staring at the stars.

"It's part of the curse." Cyrus's ambiguous tone, reminded himself that he still had trouble resigning to the truth that their fates were sealed.

"Well, your gods are the harvest gods. Do you think we can be saved?"

"It's possible. Why? Are you thinking about converting?" He took his attention off of Wayland and turned to Hill.

"Nah." The kid laughed. "We're already kinda like gods now. Aren't we?"

Cyrus laughed deep from his belly. "That we are, Shadow."

The two Shadows sat in a drug induced stupor watching the last of the flames faded into a white smoke. It was still dark and he was still high when Hill woke up on the cold patch of dirt. Staggering through the camp, he noticed Wayland's tent was closer and wasn't being used, so he crawled inside and fell in a heap onto the soft pillow. He gazed up at the walls festooned with the signs of Wayland's struggle. Even though it made him sad, he was defiant to not succumb to the same fate. He said a silent prayer as his late brother's demons and the drugs lulled him into a deep, dreamless sleep.

"Wake up, hog fucker!" Valmer kicked at the sleeping Private's rack. The sun and smell of bleach burned Hill's eyes when he attempted to open them. He stretched as much as he could, but his body was stiff and sore, and his head was so heavy, he could swear it was filled with rocks.

"The itsy dust is a bitch, but you'll get used to it kid. It's for your own good, keeps you from going all...you know." Valmer decided to distract himself from the subject by taking joy in the junior Shadow's pain. "Cheer up. For us it's free and it flows down here like wine. I bet your mother has to suck fifteen cocks to get her hands on a hit like that." He laughed at his own joke and left.

Hill still lying down, gazed up to look the canvas shrine to Wayland's insanity again. To his dismay, the walls were blank, not a mark on them. Wayland's papers and belongings were gone too. It was just Hill and the smell of bleach in an empty tent. Wayland's memory was erased and not a word would be spoken about the fallen shadow ever again.

CHAPTER 4

Cyrus stepped off the air transport terminal at New Empire City and headed directly to the high-end Empire Grove Markets. It had been a long three months of fighting the Navat for the Venolin Corporation Settlement and he welcomed the break. It had been a good victory and Cyrus was relieved that the Senate had no choice but to continue backing their operations in Kyrant.

For Cyrus, it was always astonishing how much things had changed whenever he would return to Opree. Nowhere was that change more evident than in New Empire City. Most of the city had been rebuilt directly on top of the wreckage of the old one. Silver skeletons of new skyscrapers stretched higher than ever before. New industries brought new wealth. The Middle Castes were growing leaps and bounds, making the Vistany even wealthier. Vistany fashions and culture dominated the streets. Normally, like most of those in his generation, Cyrus would gripe about the petty shallowness of the modern Opree youth, but today he sought out its novelty as a welcomed distraction.

His favorites were the stores that displayed the latest gadgets. Technology had advanced so much since the start of the war. Technology that because of the embargos, was severely restricted in the colonies. Cyrus was fascinated by these new and expensive toys but found few were practical for use in Kyrant.

Moving platforms snaked along rows of stores, rushing people along the crowded market place. By the food court, a large monitor projected the news report, showing images of the riots in Roe. Sipping on a large cup of fresh Manara apple cider (a seasonal treat never available in Kyrant), Cyrus watched emotionless as the screen played amateur footage of mobs of Irantis attacking government facilities and colonists loyal to the Empire. The familiar images and sounds of war, buildings on fire, dead bodies, and gunfire seemed alien in the backdrop of his ancestral homeland. His mind went to thoughts of loved ones still there.

He reached inside his jacket and grabbed his pocket-com. Despite technology for instant communication wherever you went had been available since he was a young man, this generation craved digital distractions like razor wolves craved carnage. He stared at it for a moment, admiring the sleek design that looked like it was just a small piece of glass that with one touch, turned into a beautiful full color display. With this he could have her in an instant, her voice right in his ear.

In Kyrant, mail was a luxury that came maybe once a month. They were cut off completely, sometimes two or three days' drive from even a radio com station. Time moved slower out there than it did in the cities, or even Lo Irant. It was as if the rest of the world was moving at breakneck speed and the aging Shadow couldn't keep up.

Before he keyed in her code, he did the math in his head. Had it really been so long they'd last spoken? He went over his calculations again. She was fifteen now, hardly a little girl anymore, and suddenly the little device he held in his hands, whose sole purpose was to enhance one's ability to communicate, made it very difficult. He couldn't understand, 2333 34 2100 all he had to tap was 6 and he'd be able to say all the things he has wanted to, and yet his finger hovered paralyzed by guilt.

He turned it off, put the device safely away back in his pocket and was able to breathe again.

A group of young girls, decked out in the latest fashions, pushed by him, fawning over their latest purchases and laughing without a care in the world. He watched them pass, bright stockings, short skirts and high boots, strings of crystals woven into their hair. Apparently this is what passes for fashion these days. He felt old.

The pocket com in his jacket grew heavier by the passing minute. Instead of making the call, he spent a small fortune on the latest clothes and gadgets—whatever the shop girls said was what all the young Vistany girls were asking for. He felt ridiculous holding the bright colorful bags and packages from stores made for teenage girls, but he couldn't remember the last time he'd sent something home. It could have been a year but in all honesty, it could have been five. It was best to play it safe when making up for lost time and money had never been an issue.

Cyrus had been wealthy from birth, the third-born son of a steel fortune heir. All of his family, save a few distant relatives, had died in the attacks. His inheritance, along with spoils he gathered during twenty years of war, would take ten lifetimes to spend. It allowed him to provide his Shadows with the things they needed that the Empire wouldn't, and paid for the damage they would sometimes cause. Whatever problems Cyrus couldn't kill, he bought and the few left over usually became respected friends.

Watching the endless masses of people shopping, working and socializing, he pictured himself in a civilian life, fancy suit, and private vehicles. Although New Empire was a wonderful place to visit, it just wasn't home. As the sun went down, the lights went on in the fountains and on the walkways. The soft orange, pink and purple colors of the sunset reflected off of the mirrored surfaces of the buildings. It reminded him of the rare and beautiful starfire stones he'd procured in Kyrant.

His eyes lit up at the thought of the stones. The last time he was in New Empire, for the Senate hearing some time ago, he had placed a very special custom order at the jeweler. It should be complete by now.

The older Kyre-born woman behind the counter opened the white velvet box to show Cyrus the completed piece. Her aged hands were covered in burn scars from the wars.

"It says here you're paid in full. I was wondering when this was going to be picked up. The sir worked for weeks on this. By far his most beautiful work." She spoke with a thick accent as she handed him the box.

The piece was magnificent, a bracelet with the three starfire stones that turned a vibrant red and purple whenever they caught the light. Surrounded by diamonds and platinum, it had a traditional High Born design that gave it a timeless look. He smiled. As beautiful as this bracelet was, it paled in comparison to the girl who was going to receive it.

"She is a very lucky lady, who receives this." The woman smiled.

Cyrus wondered for a moment how awkward it was for the under caste woman to be handing over a trinket that costs more than she would make in a lifetime.

"It's for my daughter. It matches the necklace I gave her." He said.

She smiled back at him politely. "I'm sure seeing her smile when she gets this would be worth a king's fortune. She is lucky to have a father who loves her so much. It's so wonderful to watch them grow up, is it not?"

Cyrus gave an uncomfortable nod. How would he know? The polite small talk reminded him that he could not picture his little girl smiling. He wasn't even sure what she looked like now.

She was only six the last time he'd seen her. She had cried and begged for him not to leave her. He told her that even though he loved her, he was a soldier and it was his duty to protect the Empire.

"You know what, daddy?" She screamed at him, her button nose curled up and her eyes angry, red, and full of tears. "You don't love me! You just want your whores and your dusty empire!" The words were obviously his ex-wife Regina's, but the pain behind them was all her own. She was furious at him that day. He would rather be tortured for days by Navat scouts than have to endure that look ever again.

The velvet box was tucked safely in his jacket alongside his pocket com as he walked out on to the chill of the open air market. Tired, he decided to call it a night. The bracelet and the other gifts could be shipped out tomorrow. After all, he was going to be in New Empire for a few weeks.

Sulking down the lighted walkways of the large market, now thoroughly depressed, a large window of a small boutique with live young women modeling the finest in bedroom fashions caught Cyrus's eye. The soft, sheer fabrics hung gently off of their curves as they swayed their hips seductively, as if the girls underneath the little outfits were the ones for sale.

The past dropped from his thoughts and he had someone completely different on his mind when he bought what seemed like half the store's merchandise. She was someone local, to whom he had decided at that minute to visit.

LILLY

"...The seed, pushed into the ground, buried and drowned emerges strong as she emerges, arms stretched out reaching for the glory of the sun."

The Itara, Miredel Psalms 27

CHAPTER 5

Riverlands Province was the shithole of Lo Irant. The majority of the land was once untamed wilderness. Beautiful, mountainous forests stretched down the entire continent, guiding the Gran Deavo River into the sea. However, centuries of timber cutting, mining and more recently, the introduction of chemical and refining plants, had made a wasteland of the area. The land was dotted with run-down, underdeveloped towns, populated by mostly under caste Irantis. Any self respecting Vistany lady would rather drop dead than suffer the indignity of being seen there, but it had been a little more than two weeks since Lilly first stepped foot into the Riverlands and she was looking less and less out of place by the day.

It was morning in the little mining town deep in the heart of Lindbow County, Riverlands. The run-down motel was still open even though the main highway had shifted nearly ten miles north. It was cheap so Lilly forced herself to find a sort of rustic charm in the moldy, cock-roach-infested shit box she was calling home those last few days. It was all she could do to keep from going insane. She opened the box of jewelry sitting on the table by the bed. It was almost empty.

Money had never mattered to Lilly before. She never cared about how expensive her fashions were or how big her dowry was going to be, unlike most other girls her age did. Now, however, the subject of coin and cost had become the focus of everything. She was running out of valuable things to sell and by the end of the month she would be flat broke. The thought of what was going to happen to her once her money ran out was too overwhelming. She rifled through the box for something to sell. She wanted to escape the reality of her situation, even if just for a moment, but the weight of the jewelry box kept her grounded in it. Her options were running out.

The one piece that would get her enough coin to last the year was far too special for her to part with. She carefully removed the false bottom of the small wooden box and took the piece out.

The necklace was beautiful, delicate High Born jewelry her father had sent back from Opree. It was made from the starfire stones he got while on a mission in Kyrant. She remembered how beautiful it looked when she wore it for her debut, but she remembered the pain of her father's absence for yet another important milestone even more. In Opree, he was important, not a General but close. Colonel? Maybe? Lilly could never grasp rank structure. For her entire life, he had been away in a far-off land, coming home for a few months at a time in between what seemed like an endless war. Eventually he stopped coming home at all, leaving Lilly alone with her mother, Regina. The divorce drove Regina to seek comfort at the bottom of a bottle and in the arms of various men. For a while, Lilly begged in vain for her father to take her back to New Empire with him. Since then, he faded into nothing more than a ghost who once in awhile sent her extravagantly beautiful gifts and maybe a letter or two.

She held up the necklace again, giving it another look over. There was a time she would rather cut off one of her own limbs then part with it. That was when the necklace belonged to the future Mrs. Silas Blackwell. Now she wasn't the future Mrs. anything. It was still beautiful, it just carried too much of her past in it and she needed the money to create a new future.

The walk into town took nearly an hour and the late summer air was cool, which made for a pleasant trip. To call Parlow a town would be like calling a cockroach a house pet. Towns in the Southlands had rows of beautiful shops lining the main street and a large pavilion surrounded by perfectly manicured grass for festivals. Parlow had a gravel road, a bar, a gas station that doubled as the market and a mineral exchange station. It was crappy even by mining town standards, for now however, it was home.

Vance looked out the window of his bar and saw the scrawny girl walking into town. It was a sight he had become used to in the last week or so. She wasn't the first girl to come into the town like that. Three or four times a year another wayward Vistany girl would wander into the town, stay a few days, maybe even a few weeks, then pass on through. This one was different, though, and not just because she wasn't a wretched, spoiled bitch like the others. She had a type of toughness, a fire in her belly that appealed to Vance. On her third or fourth night in town, Kyle, one of his regulars, tried to get a handful of what was under the sweet young thing's dress and he ended up with a broken thumb, a broken nose and a gash on the side of his head that would be a lifelong reminder that looks can be deceiving. The girl had just said her daddy was a soldier and went right back to drinking her beer.

Since then she had been there almost every day, getting a free meal and a couple of beers. As a separatist, the thought of corrupting the daughter of a vile Iranti loyalist solider made him smile at first, but eventually he just enjoyed her company. For Vance, people always trumped politics.

The girl would talk a lot, never about who she was or where she was from, but Vance had her pegged within first week. He could tell by her accent, but she wasn't a ruined girl, like the others. She wasn't the spoiled princess who got mad at mommy and daddy and spited them by running off to the Riverlands. He wished he would have waited a day or two before calling Camden, but no taking it back now, the man was on his way.

"The girl, you said she was good, not like the last one, no?" the well-dressed woman at the bar asked Vance. Obviously Oprian Simple was not her first language. Vance pegged her for an outcaste or refugee, as Oprian Simple was the only language legally allowed to be spoken in the Empire.

She was one of Camden's, beautiful, exotic, high-end. Vance would call him whenever a new lost little girl made her way to Parlow. It was a part of their arrangement. Vance would collect a handsome finder's fee, and Camden would collect the girl.

"No, not like the last one. This one is definitely Vistany, beautiful, a little skinny, but young and I can almost guarantee she is untouched. I'd bet good coin on that." Vance said.

A moment later, Lilly burst through the door of the bar cussing up a storm of obscenities that would make a Shadow blush. Camden's associate balked at the girls display, hoping that this wasn't the same girl Vance was talking about.

"Two hundred coin! They offered me two hundred coin for this!" Lilly yelled as she took the necklace out of her pocket. "I bet you it's worth five thousand, at least!"

Vance had a beer on the bar waiting for her before she even sat down.

"I told those assholes to shove it." Lilly told the woman, for a brief moment forgetting all her manners.

The years of etiquette classes came back to her, causing Lilly embarrassment over the bit of composure lost to her anger. She always seemed to have that problem. She took a deep breath and started to address the strange woman again.

"I'm sorry, that was incredibly rude of me. Not used to seeing anyone else in this place before lunch."

She then turned back to Vance. "But, seriously? Can you believe this shit? Because I sure as hell can't! Vance, can I get some eggs please? Ooh and bacon if you got it."

"Sorry Kiddo, but breakfast ended an hour ago."

Lilly pouted silently for a moment. The bar advertised the best breakfast in the county, it was hand-painted on the window, right under the sign that said "A Free Lo Irant," but whatever time Lilly showed up, breakfast had ended the hour before.

"Just give me whatever, then." She slumped down in the barstool.

Vance came over with a plate of leftovers and then inspected the necklace Lilly had just been flailing about.

"Nice, kid, this looks like it's High Born." Vance wanted to make sure Camden's associate heard him.

"Oh? Let me see! Very pretty, darling! Is yours?" The woman pushed Lilly's hand out of the way to grab the necklace from Vance.

"Yes." Lilly snatched it back from her. "I tried to sell it, but not for what they offered me."

Lilly was unsure why this woman was speaking to her, or why she felt obliged to tell her these things. She looked and dressed Vistany, wearing very expensive-looking Oprian fashions.

Lilly couldn't figure out why she would be in this dump. The woman grabbed her by the chin and turned her head like she was inspecting a piece of livestock. It reminded Lilly of what her Aunt Miriam used to do when she was a little girl.

"Lovely, you are very beautiful." She said, releasing Lilly's chin from the grasp of her cold, bony fingers.

"Thanks," Lilly replied. She was beginning to have doubts about this woman who was stroking her face like it was a fine garment.

"I don't have time for chit-chatty talk, I am very busy woman. My name is Elana Visky. I am a designer. I come out here to find gemstones for my new line. It looks as though you are girl in need of money, selling such pretty things. It's demeaning to Vistany girl like you." The woman pulled her chair closer to Lilly's as she delivered her pitch. "I always need girls to put on the dress, take some pictures and put in the books. I pay you well! You live in the best district in Skylands City and work for me. Sound good?"

It didn't. A voice resonating from the pit of her stomach pleaded with her to run.

"Thank you for your offer, but I don't really think so, I don't even know you."

The woman shook head in agreement. "I apologize, of course you wouldn't just go with some stranger in a bar. That would be dangerous." She cackled a screeching forced laugh that made Lilly's skin crawl. "That offer sounded too good to be true. Vance, you didn't say the girl was so smart. No, darling, I don't want you to be afraid. How about I buy your necklace for five thousand coin, as I absolutely love it." She fanned the wad of hundred coin paper notes in front of an enchanted Lilly. "Then we take a trip in my luxury transport to Skylands City, so you can see my studio and meet my girls. If you still don't like it, just give me five hundred for the trip and the rest is yours to do as you will. This way you won't be stranded in some strange city without money. Vance knows I'm good to my word, right Vance?"

Vance didn't answer Elana. He just gave a tight, forced smile.

The sparkly silver etchings in the paper notes called on her to accept the money. She did need it, badly and there was absolutely no obligation. A few moments of quiet deliberation and she decided to take the money now then just pay her the five hundred when they got to Opree. She didn't want to be Elana's doll, but she didn't want to be broke either.

"Fine, I just need to run back and get a few things." She slinked around Elana towards the door.

"I'll be waiting right here darling." She clasped her hands and she let out a brief squeak of excitement. Camden would be getting another girl tonight and would be pleased with her.

With one foot already out the door, Lilly stopped to pull Vance aside. Fishing through her bag, she pulled out the box of jewelry and handed it to him.

"I wanted to thank you for helping me so much. You were the best. I know you said you have a daughter and well, I thought, maybe she would like these. My father gave me most of these and I would feel so special every time he did. I'm sure your little girl will feel the same. You were the first person to be nice to me since I left home and never called in my tab. Thank you, Vance." Lilly gave him a hug and a kiss on the cheek.

Vance looked in the box at the glittering treasures inside. If love were coin, someone loved this girl very much. The other girls that came through Parlow would fly out of his bar, never paying him notice, even when he gave them free food and beer while he waited for Camden to come get them. He looked up at Lilly and he saw a spunky little girl, not much unlike his own. There was no way he could send her out with Elana now, whatever the consequences. He sighed, his conscience still wrestling with common sense.

"Kid, listen to me." He whispered. "Do not go with this woman. She is a snake, works for a man who sells young girls to wealthy creeps in Opree. Whatever you did, it's not worth this life. You're a good girl Lilly and you don't deserve this. Go home."

She could tell by Vance's tone that he was afraid of this woman or at least the man he worked for. Her eyes fell on money still in Elana's hand. This was so unfair. She was so close to it. Still cursing her better judgment, she flashed Elana an uneasy smile and casually walked out of the bar.

Elana sat at the bar impatiently drumming her cold, bony fingers on the rim of her glass.

CHAPTER 6

Lilly couldn't believe she was on the same road she was on two weeks ago, heading in the direction she came from. Retracing her steps, no matter how far wouldn't change anything but walking back forced her to remember what had happened before:

Two weeks earlier:

It was the evening of Lilly's engagement dinner. Her grandfather had made the arrangements almost a month before, but now it was to be official. Lilly beamed in her bright blue dress. The skirt was so big, her slight frame was nearly swallowed whole, but she felt like an Oprian High Born Princess. As she was putting on the finishing touches of her ensemble, her mother walked in. Lilly could tell she was drunk just by looking at her.

Regina had been drinking, a lot. This was her daughter's big day and everything was all about Lilly Rae.

The woman took another sip of her cocktail. It was mostly pure grain alcohol at this point, but to her it still tasted like water.

There was a jealous hatred of her daughter that had been building up inside Regina way before Silas Blackwell came into the picture, but that was the last insult she would endure. For over a year, Silas Blackwell was her lover. At twenty-nine he was young, handsome and successful. Just a month after Lilly's debut, he made an offer of marriage. Pig.

If she had known that Lilly would have stolen the affections of every man in her life, she would have smashed the little bitch's head into the rocks when her ex-husband brought her home from the war. She should have rejected the bastard offspring between her husband and some Kyre witch, but back then she wanted a baby of her own so desperately and she had already miscarried four times.

For the first few years it was as if Lilly Rae was her own natural born child. Her ex-husband had her forge a birth certificate so the child could carry their name and have rights as Vistany. At the time Regina didn't care. After so many years of her husband away at war, they were finally a happy family.

When her marriage fell apart, Lilly and she went to live with Regina's father. It didn't take him long to favor Lilly over her as well. Regina was disgusted. The one joy she got now, other than from the bottle, was keeping her ex away from his precious Lilly Rae.

Now the girl was standing there, the forever-happy Lilly Rae Mason, apple of everyone's eye, gearing to tear out Regina's heart yet again. Not this time. This girl had everything in the world and was ungrateful for what Regina had sacrificed for her.

The girl would no longer find sanctuary in the lies built around her and the wealth and privilege illegally afforded to her with falsified documents. She took another sip of her drink, a smug half smile cracking from the corner of her mouth.

The girl's tears didn't move Regina to mercy. They made her smile a bit more. Lilly Rae begged her not to make her leave, agreeing to break the engagement with Silas, if it meant that much to her. The Southlands and the Plantation was all she'd ever known.

"Momma, please don't do this to me. I promise, I will do whatever you want. I'm sorry about Silas, I didn't know you hated him so badly. I won't marry

him if you don't want me to. Just don't send me away like this. Momma, please!" Lilly sobbed as Regina packed up the girl's things.

"Don't ever call me mother again! How dare you? I cannot allow my father's wealth go to a mixed-blood daughter of a Kyre whore witch. You have left me with no choice. Are you happy now? I'm sitting here on what was supposed to be one of the happiest days of my daughter's life, packing her things, sending her off into the darkness, just to save her name from ruin. How do you think I feel? You were always so selfish, thinking about yourself all of the time." Regina spat her words with an acid tongue.

The hardest part for Lilly was taking off her beautiful blue dress while her mother barked more venomous insults at her. Her heart broke into a million pieces as she stepped out of the pile of satin and tulle. Lilly felt little of anything after that moment. She barely remembered leaving out the backdoor as the party inside went on without her.

After coming to terms with what her life had become, Parlow, despite not having been the best place in the world, had started to feel like a place she possibly belonged. She didn't even have Parlow anymore. Another world, crumbled to bits. She missed the comfortable feeling of knowing where she was, but there was something very unfamiliar about this place despite her knowing the way. She couldn't put her finger on it, whether it was the taste or feel of the air. The ground didn't feel right under her feet and the gravity was throwing her balance off. Unfortunately, there was no base to compare. After hours of wandering the old highway in the blistering heat, everything familiar seemed to escape her to the point where she didn't know if she was crazy or not. She couldn't remember her body feeling clumsy, dull and heavy, but she couldn't remember it not being that way. Her thoughts were linear and logical, every dot connected, but life still did not make any sense. She was Lillian Rayne Mason according to her birth certificate and Lilly Rae according to her grandfather and she was going somewhere far away but that's all that was certain at that point. Although she feared that if she clung too tightly to that truth, it too would crumble away with the rest of her world.

Finally succumbing to the brutality of the sun, Lilly Rae fell to the ground, hard, as if gravity had decided to spite her for some egregious past transgression. It happened too quickly for her to be positive but for a moment, however brief, there was something familiar about the feel of the dirt between her fingers as she struggled to peel her clumsy, dull and heavy frame from off the road. She probed her fingers deeper in to the mix of pebbles, dirt and clay. Even after the feeling went away, she continued to claw at the ground. The fall left a layer of dust on her face, which made her deep violet eyes seem wild and unnatural. The aftershocks of pain moved through her body like tiny bursts of electricity. For a moment everything felt right, sadly that feeling faded along with the pain and she continued on her journey.

After a while the walking didn't bother her. She ignored the pebbles in her shoes and even the vengeful sun, which seemed to focus its entire wrath on her aching shoulders. It was several more hours before the burden of her nagging thirst and the oppressive weight of her knapsack overtook her. There was no way in nine hells Lilly Rae would be walking any more today. She tossed the heavy canvas sack on the ground, stuck her chest out, showed a little leg and waited.

It didn't take very long before she saw a transport tanker make its way over the horizon. She imagined the fat, stinky driver that was inside. She concluded that he was going to have crazy stories and be boisterous, loud and possibly a little too touchy. Just like the ones in the radio picture shows her grandfather used to take her to. To her disappointment, the under caste woman that inhabited the tanker's cabin was albeit plenty salty and grizzled, was clean, quiet and offered no amusement whatsoever. After only a few hours of silence in the cab, Lilly Rae felt safe enough to drift asleep as they chased the sun that dipped just below the horizon.

The bright lights of the transport hub parking lot pierced her eyelids. The rattling hum of the engine that had previously lulled her to sleep jarred her awake as it idled. Her body ached in the cold and she suddenly remembered that she had to pee. It always seemed it took her body extra long to get used to moving. Her muscles generally were too weak and tight to listen to her brain. Most of the time they preferred to do nothing and frequently vocalized their objections to doing anything but.

The bathroom was dimly lit and the last of the working fluorescent lights were in their death throes, flickering on and off. It was relatively clean in the sense there were no dead hookers, exposed hypodermic needles or shit artistically decorating the tile walls. Having to pee that badly rendered silly standards like hygiene or not being stabbed by a casteless drifter rather trivial.

Her reflection in the mirror was smoky. It was made of that unbreakable safety mirror stuff they put in prisons and crazy houses. It made her aware of how pale she was, even for an Iranti girl from the Southlands. Her hair was not even really that blonde, like other Irantis. It was more of a dull golden copper that masked the better part of her face in unmanageable spirals of frizz. The hazy faded image seemed more recognizable than it did in any normal mirror. Maybe she belonged in a crazy house or prison. *Every mirror should leave a little something to the imagination.* Regina's words repeated in her mind. Seeing every oversized pore bursting with refuse and puss started to become too stressful. Although being only fifteen, she swore she could see lines that were beginning to form around her mouth and eyes and they were a countdown of her own mortality.

The transport driver was sitting at the counter. The woman gestured to Lilly and made room by the empty seat next to her. The waitress was a young under caste woman with missing a tooth, yet she had a beautiful smile and carried herself like a High Born. Her uniform had "Evelyn" neatly embroidered in soft pink. Lilly ordered the pancakes and was eager to finally have a decent breakfast. Despite being dry and a little overdone, they brought that small feeling of being connected to her world the way only dirt, pain and pancakes can and that made them the best pancakes she'd had in a while.

Bits and pieces of bacon stuck in the syrup and Lilly poked them with her fork, arranging them into a smiley face, but the bits just sunk down in the sweet sticky syrup into a frown. *Sad bacon*, Lilly thought and continued poking to the beat of heels clicking across the diner floor behind her.

"This is my lovely girl!" A pair of cold bony hands wrapped around Lilly, startling her. She remembered that voice, but was too shocked to speak. Elana was standing behind her with two bodyguards. Her claws gripping Lilly tight.

"I was worried sick over you. Naughty girl! Running away like that, you make your papa and I so worried." The woman was deceptively strong and Lilly struggled unable to get out of Elana's grasp. "It's time for you to go home with you sisters. My little minchka noodle."

Nobody in the crowded diner looked up from their food as Elana and the men dragged the kicking and screaming girl out the door. The waitress quietly cleared the plate of half-eaten breakfast off of the table, erasing any evidence of Lilly having been there at all.

CYRUS

"They bare his mark and have turned against their gods to join with the forgotten son, Ismarlen. The dammned drained the blood of the first father from their bodies and became an abomination."

Nez Pores, Book of Luminations 2:361 (translation)

CHAPTER 7

Mayara slumped in her chair, buried under a massive pile of medical textbooks. Her final medical academy examinations were approaching. After passing these, she would be a doctor and finally be able to open a clinic so desperately needed in the undercities. Normally, studying came easy to her. She was fascinated with medical science and excelled in her classes. This night, however, was difficult. It was beginning to get warmer out and the early summer night beckoned her. She closed the shades to try to banish the nice weather but her brain would not let her forget, not without a fight anyway. Struggling to get through every word, eventually her eyes refused to focus. Five hours had passed, five hours in her chair, reading books.

Hungry for a distraction, she turned to the tea she'd made at the beginning of her study session, deciding if the ice could, soupy black sludge was acceptable to drink. Her nose scrunched when she drained the bag against the spoon and laid it on the plate underneath the ceramic cup. She always managed to ruin good tea when she was studying. Swirling the tea around the mug didn't make it any more appetizing. A dark ring had stained the inside of the glass. Her fingertips strained to push the cup as far away from her reach as possible in a bid to rid her mind of horrible thoughts about dirty dishes and the need to wash them.

A knock on the door startled her. Her legs, stiff and sore from being in the same position for the last few hours, refused to move.

"Who is it?" She called from her chair, but could only hear a muffled answer.

"Just use the key." She yelled. If they knew her, they knew where she kept the key.

The tall Iranti-born officer stood in the foyer of her grand apartment, holding an armful of bags from several high-end stores. The older gentlemen smiled gently when he saw her still in her nightclothes under a pile of books.

"So, I'm guessing you have had a busy day?" He lifted an eyebrow

"Cyrus!" She squealed with excitement and stumbled out of the chair, disregarding the pins and needles in her legs. Her arms squeezed him tightly around his waist as she lavished him with kisses, standing on her tip toes to reach his face.

He welcomed every kiss and returned them in double. He was enchanted with his Kyre mistress, small waist with shapely hips, a caramel colored beauty with sparkling Emerald eyes and a playfully seductive smile.

"You didn't tell me you were home." She gave him a slap on the chest and started to pick up the messy sitting room. "I would have changed—." Holding an assortment of books and clothes, she remembered there was nowhere to put the stuff in her cramped apartment, so she just let it drop back on the floor where she stood. "I would have showered."

Cyrus didn't mind. After spending the better part of six months in the field with no one except his Shadows, Mayara could have gone without grooming or personal hygiene for months and she would still seem appealing. Still, his mistress insisted she take a shower, a notion Cyrus had little objection to, as long as he got to watch.

Taking in the heavy cloud of steam hovering in around the shower, Cyrus felt like he was in a dream as he watched Mayara under the stream of hot water. He tried to contain himself, hold off until she was done, but after months of fighting in the field, a man could only wait so long.

He reached into the shower and grabbed her by the waist from behind, laying a series of rough kisses on her neck. She melted into his arms as he dragged her from the warmth of the water. He turned her around to face him and pinned her against the door. He licked his lips, taking a moment to admire his next great conquest.

Everything about her was perfect; head to toe, every inch of her reminded him of the statues of Rytu, the Kyre Goddess of love and beauty. Standing there, tiny rivers of water droplets traced her bare curves as they made their way down her body. Her eyes were wild and they wanted him. Her nimble fingers grabbed at the soaking wet fabric of his shirt and she bit her lower lip too keep it from trembling out of a mixture of intense desire and the chill she got after he pulled her from the shower.

There was violence in his passion when he kissed her and that excited her even more. She stared into his eyes and saw the rage, desire, aggression and all of the other emotions he dragged back from battle that he needed to bury deep in between her thighs. She did not break her gaze as she carried her to the bed.

There was something about the way Cyrus made love to her just after he returned from a conflict that was special. It was the only time she got to experience the most real and raw bits of him, the vulnerable and tender. Cyrus dominated any room he was in, the most feared man in the Empire, yet he worshiped her, screaming her name as prayers in ecstasy. He would barely talk about who he was, but on those nights there were no parts of his soul he could hide from her. It was a power she craved.

Hours had passed and the two lovers were spent and exhausted. Both were raw, sore and extremely dehydrated. Mayara drew back the shades on the window to let the light into the bedroom. It was dawn and the beautiful and leggy Kyre woman was clad in one of the little "outfits" Cyrus had bought her. The red fabric contrasted nicely with her dark olive skin.

Used to early mornings, Cyrus was still in the bed, waiting for her under the covers, playfully beckoning her.

"Cyrus," she said with her thick Kyre accent, "I have to go to class...I can't. I can't." She giggled and pulling a wrinkled shirt over her head.

"I haven't seen you in months and I know you missed me." He kissed the back of her neck, trying to coax her back under the covers. She was tempted by his kisses and was slowly drawn into his arms. There would be no going to class today.

Despite the man being over twenty years her senior, she found him very attractive. Aside from being handsome, he was kind and good company. If it weren't for him she would have never been able to attend Medical Academy.

She'd met Cyrus at the undercity bar she worked at, while trying to save the coin needed to put a down payment on her caste debt. After one week of serving him, Cyrus insisted he sponsor her caste debt, putting his money upfront so she could register into one of the middle castes and become a doctor. Since then he had taken care of her needs while she attended school.

Although their arrangement on the outside looked immoral, she was in no way his concubine. He had made it very clear at the beginning that his financial assistance was in no way dependent upon her company. Whenever Mayara inquired about his decision to be so generous, he would just refer to it as "reparations".

She never questioned him further about it. It was one of his rules: she could ask any questions she wanted, but if he refused to answer or clarify anything, she must leave it alone. They both had rules for each other. She must be discreet about their arrangement. She couldn't have any other men over while he was visiting her. He couldn't make open judgments about her lifestyle. She maintained the right to refuse him at any time, without justification, and most importantly he could not use their arrangement as a means of coercing her to do anything outside of those agreed-upon terms. In three years neither of them had broken any of the rules.

Cyrus was spent after a day at Mayara's, a good spent. Having found comfort in the arms of his beautiful mistress all afternoon, he was reluctant to leave her bed. She was in the kitchen cooking up dinner. The aroma of the spicy Kyre food filled the small one bedroom apartment, making him hungry.

"Stay for dinner, darling," she called. It was less of a request than a demand and Cyrus was not about to argue with her. He exited the bedroom to pay a visit to the cook. He stood in the entryway to the kitchen admiring Mayara's exotic features. Her silky black hair hung right at the small of her back, dancing dangerously close to her shapely behind, which was swaying back and forth to the beat of the music Mayara had blasting in the kitchen. It was that new style, a mix of urban and tribal music. Cyrus was not very fond of it, but the generation gap didn't stop him from dancing with her right there in the cramped kitchen.

They were still embracing even though they had stopped dancing. Mayara ran her fingers down his bare chest and softly traced around his many scars, carefully ignoring the jagged one on his cheek and the large brand over his heart while he hovered blissfully in her scent.

"I need to get back home tonight. There are things I need to take care of tomorrow that I should have done today," he said, making no effort to break their embrace.

"No, stay. I will finish making your dinner then I will draw you a bath, spend the night with me. Don't make me beg." Her eyes were hungry for him and she playfully bit down on her lip, giving away her intentions.

"Even the Navat sleep woman! You sorceress! Your Kyre magic has vexed me so. I have become a slave to your beauty." He said, tickling her.

It amazed him how beautiful her mouth looked when she laughed and he kissed it. He didn't want to go back to his place, or even home to Kyrant. This apartment, nestled away in the University district of New Empire was the only space in the world where Cyrus could find the closest thing to true peace, so he let the world outside of it disappear from his thoughts while he hid inside her for one more night.

CHAPTER 8

Dear Cyrus,

I regret to inform you that upon coming to the discovery of certain truths, our beloved Lilly has taken her own life. We are devastated at such a tragedy. I have included the paperwork necessary to have the Trust set up in her name to be transferred over to her me. Please fill out the forms, my attorney has prepared and return them, so we can move past this terrible event. Once I receive the funds, I'll let you know where you can pay your respects.

Regina

The typed note crumpled under the crushing weight of Cyrus's palm and he fell to his knees on the marble floor of the foyer. Lilly's starfire bracelet spilled on the tiles when the box fell from his pocket. The sharp snap of the heavy trinket bouncing on the floor echoed loudly down the hall, snuffing out the uncomfortable silence. Barlow, his butler struggled to help him to his feet, but his feet couldn't recognize the floor. His body rejected the heaviness of what remained of his universe. His fingers tore at his coat until he pulled the small leather pouch that held his escape. Just knowing it was there as he gripped it close to his chest was enough to bring the air back to his lungs.

Barlow had received the message last week, but as pained as he was to see his master like this, Lilly had always been a ghost to him; a child with her own room in the large house, but whose face he never saw. Despite all of this, the house seemed even emptier with the news of her death. He had been with the Mason family for over forty years. Having barely escaped with his own life when the Navat attacked the city, a fate not afforded to the rest of the family, Barlow always held out hope that a family would sometime breathe life back into the estate, however it seemed that he would serve out his days as a caretaker to an empty tomb.

The staff waited in the darkness for their master to compose himself, unsure of what just happened. Barlow shooed them away.

"Barlow!" Cyrus's voice cracked and he coughed. "Get the air transport ready. I'm going out."

"Sir, you just arrived. Maybe you should rest. I'll have your attorneys come in the morning."

"That bitch isn't getting a single coin from me!" Cyrus yelled. "Get the air transport ready, I'm going to Core City for the night."

"Yes, sir," Barlow answered quietly.

It was dark when Cyrus and his guest arrived at the tall iron gates of the huge estate overlooking New Empire. The young casteless woman leaned over the slightly drunk and rather disinterested Colonel, trying to swallow the grand sight with her eyes. She had never flown in an air transport before and she definitely had never seen a place as fine as this. Lights bathed the walls, casting large shadows that highlighted the intricate carvings adorning it. Two Oprian flags, dark blue velvet banners dotted with twelve silver stars hung in front of the house. Between them flew a third flag of the same material but deep scarlet, with gold scythes behind stalks of wheat paid homage to his ancestral lands of Lo Irant.

Gaylestone was one of the largest and oldest houses in the wealthy Diamond District of New Empire. There was a time the Colonel swore he would sooner see it burned to the ground than return to its great halls and marble corridors, but after becoming the sole heir in his family after the Navat attacks, he had a change of heart. Although he rarely stayed at his grandfather's home save for a few weeks out of the year, Cyrus could never bring himself to sell it. He told himself it was mostly because it irked the hell out of the Highborns and the Vistany elite that they were neighbors with an Iranti-born.

"Dis, you home? Shit, I woulda ponced up for da occasion." She almost sung her words in a way that sounded like she was originally from the undercities of New Empire.

Cyrus had always thought the way they spoke down there had a lyrical quality. The way her red painted lips puckered when she spoke caught his attention, as did her hand on his thigh as she tried to get a better view. The streetlights caught in the new fire stone bracelet he gave her.

The sleek black transport pulled up into the brick courtyard and an elderly gentleman, prim and pressed, opened the door. Cyrus exited first. The girl was left to fumble out of the vehicle herself, uncomfortably tugging at her too-short dress as she tried to catch up to her host, who at this point was already through the front door. Each click of her heel on the cobblestone, echoed loudly in the black silence of the late winter's night. The windows were watching her and suddenly she felt so...exposed. Every inch of her wanted to slink back into the transport and go home. She sighed deeply and continued, home was too far away.

He led the young woman by the hand down the dark halls towards back of the house, tugging her gently along whenever she paused to look around. The room looked out of place in such an old house, modern furniture and art on display. The latest in novel gadgets had their spots on the shelves, next to shapeless sculptures and ancient tribal artifacts. Whatever caught his eye, he would collect and put on one of the shelves in this room. Although some of the objects were considered priceless, none of them carried any particular sentimental value to Cyrus.

The girl couldn't have been less interested in his menagerie. She tugged at her skirt before plopping down on the sofa, sinking into the thick plush fabric. For a moment she allowed her head to swim in the drinks she'd had on the flight over from Core. The warmth from the alcohol chased out the chill from the night air.

He felt heavy on top of her. His weight crushed her ribcage. No matter how much she tried to escape into the high and let herself float away, his intensity dragged her back into the moment with each angry thrust. His hands explored her with a clumsy violence before they settled, wrapping around her neck. She started to struggle as his grip tightened around her windpipe. Panic set in and she dug her fingernails into his wrists, clawing at his hands attempting to pry them off of her. His once sad, blue eyes were angry and glowed with an inhuman rage. They looked right through her as she pleaded with her last breaths.

Cyrus awoke in a cold sweat on the marble floor. It was still dark and everything was spinning. He sat up, resting his head in his hands until the room settled around him. There were so many blank moments he tried to piece together. The girl and then the itsy, the cocktails in the transport, that much was clear. He retraced his steps inside his mind while surveying the damage to the place. He didn't know how he ended up on the floor, but he remembered the sex and-

"Shit..." Cyrus dropped to his knees by the sofa where the girl lay.

Her limp, lifeless body was sprawled in an unnatural and vulgar position. He pursed his lips in disappointment when he couldn't detect a pulse. It was a shame. She was so young, so pretty. Her hand felt soft and cool as he caressed it against the rough stubble on his chin, his eyes transfixed on the starfire bracelet, the red and purple glow from the candlelight dancing in the blackness.

The steam from the tub made the bathroom a hazy dream world. He gently scrubbed the girl clean, the hot water giving some of her color back. There was no discernable reason as to why he was doing this, lost in the itsy and grief, Cyrus felt compelled. He washed away the smeared red lipstick. She looked younger without her make-up and yet, much more worn. In silence, he cradled her head against his chest as he carried her down the darkened hallway, her wet hair soaking through his shirt.

The girl, hair neatly brushed and still dead, was dressed in a modest nightgown. She felt like a feather

in his big arms. The room was a pale blue, a large four post bed, decorated with soft lace and filled with toys and treasures that have never been played with. Cyrus placed her in the bed, stroking her hair, whispering quiet apologies. He gave her a peck on the cheek before shutting off the lights.

Watching her from the darkness of the shadows, he could imagine she was sleeping, a peaceful sleep, one she would rise from in the morning. By the time the light stretched across the room chasing away the shadows, Cyrus was gone and the unfortunate girl was left for Barlow to deal with.

LILLY

"... Winter brings Death whose scythe cuts down every man, beast and stalk, but leaves the stones, rocks and mountains for Death only leaves the strong. So Tryn, tired and worn from his ordeal, prayed to the gods to spare him from Death, they heard his prayers and he became a stone. He felt no cold, no pain, none of Death's blows penetrated Tryn the stone. The sun rose in the spring, as it did, but Tryn could not feel its warmth. His wife returned from their winter home and he could not touch her. In his despair Tryn prayed for death, but his gods could not hear him for he was no longer a man, but a stone."

-The Story of Tryn the Stone (a Northland Fable)

CHAPTER 9

Lilly languished on the hard wooden bench, chained to the crumbling plaster wall. The last three days had been a miserable and painful blur. From the moment they dragged her into the transport, Elana had been forcing pills down her throat. The heavy shackle on her leg dug into her skin. Lilly pulled at it attempting to give her raw ankle a reprieve.

"If you stop dey won't lock you up like a mongrel dog," the girl sitting next to her whispered. It was the first time anyone had spoken to her since she was dragged from the diner. Lilly couldn't form a response.

"I'm Rebecca." She spoke with a subtle confidence. "I've been here a long time. If you just listen to dem it's so much better, I promise. We're lucky, if dey like you here you get you own bedroom, and de men bring you presents. Odder places are much worse."

"I don't understand." Lilly scratched her head. There was enough pins and product in her hair that it was more structurally sound than most bridges. She wasn't sure what it looked like, but it itched something awful.

"Tonight's gon be you first night. I'm gon to give you advice. When dey line us up, stand up straight and smile. You don't want dey to know it's you first night or you'll be working til de sun come up." Rebecca was the only person to speak to her with an ounce of kindness and warmth since the diner.

She was about sixteen, though her eyes she looked fifty. There was a hollowness about her. All the girls had that same look: thin, young, beautiful and not one of them looked her in the eye. They just had these stares, like they were focused on a place far away from here. Lilly wish she could be any place far away from here.

The sound of heels clicking on wood floors caused the girls in the room to stiffen up. Elana appeared from behind the beaded curtain with a clipboard, her two oafish bodyguards standing behind her.

"Her," she barked with her red tipped, bony finger pointing harshly at Lilly. The two lumbering bodyguards complied and followed Elana back behind the beaded curtains, dragging a reluctant but obedient Lilly with them.

The parlor of Camden's brothel was dark and dirty. Through the dirt, Lilly could tell the faded wallpaper had once been expensive. Dust flew up when she sat down on the old velvet-covered chair and floated back down like a light snowfall.

"I have special night planned for you." Elana sang her words and clapped her hands in excitement."Tonight, you will make me enough money, I forgive you the trouble you put me. Wait here."

Elana left Lilly in the room and the reality of what was about to happen settled in as she sank deeper into the dusty velvet couch. Her first thought was to run, but the sore on her ankle told her it would be a bad idea. There was a window, the glass crudely covered in black paint so there was no way to know how high up she was. The minutes seemed to drag on. The clock on the wall had stopped and judging by the thin white lines etched on the dusty gray face just underneath each of its golden hands, not a minute had gone by on that clock since before she was born. She could hear the muffled music and laughter coming from downstairs. Even her imagination, usually a reliable sanctuary, betrayed her as she pictured time moving quickly everywhere else except that room. A hundred years could have passed, everyone who ever knew or cared for her was long dead and she was forgotten and nameless. Part of her wondered if the anticipation of her fate was worse than succumbing to it. Maybe she wanted to stop time, let herself stay forever in this magic timeless room.

Unlike the crazy house mirror at the truck stop, her image in the broken mirror hanging on the wall just above a dilapidated vanity, looked flawless, almost uncanny. It was a porcelain version of herself that she could not recognize.

She felt that in the candlelight she looked so much older too, red lips, soft pink silk dress that was much too small and heels that were much too large. She tugged at the hem of the dress to try to feel less naked, but it wasn't a forgiving fabric. She remembered how beautiful she felt in her blue engagement dress. Her beauty shining through the dusty cracked mirror brought a sickness to her stomach and she spat a vile curse at the stranger staring back at her.

Heavy thuds of footsteps flowed by sharp clicks of heels were becoming louder as they approached. She pleaded in vain for a few more minutes alone. Panicked fingers reached for the broken piece of mirror on the vanity and held it to her throat, but she couldn't get herself to apply the right amount of pressure to end herself entirely. Her lips quivered as the footsteps got closer and her legs began to shake, her back still to the door afraid to turn around. She wouldn't dare let the tear that was forming in her left eye fall. She swallowed the razor sharp ball of despair that formed in the back of her throat and became a stone.

"It's time, your prince awaits." Elana squealed and kissed Lilly on the forehead. "I'm so proud of you! You'll be my number one girl."

Another girl, one Lilly had not seen before wandered listlessly into the parlor, her hair already a mess, make-up smeared, holding together the ripped fabric of her dress. Blood poured from her nose. She didn't seem upset or sad, just blank. An older Vistany gentleman, who was visibly irate, quickly followed her.

"One of your little whores just bled all over me. Fuck, Elana, when I pay for a girl, I expect her to be in one piece!"

The iron grip of Elana's fingers on Lilly's shoulders momentarily lifted as she addressed the angry customer. Lilly looked down at the girl with pity. She just stood there, blood soaking her silk dress, black eyes focused on a place far away.

Still holding the shard of mirror, Lilly squeezed it hard until she felt it penetrate her skin. The pain killed the fear as she watched her blood drip onto the floor like drops of wax from a candle. Looking right into Elana's eyes with defiance and a fire that burned from deep inside of her, she flung herself at the glass window.

Cold, wet air graced her skin, followed by the sharp pain of pavement. It took a couple of drops of rain falling on her face before she realized the pain she felt wasn't death but just the opposite. Elana's burning rage glaring down at her from the second floor.

"Get her!" She screamed, face twisted and red with fury.

Lilly scrambled to her feet, but the pain was too much to get her very far past the alley. She saw Elana's bodyguards barreling towards her from the corner of her eye. Pain pushed through her shattering her courage. She stopped and collapsed onto the street, cursing herself for her brashness and waited for Elana's goons to retrieve her.

A hand reached out in front of her face from out of a grate in the street. "Looks like you could use a little help." A young man said as he dragged her down under the street.

Elana's men were too big to follow. They fired their weapons into the dark hole and eventually gave up. Lilly fought to catch her breath as it became clear she was safe for the time being.

"Shh, you're okay. Don't be afraid, now." He ripped a piece of his shirt and wiped away some of the blood coming from Lilly's forehead. He was tall, thin, older than Lilly but only by a few years.

"I'm Caleb and I will be rescuing you today." He smirked, brushing his blonde hair off of his face.

"I'm Lilly. Thank you." She stumbled onto the cold wet cement. Although the stench in under the street was foul, it seemed sweeter than in the brothel.

"You picked a helluva way to quit your job at Camden's."

"I don't work for Camden. That stupid bitch kidnapped me." Lilly snatched the rag from Caleb's hand and tended to her own wound.

"Whoa, spitfire, I know what kind of game Camden runs. He's a slaver, scum of the Earth."

"Wait, what did you just call me?" Her father used to call her his little spitfire. It was weird hearing someone call her that after so many years.

"Spitfire? Why, does that offend you?" He smiled a smile that her mother would describe as trouble.

"No, my father just-nevermind. Where are we?"

"Our own private entrance to the Core City under-city." He pulled a plank off of the boarded up doorway covered in graffiti. It opened to a dark alley.

Lilly was hesitant to follow a stranger, especially after how her luck with strangers had been lately. She looked back to the unfamiliar streets of Core, packed with strange faces, and back to Caleb. His eyes were gentle and he had just saved her. She put her hand into his. If she was going to get ax murdered by a psycho killer, at least this one was handsome.

Caleb led her down a narrow stairwell into the underground city reserved for the under castes and outcastes. Every city in Opree had an undercity. As the population grew, the cities just built up when they could no longer build out, using the decaying bits of building as foundations for the sparkling metropolises built by the Vistany's ever growing wealth. The undercities were a place where the poor and outcastes lived, under caste laborers, convicts and whoever the Empire deemed unworthy of a life on the surface. Core had the only undercity in Lo Irant but unlike in Opree, the difference between the city and the undercity was slight. A popular trading post and way station that ran along the entire length of the border between Opree and Lo Irant, Core was built out of shipping containers to accommodate how quickly it grew. Most people in Core there were transients; businessmen, traders, or thieves, and those who lived there rarely saw the wealth that passed through stay for very long. Garbage piled up around tin shacks stacked on top of each other, vendors selling their wares, out of cardboard boxes on dirt streets, the streets above criss-crossed blocked all but small pockets of sky.

Lilly struggled to keep up with Caleb. The heel of her shoe broke and she tossed them both, a decision she immediately regretted due to the dirty, broken glass covered streets. Caleb saw her limping and called over a rickshaw.

"Let's get you something to eat. I have a place you can stay for the night." Caleb put his arm around her as they sat down. Lilly was glad it was much more comfortable than it looked. She felt safe around her mysterious rescuer, like she had known him her entire life. Finally relaxed, she dozed off on his shoulder.

"Sleep now, Miss Lillian Rayne Mason. I have big plans for you," Caleb whispered to himself and stroked her hair as she slept.

In the atrium of Camden's brothel, Elana was scolding her inept guards in a language the client couldn't understand. He waited in the hallway, tapping his shoes on the black and white checkered marble floor. The horrible florescent light brought out every flaw in the dark purple room. There was a charm to the place. The rundown house of ill repute had a vintage kitsch that made the place feel homey, like he was visiting an elderly spinster aunt with entirely too much money and not nearly enough taste. The holograms of dancing girls flickered in blues and purples. It was a menu. Although banned in the colonies, he wasn't surprised the brothel had them. Tech restrictions always seemed more lax whenever the authorities were tempted with something that made them look the other way.

Upon hearing the dry cough of the client, Elana's demeanor changed on the head of a pin, her unnaturally pearly white teeth hiding her acid tongue. Her grin bordered on sinister.

"Darling, you're here." She greeted him with two pecks on the cheek.

"Hello, Elana, I called before, you said you had a girl for me?"

"Why yes, just hold on a moment." She scurried to the back and returned with Rebecca, who had a smile that was more plastic than Elana's.

"I thought you said she was a blonde," the man said.

"So she not blonde, the other girl got sick! Rebecca, my best girl. Take her or leave her!" Elana hissed.

"Very well, she'll do." He mumbled and extended his arm with a disappointing sigh. She took it after some cajoling from Elana.

The man pulled a white velvet box from his pocket. "A beautiful girl deserves a beautiful gift," he muttered. She tore the shiny bracelet out of the box, letting it fall to the ground as she slipped the bracelet onto her delicate wrist.

"It's beautiful, luv." She kissed his cheek and slipped it onto her delicate wrist.

"It's starfire stone, very rare. It's one of a kind," he grumbled and opened the door. "My name is Cyrus. Get in."

CHAPTER 10

The temple spires stretched out to the sky like the boney fingers of an old man reaching for the heavens. Its charred skeleton contrasted against the red haze of the setting Core City sun. Lilly tip-toed carefully on the cracked marble steps that seemed to quiver under her slight frame. Grace was a gift the gods saw fit to deny her and there was at least a five-foot gap between the door of the temple and the steps, below laid fifteen feet of crumbled granite and jagged metal. Her toes curled around the edge, hesitant to make the jump.

"Don't be afraid. It's not as bad as it looks." Caleb took what look like an effortless hop over the gaping canyon and reached out for an apprehensive Lilly. "It'd be a terrible thing to let such a fine lady fall. May the gods strike me down if I ever did" He smirked and beckoned her again.

Taking a small running jump, her cold bare feet landed close to the edge across the gap. Caleb, true to his word, carefully guided her into the safety of his arms.

Something hard and sharp dug into the sole of her left foot, but she ignored it.

The heavy wooden doors creaked when they opened. It created an echo that made for a rather unsettling welcome as it bellowed through the barren, crumbling walls of the old temple. "And for the faithful, they provide..." he called out into the darkness.

"...And to the righteous the glory of a thousand suns." A voice sounded from the rafters. It was hard for Lilly to tell where it came from exactly.

"Be he Azel, the First? Who does call to me?" the voice sang out again.

"Caleb, Prince of the Gutters, King of a Free Lo Irant. Glory be to me, mother fucker!" Caleb smiled and bowed to the darkness before flashing a series of obscene gestures.

Crack. The sound of the bullet reverberated off of the decaying walls, lodging itself in the floor just inches in-between Caleb and Lilly. Her fingers dug into his shoulder. Embarrassed, she pretended she was just brushing something off of his jacket.

"Fuck! By the father, Grant!" Caleb's jovial tone turned dark on the head of a pin and his accent disappeared completely. "You could have taken my foot off!"

"And it woulda been your pride that angered the gods enough to move the bullet that strike you, cause I always hit my mark." The voice appeared from behind the pillar.

He was about the same age as Caleb and wearing the same drab olive green jacket with a crudely made Iranti flag sewn onto the left shoulder.

His smile softened Caleb's scowl and the two friends embraced. From the shadows emerged the others, kids mostly, not much older than Lilly herself. Four dozen bright blue eyes piercing through dusty faces all happy for Caleb's return. He reached into his large knapsack and dropped bread, cans of food and even some candy into the outstretched palms of his flock. The children squealed and disappeared back into the darkness, except for ten of them. Grant stood with six other boys behind him. "Lilly, I'd like to introduce you to my most trusted disciples. This is Grant and the Six. They are our protectors." Caleb introduced them. Lilly curtsied politely, not knowing what else to do. Grant took her hand and gave it a gentle kiss.

"So ya bring a bloodsucking Vist to our holy place, Caleb?" One of the girls scoffed as she approached Caleb. She was wearing a black and red painted canvas tunic over her clothes, her sandy hair was braided with colorful bits of string and yarn that cascaded down her shoulders. It was an old Riverlands tradition to honor clans and family names. Her lips curled with contempt when he put his hand out to prevent her advancing closer to him.

"Enough, Nev." His said curtly. "Lilly's not a threat. I'll be less surprised to see a damned soul welcome in a holy temple than this one falutin with the Vist. Saved her

I did, from a right particular grimy old bastard over at Camden's."

Lilly waved sheepishly as Caleb introduced her to everyone.

"This is the twins Arial and Nara. Don't be fooled by their slightness, together they once took out the Atura Chemical communications tower. Seen it myself, was quite a sight, two little lambs giving those Empirial rats a good and proper fucking." The twins were about eleven, skinny things, long and spindly, covered up by what seemed like a half dozen sweaters crudely patch worked into oversized shirts. Their large round eyes hidden by unkempt nearly white hair.

"Nara doesn't speak, but if Caleb likes you she will too. It's nice here you'll like it." Ariel gave Lilly an enthusiastic hug, Nara looked to her twin for reassurance before joining her in the embrace.

Nev looked past Lilly letting her hand hover awkwardly alone. "Caleb, that situation from Errold County, it can't wait."

Caleb's smile faded into a grimace. "Right, I'll meet you upstairs in a moment." He turned to Lilly. "I apologize Lil, but my attentions are needed elsewares at the moment. Grant will see to you."

Nev pushed passed Lilly and followed Caleb into the darkness, rambling on about places and names Lilly never had heard of.

"She seems charming. I can see why Caleb likes her so much." Lilly huffed under her breath.

"What Nev? Pay no mind to her," Grant sat down in one of the broken pews, his knife carving into the unbroken flesh of a fresh green apple. "She's been here with Caleb from day one. She does this with all the new ones, even me. She's quite sweet once her claws go back in. Caleb never turns away any of the Core City street children, Iranti ones at least. We don't trust loyalists, colonists or refugees only our own kind."

The slice of apple stuck to the tip of his knife waved in Lilly's face. She hadn't eaten all day and it was a welcome treat.

"So there are more of you? She said, her mouth still stuffed with fruit.

"Lots, we call ourselves The Children of Azel. We recruit those in the undercity to our cause."

"Cause?" Lilly choked on the last piece of apple.

"It's not enough to survive as outcasts. We are told what we can do, where we can live and whom we can address. It's not supposed to be like this. All of this land was our land until the swines took it from us and forced us into castes. The Iranti people need to be free, the gods gave us that right. Caleb wants to free us from tyranny and give the lands and their lives back to the people."

"Caste isn't permanent though. Irantis aren't slaves. You can buy your way out if you want it badly enough."

Her words sounded like they came right out of her grandfather's mouth.

Grant scowled. "Right, we get the privilege to pay Empire run corporations for the right to work in their factories, breaking our backs for the rest of our lives just to cover the interest on a debt that our grandchildren will be paying off. Better not let Caleb catch an ear of that shit. I'm not selling my name and my banners for golden shackles. Open your eyes Lilly, we are all slaves. The Empire decides who is useful and who is garbage. People like us, the garbage, are forced to work in the mines and factories. We get our little shack we rent from the corporation and pay them to slowly work us to death. We get no say, no choice. We're gonna stop it though. Caleb is gonna lead us to a free Lo Irant."

Lilly had never looked at things like that before. Back home, her world had been the plantation. She wondered if the servants and field hands were forced to work and it made her very uncomfortable. She loved her nanny, Maddy. Rick, Todlyn and Morrisy taught her how to ride and shoot. Since as long as she could remember, they had been a part of her family. The thought sent her stomach sour and a wave of truth came pouring on top of her. Not once did she ever concern herself with their lives. She didn't know their family names or even if they had family. Her cheeks flushed with a quiet shame. She fiddled with the blood caked makeshift bandage around her hand unsure what else to say.

"I didn't mean to snap." Grant put his hand on her shoulder. "It's not your fault you grew up a middy in the Southlands. It's how they win, divide us."

Lilly froze. Caleb went off about the middle castes in the rickshaw. He called them traitors among a slew of other vile names. "What makes you think I'm a middy from the Southlands?" she squeaked.

"Honestly, I thought you were Vist when I first laid eyes on ya, but Caleb would have killed you before letting a loyalist come here. You've had proper education. You curtsied when I kissed your hand. A Vistany girl woulda slapped me and if you were from the Northlands you wouldn't know what to make of it. Don't worry. Your secret is safe with me. To leave a life of comfort to live down in this shit hole, musta been sometin outrageous. Nevertheless you're one of us now, a Child of Azel, a castaway. Make no matter who you were before." He winked.

"Where are you from?"

"I was born in the foothills of the Idlevale. My father kept his own lands and his own business, until the Empire came and shut him down. They forced my family into the mining camps. My mother died in the first year from the dust, my sister followed. I ran first chance I got. Did what I had to until I became a soldier in Caleb's grand army."

"You really believe in him. Don't you?"

"Caleb? He's a great leader and believes in the cause. He inspires the people. The noblest of causes ain't shit without a leader to inspire the people to believe in it or something like that." Grant fumbled. "It sounds better when Caleb says it. I just fuck it up. It's why he does the talkin and I do the fightin."

"You've actually fought- in battles?"

"No, not really. Mostly we just do jobs, vandalize Empire equipment, mess with communication lines, pro-quire food-"

"You mean procure?"

"Yeah, pro-cure the food, supplies from wherever we can get them."

"So you steal?"

"It's not stealin when they starvin you to death. Fuck, princess you sound so high and mighty. Like you never lifted anything in your life, spend two weeks out there on your own and your airs will be faded."

"I didn't mean it like that. I mean- it's not.... I'm sorry."

"Look, you seem nice and obviously Caleb sees some-thing in you, but now you know the way things are. You need to be makin a choice and right quickly. We can't risk weak hearts. Tomorrow is the Sabbath, Caleb does his talks then. If you don't see the light after that you never will and it best you leave." He handed her a small hand-bound book, the cover torn off. "I'm turning in for the night. Be careful with this, it's banned throughout the Empire. Some stiff in the Province wrote it, now there is a bounty on his head. They were doing a reading of it at the pub, but the authorities came and arrested nearly everyone in the room. I made it out with this. Caleb isn't fond of any print that's not the Itara. I've got the thing memorized, so it doesn't do no good sitting in my pocket. It will show you the truth, the ones I didn't tell you."

Lilly flipped through the tattered pages.

"Why are you trusting me with this?"

"I have a secret about you, it's only fair you know a secret about me. Plus, if you betray us, I'll just kill you," he called as he walked into the darkness.

Lilly sat alone in the pew as the candles danced to their deaths. A few more children came off the street and made the slender makeshift benches their beds.

The benches were hard. Lilly couldn't think of a substance harder than stone, but these benches must have been comprised of it. Even at Camden's she would have had a mattress and a pillow. The cold was just as unbearable as the hard bench. The balled up the canvas miners coat Caleb had given her that she was using as a pillow provided little comfort. For a moment the floor looked like an attractive alternative. The scurrying shadows of rats quickly eliminated that option. Frustrated, she sat up and listened to the melody of the city noises and the soft breathing of children sleeping.

They're not complaining, she thought. Most of them had soft smiles on their faces. She pleaded softly, praying for the gods to restore her old life, her warm bed, her blue dress, shit-even Regina. She would welcome it all back and be grateful for every down feather in her comforter. *I've learned my lesson. Please, let me come home.* She silently begged.

The stone floor was ice against her bare feet as she made her way closer to the candles at the altar. She pulled the book Grant gave her from her pocket in hopes it would help her fall asleep. Reading was always so boring, but it beat thinking about how cold, hungry and tired she was.

She strained her eyes in the darkness to read.

Chapter One: "Freedom as a Birthright"
Every single Iranti, Kyre and Oprian carries the one bloodline inside of themselves. We were made equals under the Gods who gave us dominion over the lands. No individual or group carries an exclusive right, by birth to hold dominion over his fellow man.

The words captivated her as she read further. Each page opened another window to a world she had never known. When the candles burned too low, she sat by the barrel fire for light. She was sleepy but enchanted. Her eyes burned from the smoke, but she dare not deny her hungry mind from a single morsel.

Dawn chased the stars from the sky as she struggled to finish the last few words and she went to sleep a completely different person than when she'd woken up the morning before. The Southlands faded into a hazy dream and the familiar faces of her past drifted into obscurity.

LO IRANT

"Like the trees bows to the wind, and the earth moves for the plow, you are subject to his will."

–The Itara, Ihlandria Voc, 34:12

CHAPTER 11

It was almost sunset in the town of Roe in Shallow Brook County, Riverlands. Despite the cold, people from all over the county swarmed outside the small brick building to get information as to why the gates to the mines and the chemical plants were closed this morning. Atura Chemical, an Oprian corporation that owned all of the chemical plants and three quarters of the mines in the Province had shut down its entire operation overnight without warning, leaving tens of thousands of Irantis without jobs.

They were waiting for answers. Rumors had spread like wildfire and the mob began to grow restless. So far the row of armed guards positioned in front of the still vacant podium have been enough to stem any violence, but as the sun slowly crept behind the mountains the tensions continued to rise.

Already diminutive Bernard Fint looked even smaller set against the pillars of the town hall as he approached the podium. He was contemplating how he'd gotten himself into this position. As public relations executive, he figured he had landed himself a pretty safe job. Atura Chemical was a well-respected Corporation in Opree. It had been around for almost a century and the operation in the Riverlands of Lo Irant, had been rather successful for over forty years.

He'd gotten the call a week before. The operation would be closing and he was responsible for the PR campaign that would mitigate any negative reactions from the Iranti workers and their families. He thought he had months. He requested a year to set up informational sessions, programs and buyouts. Shutting down the economy of an entire county was a delicate process. If he hadn't stayed late the night before working on the project he would have never noticed the company loading all of the expensive equipment, paperwork and anything else of value not attached to the foundation into trucks. An official from Corporate left him a folder with a few bullet points of information but nothing else.

There were Empire-born colonists, bankers, shop owners, doctors, and entire families left behind with no way of getting back home. They'd been left in a quagmire of anti Imperial sentiment. Fint was given the job of stopping this firestorm from burning the image of the corporation, at the moment, however, he was worried more about the firestorm burning him.

He nervously approached the crowd packed behind the metal and concrete barriers, crying out for answers. There were thousands now gathered in front of hall and hailing from all over the county. The paper with his talking points was already a crumpled up ball in his hands.

"I know everyone has their concerns and trust me, Atura Chemical has not forgotten you." With his hand shaking uncontrollably, he took a sip of water in an attempt to calm his nerves, barely managing to avoid spilling water all over himself. Thousands of faces were staring at him, their fate dangling in his unspoken words. Fint had never felt so powerless. He had nothing against Lo Irant. His cousin had married an Iranti-born and she was lovely. In the crowd he saw fathers, just as worried for their families as Fint was for his own. In the eyes of the corporation however, they were commodities, assets that needed to be liquidated. In the eyes of the crowd, he was no longer Bernard Fint, mild-mannered family man who enjoyed collecting stamps and fine wines but Atura Chemical, destroying their lives.

"While Lo Irant has been the home of their chemical and mining operations for over forty years, operations at this plant, as well as the five other plants and seven mines owned by Atura, have been hereby suspended indefinitely." He paused to allow for the reaction of the crowd to subside, but it didn't.

"Also..." the crowd was still too loud to speak over. "Also, all company-owned land, property and ventures are to be liquidated. There will be a five-day grace period and the office of relocation services will be able to help those having difficult time finding residences."

There was a roar from the crowd after they heard that not only did they just lose their jobs, they were also being evicted from their homes. The company had owned the majority of the land in the county, most of the workers' houses were company housing. Fint stood in horror as civility was torn from the crowd.

"Now, if we can just stay calm." He protested into the microphone, his voice drowned out by their rage.

A bottle crashed against the wall beside his head. Bodies shoved against the barriers to the point where either the barriers or the people were going to break. The frenzied mob wanted blood, Atura's blood, Fint's blood. He crouched behind the podium, wiping his brow with his handkerchief. It was all he could think to do. The training film had no procedure for this. Yanked up from his belt, he was dragged by a pair of Atura's armed guards through the crowd. They made their way to a waiting transport. He could feel the mass of people coming down on them, squished against the guard's bulletproof vest.

It was quite a few minutes before they reached the air transport waiting a few blocks away, but Fint swore he didn't breathe until they were in the air. On that clear winter night, he could see the fires already raging from the riots as they flew overhead. He prayed to his gods for the Empire-born colonists on the ground, for there were no air transports coming for them.

CHAPTER 12

Dear Governor,

Our families have been in Shallow Brook County for seventeen generations. It was our land before it was confiscated and made into an environmental preserve forty years ago. We were then forced to rent it back from the Atura Chemical Corporation when they took over the mines and built their plants. Two days ago, the plants and the mines were shut down and without warning thirty-seven thousand of us lost our livelihoods. We were told we had five days to vacate our homes.

Most have complied with the order of eviction; however, those of us who remain are challenging the original sale of property stolen from us by the state. We are the families who have no homes to go to, families with small children, elderly Irantis who have dedicated their lives to their communities, veterans with decades of honorable service cast out into the wilderness. These towns that make up Shallow Brook County belong to the people who have invested their lives and the lives of their children, not a foreign entity that saw opportunity for a profit.

We respectfully ask for a stay of the eviction from our homes until we can be granted due process and our case heard before a judge. The Iranti people should never be second-class citizens in their own land.

For Father, for Family, for Flag,

Sincerely,

The People of Shallow Brook County

A dense fog hung on the grass and although there was a chill in the air, it was nothing a heavy sweater or scarf couldn't keep out. Normally it would have been a beautiful fall day in the small town of Roe, but the silent tension and anticipation overpowered the serenity of nature that morning.

The heavy armored vehicles rolled over the Shallow Brook County lines just before dawn. Roe was the last holdout of former Atura Chemical employees. Their time had run out and it looked as though there would be no government intervention.

A few hundred men, women and children had gathered at the town's center. All were members of the under castes. The Empire-born colonists had fled in the riots. Over the last few days the rioting had calmed and turned from chaos into a unified defiance. Though armed, they were far from an army. The holdouts comprised mostly of laid-off miners and plant workers, husbands, wives, mothers, fathers, school children, even the local priest. After three days of riots, the last thing the people of Roe wanted was any more trouble, but they were not going to let foreign invaders take their land, land granted to their ancestors by the harvest gods.

Twenty-three year old Evelyn Jacoby was drumming a patriotic beat with her fingers on the butt of her rifle, whistling through the gap where her front tooth used to be, waiting for the inevitable confrontation. She was sure the suspense was worse than the standoff was going to be. The young mother of four small children was tired but resolved. She didn't work three jobs so her children could be raised in the slums of Core City, living out of those shelters converted from shipping containers the government had offered them. The Empire wished to take the four-bedroom house her father had built and in return they would give her a windowless metal box in between a landfill and a chemical plant. For this, of course, she was supposed to be ever thankful to them.

The transports appeared over the horizon escorted by a small army. They resembled Empire troops, however, they were a part of Atura Chemical Corporation's Security Division. It wasn't unusual for an Empire-run corporation like Atura to have their own private military when dealing with the colonies, especially since the Senate had ruled that it was perfectly legal.

"They are armed sir, but they are outnumbered almost five to one. This shouldn't take long. They just sent someone out to speak with us." Lieutenant Calis called into corporate headquarters.

"Original orders stand, Lieutenant," said the voice over the radio.

"But sir, I'm sure if we just..." Lieutenant Calis protested.

"Original orders stand, Lieutenant. Did I make myself clear?" the voice repeated.

"Crystal sir, we will proceed with original orders." He replied dryly.

He didn't know why he was in this shit box or why the company would care so much, all he did know was that this under caste mob of peasants were the only thing standing between him and a nice four-day vacation with the wife and kids. He didn't want to this to drag on all morning.

Twelve minutes into the standoff, neither side had yet to make a move. The residents were used to Atura flexing its muscles, but usually this pageantry was followed by arbitration. Union representative, Brandon Malkner, had helped keep his people calm. In his hand was the list of demands he helped draft the night before. Malkner walked down to hand it to Atura's eviction enforcers. He was used to the procedure.

There was a strike several years ago that had lasted for months and ended without any serious violence. Atura was his family. They gave him his first house and helped with the funeral costs after his daughter died from well plague. All his life they had been willing to work with him. Once he showed a little bit of strength to show he wasn't going to cave, he was certain they would come to a peaceful solution.

Gesturing to Atura's army that he was unarmed, Malkner stood just paces from their guns. Confident, He waited for several tense minutes for them to send out a representative. The silence and Malkner's faith in Atura was broken by the roar of the transports starting up. Malkner waved the list of demands at them.

"I'm unarmed. Stop! There are women and children here." He looked back at the crowed of his neighbors, family and friends.

Only some of the holdouts scattered when the transports rolled over Malkner's bullet ridden body, most stood their ground, firing back at their attackers. The chaos lasted only a few minutes and left three hundred seven people dead, all but six of them Shallow Brook residents, men, women and children.

Lieutenant Calis hopped out of the transport and surveyed the damage; six dead, nine wounded, an acceptable loss. The medical units were already treating his men.

"Get a team on those bodies. I want them dumped in the mine and on fire before noon," he barked.

The Lieutenant lit a cigarette and leaned against the doors of one of the transports. His eyes focused on a commotion in the distance.

"Help! Help me please!" The shrill cries of a woman broke through the morning air.

Evelyn Jacoby was running up from behind one of the buildings, carrying a small child in her arms.

"My little girl, Nora, she's shot, please help her." The woman begged.

The child had been hit in the stomach. She was conscious but in shock.

"Please sir, she is only seven. Save my little girl," Evelyn pleaded again.

Lieutenant Calis looked at her with pity, this hysterical woman, begging him for mercy for the life of her child. He took a calm breath and gave the woman a reassuring smile, and then he pulled his service pistol from its holster and put two rounds into the little girl, never breaking his gaze with the crystal blue eyes of the horrified mother. He waited a beat to take another drag off of his cigarette and then fired his weapon into the skull of the mother three times.

Walking over to the transport, he radioed into corporate.

"This is Lieutenant Calis. Objective complete."

NATHANIAL

"And your blood ties you to your brother. Honor him above your banners, for that is our way."

- The Verinat, Proverbs

CHAPTER 13

It was late when Nathanial and the Princes Malcolm, Elliot and Arryn returned to the palace from a game of Marrotat, a popular horseback sport among High Borns. The four young men came in dirty and worn. Nathanial hobbled across the grand marble floor towards the grand staircase, sore from the game. It had been weeks since the Arbinger, but his leg was acting up after Elliot took a cheap shot at him on the field.

"If you would just rest it, it would heal," Arryn scolded, dropping his soiled helmet into the hands of Gerald the footman, who struggled to hold it among the rest of Arryn's gear.

"It's healed." Nathanial grumbled. "If Elliot hadn't struck me with the mallet, I'd be fine." He carefully folded his pads and gloves, handing them to the new footman, whose name escaped him.

"Don't be ridiculous Nate, I barely grazed you. To think you'd learn to ride better by now." Elliot picked the dirt out of his nails while his valet removed his pads and helmet.

The mid-winter holidays were winding down in the Royal Palace at Ivory Castle, an ancient city that was once the jewel of Opree. The High Born Caste, the Oprian aristocracy, had been out of power for almost three hundred years. The twelve families who used to rule over the twelve great kingdoms were in shambles, many having squandered their once great wealth while others had adapted, merging their estates with the new money of the powerful Vistany Caste, who controlled the government and the economy, owning majority of the empire's corporations.

The beautiful white marble city carved into the Pirachni Cliffs looked frozen in time, save for the transports lining the streets and the modern fashions of the wealthy citizens who lived there.

Nathanial had spent every break and holiday at the Palace since he'd met Arryn, during his first year at Penderghast. The King greatly respected Nathanial's father. It didn't take long before the majority of the royal family adopted Nathanial as one of their own. The prospect ruffled many feathers in the High Born Court. Even though Nathanial was from a prominent family who bought their way into the Vistany caste over two centuries ago, he was not Empire-born and was always going to be an outsider; his money would never to be able to change that.

"Arryn, when are you leaving for Penderghast tomorrow?" Malcolm inquired.

"We're taking the rails just after breakfast. Why?"

"The rails?" Elliot interjected. "Not you too Arryn, I don't know why this family is so insistent on acting like commoners. Why not just have father arrange for a private air transport? It's so much easier. I'm sick of living like a peasant because father believes we should appear more accessible to the people."

"I know, our life is just so terribly pedestrian," Malcolm shot back rolling his eyes. "Anyway Arryn, I was wondering if you wanted to push it back to come to a Senate hearing with me. They're discussing a possible vote on mandatory well plague vaccinations for Lo Irant. It should be pretty interesting."

"Yes, a very interesting prospect. What a shame it would be to miss it, but I think I'd rather have my teeth drilled out by Larnder Monks."

"Arryn, you should start attending hearings." Malcolm frowned. "Although we don't make the laws, it's important for us to be knowledgeable about what's going on in the civilian side of the Empire."

"Not my arena, thank you. I'll let you and Elliot deal with the affairs of state when father is gone. Politics is not a particularly good color on me. It is boring and I am exciting and therefore ill-suited for it," Arryn retorted.

"It's time you grow up, Arryn," Malcolm scolded. "You're third in line to the throne. You should at least be prepared if..."

"If Kyre concubines begin washing the temple walls? Maybe if the plague hits? Malcolm, I have no illusions to what I am, the third born son of an impotent King. I am superfluous and exceedingly happy to be so. Besides, the crown already lost to the rebellion. THREE HUNDRED YEARS AGO! In my opinion, we High Borns need to get over that fact and move on. Who would even want that job? There are too many headaches and not enough perks."

"You're right. There is more of a chance of Nathanial being king than you." Malcolm nudged Nate so hard, he almost choked on his own tongue. "The sad part it I'm only half joking. Lo Irant is getting restless. The situation is bad."

"I read about Roe, but that was Atura's fault not the Empire's. Surely they know justice will come. We don't support murderers." Nathanial had worried the incident would further strain relationship with Lo Irant. He couldn't help but notice how tensions rose around him whenever there were problems in the tumultuous colony and that irked him. He never once set foot on Iranti soil, could never remember a time where he ate a traditional

Iranti meal nor did he associate with any other Iranti-borns, save for religious services that, because of the insistence of the Queen, he attended regularly since he was a boy. It wasn't that he was ashamed of his heritage, he just felt his loyalty was to the Empire first and foremost and was uncomfortable when being both Iranti-born and loyal to the Empire were deemed somehow mutually exclusive of one another.

"It's not just Roe, Nathanial. Irantis want a voice. They want citizenship. There are still parts of Lo Irant that are bad off. It's important we keep communications open and let them know we want to help." Malcolm continued the discussion as they entered the large sitting room. Like his father, Malcolm was a diplomat. He worked closely with the Senate, the corporations and various Iranti groups to try to keep tensions low. He championed causes like educational programs, food and medical aid, as well as pushing for an ease of tech restrictions. His latest cause was developing a vaccine for well plague, a water and food borne illness that claimed hundreds of thousands of lives every year. He had his father make a rather large grant to the Venolin Pharmaceutical Corporation to raise awareness for the disease and he was thrilled that there was progress being made.

"That's a fairytale, Malcolm. The Irantis don't want help, they want independence. They know the Senate won't grant them citizenship. The Irantis think they can have us over a barrel once they control the resources. It comes down to simple economics." Said Elliot, thumbing through the paper.

"So why not give them citizenship? It seems fair enough. Call their bluff and end of issue. It's taking months for the Senate to deal with this? And they say a government by the people is better. If I were king, a real king, with the power we once had, I'd have all of the Empire's problems solved in a day." Arryn proclaimed quite smitten with himself.

"Not so fast, your highness." Elliot retorted with his face still buried in the paper. "Think of the burden that puts the state under now we have an extra, let's say, three hundred million citizens. The coffers are tapped as it is. Plus we give them seats in the Senate, diluting the power of the voices of those born in Opree. There is a balance that needs to be maintained."

"That's a little extreme Elliot, but you see Arryn, he has a point. There is more to it than just making decisions. We as the royal family have a much more difficult position. We are still the face of the Empire and need to keep relations strong, especially when the Senate acts against the common good. Ivory Castle isn't even safe. We need to assess threats like the Lo Irant situation every day." Malcolm was always the voice of reason and balance, reminding Arryn a lot of their father.

"Well, if Lo Irant succeed at infiltrating Ivory Castle, it won't be too difficult to point out the traitor." Arryn chided pointing at Nathanial.

Nathanial stood paralyzed in the awkward silence. The three brothers stared at him, waiting for his reaction. For a moment they had lost all familiarity, three pairs of slate gray eyes peering out of porcelain skin, void of any imperfection. For the second time since he became friends with Arryn, he felt unwelcomed at the palace.

"He has a point, Malcolm." Elliot said, folding the paper over so just his eyes were showing. "Maybe it's harsh, but it needed to be said. Nathanial is Iranti-born. It's wise for Arryn to get used to questioning everyone. I'm not saying Nathanial would betray the crown or the Empire, but gods and blood hold thicker bonds than friendship." His eyes went back to his paper.

The sudden chill in the room became too much for Nathanial to bear and he quietly stormed out of the room.

Arryn threw his arms up into the air, "Well this is just great! What's wrong with you Elliot? Nathanial would die before betraying me!" he shouted. "He would die before betraying any of you either. He loves this empire and we are the only family he knows."

Malcolm put a calm hand on Arryn's shoulder. "I know. I look to Nate like a brother too, so does Elliot. If anything Nathanial is loyal to a fault. That's why he is father's first choice for Captain of the Ivory Guard." Malcolm couldn't catch the secret as he let it carelessly slip out of his mouth.

Arryn looked down at his feet and let Malcolm's words sink in. "Father wants Nathanial to be Captain of the Ivory Guard?" It wasn't much of a secret that he and his father rarely saw eye to eye, but the notion that the King would pass him over entirely was a thought that never once crossed his mind.

"Don't seem so surprised. For years you complained about being 'forced' into service to the crown. Father assumed it would be for the best." Malcolm began to regret ever mentioning the subject. He should have known Arryn was going to react poorly to the news. It was it was typical for his youngest brother to be completely oblivious to anything, until someone told him he couldn't have it. Arryn was accustomed to getting whatever he wanted, mostly because he would burn down the heavens to get it and giving in to him was significantly less painful than arguing with him. Malcolm was certain this wouldn't be the last time the subject would be brought up.

"We figured you would be better suited for brothel inspector." Elliot muttered.

"Don't tell Nathanial yet. I don't believe father has told him anything," Malcolm added, working hard at damage control.

"I hate to disappoint you, but Nate would never accept. He is going to be my second in command. That's the way it has always been and that's the way it will always be." He excused himself and sauntered out of the room.

CHAPTER 14

The nervous four-year-old cautiously peaked around the corner of the old house following the sounds of his older brothers' laughter. They were hiding from him again.

"Devon, Gregory? You're not 'upposed to be down here." He whispered down the hall, hoping he was loud enough for his brothers to hear, but not loud enough to whatever lived back there or alert his parents that they were playing in a forbidden part of the house.

Faint whispers and giggles drifted through the stale silence and the hairs stood up on back of the boy's neck.

The hallways of the old servants' quarters were dark and winding and had always frightened him. Mr. Fielding, the butler, kept a room in the main part of the house and Mrs. Potterfield had lived out since she remarried so the small rooms in the large townhouse were mainly used for storage. The warm orange light of a late winter's afternoon poured through the dirty window, casting its dusty glow over the piles of covered furniture in one of the rooms. He dragged his fingers across the white sheets as he peaked over the boxes looking for his siblings.

It's just boxes and sheets, he thought, the fear slowly simmering inside of him. The house was eerily silent aside from the occasional giggle and boom, although they both seemed equally far away. He was alone. Frozen with fear, the monsters in his mind crawled about. He was unsure if screaming would bring his mother, or draw unwanted attention from anything else that could've been lurking in the dark.

"Gregory, hurry up, come over here!" He heard the tiny patter of footsteps and his brother, Devon, whispering from down the hall.

The boy turned around just in time to see ten-year-old Devon turn down the corridor after eight-year-old Gregory.

"Wait for me!" He chased after his older brothers, trying to follow their whispers and laughter but the house fell silent again.

The wooden door, painted over one too many times, had a decorative glass pane. It was his mother's painting room. Before baby Grace was born, she would take him down there while she painted beautiful pictures. Devon and Gregory weren't allowed in the painting room, just him and it made him feel special.

Another boom, this one a little louder, shook the house just enough to rattle the glass jars on the shelf. He was pleasantly surprised to see his mother in the room, sitting at her easel, brush in hand. After Grace was born, she was all his mother seemed to care about. "All she does is poop and cry, and they think she's so great," he thought, stewing in his jealousy.

He leaned up against the doorframe watching his mother sing to herself while she painted. In his mind there was nobody as pretty as his mother. She had straw-colored hair and skin that was the color of milk, just like the pictures of the princesses in his storybooks. She was kind and funny, and her nose crinkled when she laughed.

She didn't break song or stroke when she allowed her youngest son to crawl into her lap. He snuggled up to her, hypnotized by the rhythm of her breathing and brush strokes and the melody of her song. Even the commotion from the outside storm seemed to follow to the beat of the tune. He listened to the symphony, fabric of her soft silk dress twisted in his tiny fingers, as he drifted to sleep. His last thought was how she smelled of flowers and fruit pies.

A bright white flash and a loud bang that blew out the windows interrupted the child's peace. The room was dark and empty, no sign of his mother anywhere. Panicked, he climbed over the debris caused by the explosion, protecting his ears from the noise of the sirens.

In the darkness two glowing orange eyes of the creature that lurked there peered down at him.

Nathanial opened his eyes to darkness and rolled over onto his back, letting the strange black shadows form into the familiar shapes that made up his bedroom at the palace. He couldn't remember his bedroom at his family's house, not in detail. It was blue, he thought, maybe? He did remember his room at the orphanage, oddly enough. Despite being there for only six months, he could never forget the yellow walls and the rows of bunk beds.

The nightmares generally didn't bother him. It was his memories that kept him awake. On the edge of the bed, holding his face in his hands, he waited for this one to wash over him. It seemed like they were from someone else's life. He could remember his mother's voice singing softly, but it felt unfamiliar. After the Navat attacked New Empire, there was hardly a family who didn't lose someone. The wealthiest districts caught it the worst. Families as old as the first father completely wiped out. It was a reality for everyone, a black streak across the past so devastating, the world needed to begin again. Time had always divided, before and after the wars. The time behind the wars was better left erased in Nathanial's mind. That small child, the third son of General Alexi Harker, was dead. Nathanial's life began after he took those first steps away from the orphanage, holding hands with a distant uncle who dropped him off at Penderghast that very day.

The mattress was soft enough, and he was tired, but Nathanial couldn't find a comfortable position. If he closed his eyes, the screams inside his head would only start again. Punching the pillows didn't make them any easier to sleep on. He just couldn't think of anything else to do and it felt good.

Finished, Nathanial flung himself back down onto the bed. The hot tears built up in his eyes. He bit down on his lower lip taking several slow deep breaths until the feeling went away.

The silence in the room was suffocating and the echoes of the nightmares just lingered over the headboard. Although his body craved sleep, his mind needed the walk.

CHAPTER 15

It was well past midnight, but after the argument he'd had with his wife, King Jonathan couldn't sleep. He was accustomed to roaming the palace at all hours of the night. He did his best thinking at night.

After fifteen years it still felt like he was merely a caretaker for the throne. The High Born aristocracy was already dying before the Navat attacked Ivory Castle; five of the twelve families were wiped out almost entirely. For a time Jonathan felt that the title should have died with the last family to hold it. Thirty-three people were murdered, whole families, before Jonathan was offered the throne. He refused it at first. What honor would that crown have brought? What right that came out of so much death and destruction could ever possibly be considered Divine? Andrea spoke of him as a great unifier, who brought back the pride and spirit of the High Borns and Oprians alike. Appearances had power, according to Andrea, even hollow thrones and empty gestures could move the hearts of a broken people desperate to cling to something. She was right. She was always right. Still, it frustrated him that he couldn't do more. There was a time when hosting parties and fundraisers were all they could do to lift spirits during the wars, but the wars were over and a new one was on the horizon. He always wanted to do more with his position, although he was beginning to realize that his crown might as well been made of paper. It was just a pageant, a bright candle that flickered during dark times. It wouldn't illuminate an entire people or cast light on the corruption of the Senate. He was merely the ceremonial head of a body that was rapidly decaying.

The south veranda overlooked the gardens, the fountains made it a favorite spot for the King to think or just relax. He was surprised to see Nathanial there so late in the night, sitting by the fountain, with a heavy scowl, poking at the water with a stick. The King thought Nathanial always had a sadness about him, a troubled gaze that inevitably found him in times of quiet. Even now that he was a grown man, that expression saddened Jonathan the same way it did when Nate was a young boy.

"When you wear your troubles on your face, you will never be able to escape them." Jonathan interrupted Nathanial's pondering with the old proverb. It was something his wife would say to him from time to time and the only thing the sleepy King could think to say.

Nathanial was startled and he fumbled a courteous bow. "Sorry. I-I didn't think anyone was up. I-I'll leave you to your peace."

"Nonsense my boy, you're just the person I want to speak to." Jonathan let out a grunt as he sat down beside Nathanial. "What troubles you enough to keep you up this late?"

"Nothing really, I was just thinking."

"And terrorizing my fish," Jonathan pointed to the stick still in Nathanial's hands.

"Sorry, I wasn't poking at them." Nathanial resembled a child with his hand stuck in the cookie jar. "I-I didn't even realize..."

"It's okay Nathanial," the king gave out a gentle quiet laugh.

"You had something to speak to me about, my lord?"

"Yes," Jonathan coughed and took a serious tone. "You'll be graduating this year and I was wondering if you had put any thought on where you intend to go after."

"Well, I guess I just planned to serve under Arryn in the Ivory Guard." Nathanial scratched the back of his head. In honesty, he hadn't given it much thought. Penderghast had been his home, his life for so long and he didn't want to think about having to leave.

"Nate, you are the top of your class, a son of a General with the makings of a great soldier. Do you honestly think you could be happy serving as second in command at Ivory Castle?"

Nathanial bit the inside of his cheek hard. He couldn't believe what he was hearing. Did the king want him gone? When he thought about it, however, it did make sense. Having an Iranti-born living like a prince in the Ivory Palace never lost its controversy. He wasn't one of them, as much as the Royal family treated him like their own. Still, after Penderghast, this was home and the prospect of losing both made him uneasy.

"Probably not," Nathanial muttered. "I guess, I just don't know anything else, but I understand if you think I'm best suited elsewhere. You and the Queen have been more than generous to me."

"That's not what I meant. You always have a place here with us, if you want of course. Although I hope you stay. What will the over-stuffed bags of piss and hot air at court have to talk about if you leave?" The King laughed again.

Nathanial was less amused. He was proud to be Iranti-born, yet he was tired of it being a constant topic of conversation.

"What I meant is that the High Borns have nothing better to do than try to salvage outdated tradition and spend money they no longer have. I have always pegged you as someone who was above that. Although, selfishly I hope you wouldn't sense your own potential greatness and come on as the Captain of the Ivory Guard."

"Wait?" Nathanial choked. "I'm sorry my Lord, but did you just ask me to be Captain of the Ivory Guard?"

"I did. So, what do you say?"

"But, what about Arryn?"

"It's become clear to me that Arryn has little interest in anything beyond Arryn. He has unlimited potential as a leader, but it's all still a game to him. I want to bring respect back to the crown. We can still be a leader of the people, but we need to gain our legitimacy back and I thought I would never say this but, having an Iranti-born serve as the captain of the Ivory Guard would bring less scandal than Arryn would."

While the king spoke the truth, he knew well and good that his decision to bring Nathanial on was to ease tensions with the half a billion Iranti-borns living in the Empire. It killed his wife that Jonathan wanted to pass over Arryn but the decision was best for the Empire.

"You underestimate him," Nathanial protested. "Arryn is a phenomenal leader, my biggest competition. I wouldn't feel right taking this away from him."

The King put his hand on Nathanial's shoulder. "It was never Arryn's position to begin with. Yes, it's tradition if the king has a third son, for him to serve as Captain, but it's my decision to make and I choose you. Your fierce loyalty to him only proves why my choice is correct. You too often allow yourself to sit in his shadow Nathanial.

You must have the confidence to be your own man. I love my son, but it is you who will be great."

Nathanial shifted uncomfortably on the bench. "I am grateful for this opportunity, but I need to think about this."

"Of course, my boy." The king grunted as he stood up and smiled. "I'll leave you to your fish terrorizing. I'm going to bed."

CHAPTER 16

It was sunrise in the Ivory Palace. Nate opened a sleepy eye at the approaching day and cursed it. He only got to sleep what felt like a few short minutes and he had a long rail ride ahead of him. He peeled his head from the pillow and planted his feet on the cold floor. The light bleeding out from behind the curtains was a hazy gray and he could hear the gentle beating of the rain on the window.

An empty suitcase sitting in the corner reminded him that he had neglected to pack. He buried his face in his hands for a moment, hoping the task would go away if he ignored it, but when he looked over, it was still there. He could easily do what the princes did and call for a servant to pack, but they never did it right and he would just end up having to redo it anyway. He grumbled and plodded his way to the small altar in the southwest corner of his room.

Despite being raised among Oprian High Borns, Nathanial was encouraged to keep the gods of his ancestors. The Oprians believed that the gods were gone, never to return and that man honors their gods through expansion, innovation and human achievement. Iranti's believed the gods would return again; that they should keep the world as it was and their lives should be one of devotion to them over worldly or personal pursuits. Although Nathanial believed that one day the gods would one day return, he was like most Iranti-borns in Opree and didn't take the scripture literally. As a child, Nathanial would have preferred to passively worship the sky gods like everyone else he knew. Instead, Queen Andrea ensured he received strict religious instruction by an Iranti priest. As a young man, Nathanial appreciated the connection to his ancestors that his gods gave him. There was something about the stories that he loved too, tales of sacrifice and battle. The gods were nobler than men and when he was younger he would often imagine what it must have been like when the gods still walked alongside man.

Kneeling, he lit the candles one by one reciting his morning incantations. The small wooden altar draped in deep red velvet was adorned with bits of grain, idols of the gods and various trinkets symbolizing prayers and offerings to the harvest gods. Usually he just rushed through morning prayers. It was supposed to be an hour of quiet reflection, thanking the gods for what he was given and asking them for guidance. Most days he used it as an extra hour for training, studying or tidying up. This morning was different. He needed the counsel of the gods. A hologram of his family hovered over the altar, he tried to remember them as they were in the flesh, not as images projected in a ghostly blue light, but it was difficult.

Studying the image of his father, clean-shaven, stiff in a crisp Oprian military uniform, Nathanial wondered how he felt being an Iranti-born serving as General. For many Iranti-borns living in Opree, it was a challenge to shed the stigma of being foreign born and therefore distrustful. With the unrest in Lo Irant, Nathanial felt that everyone looked at him with a little more scrutiny. Could he really be taken seriously as leader of the Ivory Guard? Should he accept command under Arryn, throwing away his potential as a military leader? Should he leave the only family he had to venture out on his own? How could he prove himself loyal by betraying his best friend? The questions kept coming, however, the gods seemed content to deny him any answers.

He left the candles burning at the altar, his mind more clouded than when he started. The suitcase sitting in the corner seemed to stare at him, its emptiness menacing him with the threat of a simple task that for some reason he could just not bear. He avoided looking at it as he got dressed to train. He preferred training at this time of morning, when the castle was still quiet and the air cool. He stepped out onto his balcony. The rain had made everything soggy and gray. His hands wrapped around the ornate iron railing as he scoped the grounds two stories below. His eyes focused on a large patch of moss just next to the stone walkway directly below him. He calculated the distance in his head and wondered how far he'd have to launch himself to clear the walk way. He leaned on his injured leg. The pain was bearable, nothing he couldn't overcome. Without another thought he stepped back and got himself a running start before vaulting off the railing. He landed with a soft thud on the wet moss. Still on the ground he smiled as the adrenaline surged through him, fat drops of rain falling on his face. He knew he could do it.

The gardener who was already busy at work caught the stunt and shook his head. *At least he didn't land in the rose bushes this time*, he thought and continued his day.

It was almost time for breakfast. Nathanial was packing up the last of his things when Arryn came in the door and plopped himself on the bed, messing up the neat pile of clothes Nate had just folded.

"Guess what I just found out?" Arryn said with a grin, poking around on his pocket com.

"What?" Nathanial asked curtly, annoyed that his clothes were getting wrinkled and dirty under Arryn's boots. He was still upset about Arryn's remark the night before, right now though, that bothered him less than Arryn's dirty boots.

"You have to guess," Arryn insisted.

"Just tell me, Arryn."

"Nope. You have to guess at least once. Dammit, Nathanial, why do you always have to be such a tiresome bore?"

Arryn rifled through Nathanial's suitcase. Everything neatly folded in its little space. It always confused him how Nathanial could be so obsessive about the care of his belongings, but so reckless when it came to personal safety. Arryn was convinced Nate would be happy to fight a pack of ravenous razor wolves barehanded, but would rather face torture than wear mismatched socks.

Nathanial pulled the suitcase away. Arryn was not about to stop until he played this stupid game.

"Fine, you found out the mystery woman whom your father plans to be your betrothed. It's Duchess Vargas of Gailenai. You two will be wed by the sea in the Fall and there will be two cakes, lest she eats one before the ceremony," Nathanial said curtly, unpacking and refolding the clothes Arryn had messed up.

"Duchess Helga Vargas? That bridge troll? Nathanial, don't even joke about such terrible things. No, still no word on my mystery bride, but I received the announcement for the Generals of war games next week." Arryn waved his pocket com in Nate's face.

"What big news!" Nathanial said sarcastically. "It's you and Donovon. You shall play for Silver and he for Blue. We will take him and his men with the Kirland strategy as we have for the past three years. You interrupt me for this?"

"It's not me and Donovon this year."

"Not you and Donovon?" Nathanial was surprised. "I can see Donovon, he is an idiot, but Arryn, you're top of the class. I can't believe they wouldn't pick you."

"They did. I am a general this year." He dangled the announcement on his pocket com in Nate's face.

"Well, who is replacing Donovon?" Nathanial tried unsuccessfully to grab the pocket com from Arryn.

"They replaced him with you!" Arryn sat down and put his feet up on Nathanial's bed again. "They made you Blue general. Why didn't you tell me you submitted?"

"Because if I wasn't selected, I'd never hear the end of it from you," Nate said, pushing Arryn's boot away.

Arryn looked disappointed. This was their last year at Penderghast and he was looking forward to handing Donovon his own shirt to eat after they took the title in the war games again.

"I wish you would have told me. I wouldn't have discussed strategy with you for the last month. You know all my secret strategies."

"Because I developed them," Nathanial scowled. "I think I'd make a decent general, figured I give it a try."

"You'd make an excellent general Nate, that's not the point. We just work so much better as a team." Arryn sulked. If he went up against Nathanial, there was a chance, however slim, that he might lose the war games. Something that had not happened in the three years he had been general. "What has gotten into you lately? You've always had a taste for trouble making, but you never had a problem with serving under me before."

"Well, maybe for once I don't wish to be second in command! Despite what you may think, Arryn, the universe does NOT revolve around you— and for the god's sakes get your damned boots off of my things!" Nathanial snapped as he removed a shirt from under Arryn's foot and wiped the bits of dirt off it.

"Sorry, I'll buy you a new one. No need for tempers, now. We will discuss the issue later at Madame Q's. There is a delicious little bunny named Cassandra I've been meaning to visit and luck would have it she has a twin sister with a thing for blondes. I was going to surprise you..."

"Are you trying to buy me off with whores?"

"It's an offering of peace, no need to be crass about it and besides, I've covered your debts with Madam Q on multiple occasions so don't act too indignant. It's stupid to be at odds with one another. It's better we work together and crush Donovon, like we always have. Why mess with success? You don't want to suffer the embarrassment of going up against the man who holds the record of war games won as a General. You need me. I'm the best."

"Right, the best," Nathanial rolled his eyes. "That's why your father asked me to be Captain of the Ivory Guard instead of his own son!" The words flew out of his mouth faster than he could catch himself.

Arryn said nothing, just cringed.

"I was wondering whether or not I should accept, but I'm beginning to feel that *YOUR* family would be safer with me protecting them than to have a spoiled selfish nitwit in charge! Yes you are the best, but only because you've had me to stand on. Well, not anymore." He practically threw his suitcase at the young servant standing in uncomfortable silence just outside the door.

"Make sure these get down to the station in time for the next rail transport out."

The stunned young man, nodded. "Yes sir, but the breakfast is out and the King is wondering if you would be joining them."

"I apologize, Robert, is it?" Nathanial calmed himself. "Let His Grace know I'm sorry, but I will be unable to join them for breakfast. I just have no appetite this morning and I prefer to take the early rail out." He glared spitefully at Arryn, who just stood there mouth gaping open like a fish gasping for breath in the open air.

LILLY

"Follow not these false prophets who bare false witness against me. We are all children of the harvest gods who will one day return triumphantly. It is our faith that will bring them home and a new peace will fall over our people."

The Itara, The Gospel of Azel, 21:16

CHAPTER 17

The streets of Londallin reminded Lilly of a carnival. They were decorated with banners honoring the Provinces, the clans and Lo Irant. The last of the victims of Roe were buried, and the somber remembrance of the tragedy had melted into the celebration of all things Lo Irant. Lilly and Grant had perched themselves on the roof of a gutted warehouse to get a better look of the festivities. Nev, Arial and Nara watched as Samrael and the rest of the six made a game of kicking a can across the rundown tar roof while they waited for Caleb to be done with his mid-afternoon prayers.

"It's like everyone in the Riverlands is here." Nev turned her attention to the crowd.

"A strike was brewin since before Roe, but the corporations decided to call it a holiday, a day of mourning, to save face," Samrael said as he punted the can over the roofs edge ending their game.

Grant sat at the far side of the building, his legs dangling over the edge. He watched with hesitation as the crowd grew into the thousands. "I didn't expect the Empire's cameras would be here. The whole world is really watching! Roe was a wakeup call." He nudged Lilly, who took a spot next to him on the ledge.

Lilly spotted an older middy walking around with Scarlet and Gold armbands. She was concerned at first. The majority of the crowd was the under castes, but the traditional hatred between the castes was absent. Everyone felt bound together. For the first time there was a sense of unity between Irantis. She was glad to be there for it.

Grant read from a separatist newspaper. "The usually modernist middle castes felt a freedom to express their love for their homeland without worry of being 'unfashionable.' In the two weeks since Roe, many university students have shocked their loyalist parents with everything from wearing traditional dress or hairstyles, speaking in forbidden dialects to reverting back to clan names, offered up to the Empire in exchange for their status. Loyalist Governors tried desperately to reign in the retaliation against the Empire, but their efforts of stifling the demonstrations have failed miserably."

Even though Grant was glad to see attention paid to the movement, something was just not right about this rally. Until two days ago, no whispers, no home press fliers, nothing was being said about this. Now, it was on the lips of everyone in the Riverlands and probably Lo Irant.

Most of the Resistance was steering clear, and though Grant begged Caleb not to speak, he just kept repeating that it was his "divine mission."

He fumbled in his pocket for his grandfather's watch. Caleb was late. Muttering curses under his breath for allowing the stubborn prophet to do his prayers alone, he crushed his hand around the watch, letting it dig into his palm a bit. The old beat-up piece of copper and tin had survived the Empire's assault on his father's homestead, his escape from the mining camps and it had never once stopped ticking. He felt it under his tightly clenched fingers like a small fluttering heartbeat before shoving it back into his pocket.

"They have to listen now. How can you ignore this?" Lilly grinned. "I want to go down there. We should be down there."

Grant wrapped his arm around her. He took the moment to admire her beauty as he brushed a stray hair from her face. The sun brought out the gold in her strawberry mane as it sat in a mess of loose curls that fell freely down her back. She couldn't sit still long enough to have it braided properly. Grant preferred her untamed.

"I'm not quite confident you're ready for that yet, Princess. If the IRG, or UMI show things will get rough. I don't want to even think about what will happen if the Empire sends its dregs out here. When Caleb gets back with the others, you should stay here with Nev and the girls. You got a great view up here. I promise you won't miss nothin."

Lilly was learning all of the new vocabulary of the Revolution. IRG, The Iranti Resistance Guard was the elite faction of, LIRA the Lo Irant Liberation Army, they had a reputation for violence. United Miners of Lo Irant, had vowed retribution for Roe, and dregs, was short for deregulated military forces. They had all of the power of the Oprian military and were financed by the corporations acting under their direct control. She cringed when she thought about the footage of Roe, taken by LIRA operatives, the bodies burning in the mines, with no funeral rites, no monuments to honor their names. The tragedy forced her to see the Empire for what it was and for that she was grateful.

Grant hated to see her bright, beautiful smile face fade to disappointment after he told her they couldn't join in the festivities. He admired her hunger for the cause. For the last two months they had kept their readings secret from Caleb. Traditionally, under caste women didn't read beyond primary level. A tradition Caleb had recently become infatuated with keeping. According to him, too much Oprian literature was out corrupting young Iranti girls turning them into exotic whores for the lascivious and sinful Empire. Grant disagreed with Caleb that a free Lo Irant had to reject modernism and technology, but

Caleb insisted that it was important to drive the righteous Irantis to the cause.

Caleb interrupted their moment by plopping on the ledge in between the pair. "My Lilly is a big girl. She should come." Caleb snaked his arms around Nev and Arial, binding them in a quick but constricting embrace they were all too happy to receive. "In fact, I want all of my girls with me. Nev, Arial and Nara too."

Lilly bubbled with excitement as he helped her off of the ledge.

She bit her tongue and flashed Grant a cocky grin. "Worried I'll ruck 'em up worse than you could, Grant?"

"Pride, love," Caleb corrected her sternly.

"Sorry." Her eyes cast towards her feet in embarrassment.

The prophet placed a gentle finger under her chin and smiled down at her with all the grace of the angels. "I forgive you."

"Well," Grant coughed, interrupting the pair. "Might as well be gettin' a move on it then, there is no use wastin' time up here."

Grant held the door open for Caleb. "Somethin still don't sit right with me. I think we should hold up here for now."

"Don't worry my brother, the gods have spoken to me. We need to be with our people."

"My blood, my bones, and my body." Grant spoke the beginning of their sacred oath. It was more to keep his own frustration with his leader in check than to pay respects.

"My honor, my heart, and my heritage," Caleb replied and bowed as he walked through the door.

The old cobblestone streets were packed with folks from all over the Riverlands. Vendors were handing out food, instead of charging, they asked for donations for the families of Roe. Their tills overflowed. Fiddle and drum music played while old miners sang the songs that even after two hundred years of oppression still could never be forced out of their hearts.

A young middy, dressed in a miner's tunic over her regular clothes, approached Lilly and the girls with a friendly smile and a hug. The girl was painted in the symbols of the ancients in bright scarlet, gold and black.

"Afternoon my sister, show your support for our people?" She asked, holding out a paintbrush, a gob of fresh paint dripped onto the ground by her feet.

Lilly allowed the young woman to paint **Ah'Lih Mirah**, Iranti oldspeak for "one under the gods." There was no way she could tell whether it was cold pigments touching her face or the proud defiance of marking herself in the words of the forbidden language that gave her chills. Nev and Ariel politely passed, but Nara let her cheeks be adorned. She smiled deviously at a disapproving Ariel, and made a gesture in the twins' own language. Judging by Ariel's furrowed brow, Lilly and Nev determined it was an offensive one.

"What in the seventh hell is this?" Caleb grabbed Nara's arm with such force she almost lost her balance as he spun her around into the empty alley.

"What's what?" Lilly threw her hand down on Caleb in defense of the frightened child, meeting his angry eyes with her own fury.

Caleb's finger shook with anger as he pointed to the painted markings on Nara's face. Her cheeks puffed out from where his hands held her jaw with a steel grip, her eyes filling with tears.

"This blasphemy! Marking your body! Are you serious?"

"It's just paint, Caleb," Nev spoke in a sweet calm voice. She seemed to be the only one who could get Caleb to come down whenever he went over the cliff in anger. "It comes off, no harm." She gently kneeled down and wiped the paint from Nara's face using her own dress. He released her and Nev comforted the sniveling girl.

Lilly had never seen Caleb so angry before. She didn't flinch when he raised his hand again, despite being almost sure it would meet her in violence. It didn't, however. His rage faded as quickly as it came and he regained his composure as Lilly lost hers.

"I'm sorry. I can ignore a lot of your willfulness Lilly, but this is too far and it's because I care about you, about your soul. It's a mortal sin to mark your body. Even scars earned in battle can leave your soul abandoned outside the Great Fields. It's the erosion of our treasured beliefs that the empire uses to weaken our resolve. Please tell me you understand." Her head came to rest awkwardly on his chest and he stroked her head. "My little spitfire, I swear you carry the blood of the Ancients inside you. Wild and filled with the spirit of the harvest you are. I didn't mean to give you a fright."

Lilly pushed away. "I apologize for offending you, but it wasn't Nara's fault. It is her you should be apologizing to."

Nara peaked out cautiously from behind Lilly. Her face was bright red, partially from the paint and partially from Caleb.

He dropped to one knee and threw his arms open. Nara ran to him and he showered her with small kisses. "How can I stay mad at you, my pet?" He laughed and signed, "Forgive me?" She gave him a peck on his cheek and a pat on the head.

"The Gods are likely to test us, my children." Caleb stood up and addressed the others. "We're a family, and must be sure to not be broken. Even I have times of weakness. Let's give thanks to the Gods for giving Lilly the strength to keep me on their path." He greeted the sun with a smile as he stepped out of the shadows and back on to the streets.

"Best not be challengin Caleb," Grant warned Lilly, pulling her back into the alley. "He'd die before he'd go over with a crowd watchin', but he never forgets a transgression."

Her brow dropped disapprovingly. "What exactly are you trying to say, Grant?"

"I'm sayin' everyone has things that irritate them, Caleb's is being challenged. Not tellin you to bend to him like Nev, but don't correct him openly. It would be bad for you."

Lilly laughed it off, her nerves betraying her true fear. "That was supposed to be anger? Ha! I've taken beatin's from field hands ten times bigger than that. I'd deck him in the jaw if he had raised a finger to me."

"You're fearless Princess, but yelling at the gods saying you're unbreakable, will only call down their wrath. Use your head." Grant eluded to a story from the Itara Caleb had used in his last sermon. He was half sure it was directed specifically at Lilly for her boldness.

Caleb moved effortlessly among the flood of people. It wasn't long before he held a growing captive audience of protesters right in front of Wellsly Fountain. Lilly danced her fingers on top of the water as he spoke, lost in his words.

Grant stood at the edge, keeping his eyes on the rest of the crowds. A few hours had already passed, he was still sore at Lilly and it was distracting. He barely noticed the several large transports that pulled up, filled with IFR and the United Miners of LoIrant. Instead of carrying signs or banners they had bats and chains. He felt a pit form in his stomach and he motioned to Caleb to cut it short.

"Caleb, wow! You are a legend out here." A young man ran up just as the group was about to leave. He was a member of the middle castes, wearing the canvas jacket of a miner and he had a Free Lo Irant sticker on the clipboard he was carrying. "I'm Danner, director of Youth for a Free Lo Irant at the University. The people are ready to hear you speak."

Grant fought the urge to punch the middy fake. What did he know about the suffering of the Iranti people? Sure as hell wasn't from his Empire-sponsored Education. Caleb spoke daily about the danger of middys diluting the cause, turning it into a fashionable folly. His jaw nearly dropped to the floor when Caleb agreed to follow this pompous ass.

"Caleb, you can't be serious? This floundering trop?" Grant protested, not caring if present company heard. "UMI and IFR just bussed in their soldiers, they're fixin' for a fight."

"This is a peaceful protest to show the Empire that a Free Lo Irant is the will of the people. The Empire doesn't want or need any more blood on their hands. The press is here. They want our story. The Oprian people are listening," Danner exclaimed.

"Listening, my ass! The Oprian people want a sideshow, and they are about to get it. Caleb, don't listen to this sniveling tit. Let's get the girls out of here. Empire owns every camera here. As soon as they go off, they'd love to get a piece of you, of all of us. He's a piece of shit Caleb. You yourself say the likes of him ain't to be trusted. Let's go."

Caleb laughed, brushing Grant aside. "Ignore, my man. Won't find a purer heart nor a hotter temper than Grant. Point the way, Danner."

Caleb's words pinned Grant under an avalanche of disbelief. For a moment, he got a glimpse of Caleb he was never meant to see. The lowborn accent faded and his demeanor softened into that of a perfect gentleman.

He wanted to storm off, save himself and leave the great prophet to his people, but Lilly and the others had followed Danner and Caleb towards the stage. He huffed and followed after them.

The stage was a simple one. Donated by the local builders' guild, their banner hung right between the Iranti flag and the banners of the ancient Riverlands Clans. Samrael and The Six joined Lilly, Nev, Arial and Nara on the stairs as Caleb took the stage. They cheered with the crowds.

"Isn't this amazing, Grant?" Lilly was beaming.

Grant was the first to notice the gray and blue transports pull up behind the square and his anxiety fell away to straight fear. "Lilly!" He yelled and twisted her head to face the transports. "They brought in dregs! We need to get out of here, now!"

Lilly's expression didn't change. She was still drunk off of the crowd. "They can't touch us now. We are invincible, don't you see?"

"I've seen what the Empire's bullets can do to the invincible Lil. We need to get out of here." He pulled her arm, but she dug in her heels.

"No, Lilly, I think Grant is right, look!" Nev pointed at the swarm of black uniforms amassing up the road. "We should get everyone out of here."

"Okay," Lilly said, the sobering reality still setting in. "By the fountain, there was a storm drain. I bet it leads to the River. Even if it don't, nobody will find you there. I'll get Caleb and meet you."

"I'll get Caleb. You go with the others." Grant spoke softly, but stern as he stroked Lilly's cheek.

"No way! I'm not leaving! I can fight!" Lilly pushed his arm away and stormed the stage.

He stood there for a moment and just watched everything unfold. The IRG met the dregs throwing their bricks and firing their rifles into the cloud of tear gas. Fiery bursts flashed in the gray mist and the first of several large explosions shook the ground.

Grant was hit by what felt like a rail transport. It knocked him to the ground and all he could hear was a high-pitched ringing. The dust made it harder to figure out which way was up, as he tried to catch his bearings. Blood trickled out of his right ear and poured from his nose. He couldn't see anything except some feet in the smoke.

A figure appeared in front of him. A dreg completely covered by his black uniform, save for his brown eyes that glared at Grant hatefully. With his ears still ringing, there was no way for Grant to tell what the bastard was saying, but his eyes said enough. The soldier's finger caressed the trigger, savoring the moment. Grant was transfixed on them as he realized that the last thing he was going to see were the shit-colored irises of an Oprian mercenary. No matter how much he tried to think of Lilly when he closed his, all he could picture was the dreg's hateful stare and though he glanced down for a brief moment, Grant decided to meet death's glare with a defiant pride.

He waited in silence, long enough to wonder when it would come, but narrowed eyes of the hired soldier ready for the kill shot open wide like a frightened doe. Blood, red as the Iranti flag sputtered out of the his mouth. Grant refused to break his gaze as the dreg fell to the ground, his hate burning on the back of the dying man's retinas.

Lilly was frozen, still holding up the smoking rifle, when Grant stood up. Her expression was just as frightened and pale as the mercenary's when she looked at him with tears raining down her cheeks. She had just killed a man.

"It's okay, It's okay," he whispered, taking the rifle from her and as soon as it left her hands, she became Lilly again.

KYRANT

"Malrus spilled the blood of the first father across the plains in Kyrant staining them a dark red. Ismarlen knelt down and asked for forgiveness for turning his back on him, but the first father could not recognize his son painted red with his blood and died leaving Ismarlen un-absolved."

Nez, Porez, Creations 16:2 (translation)

CHAPTER 18

Askryne Province was one of the first Oprian Settlements in Kyrant after the Navat Wars. Oren Feller had been there since the beginning, having earned the land after being wounded in the war. During the last fifteen years he'd developed a successful ranch, owning more land than a under caste legally could over in Opree or Lo Irant. Feller Ranch was his great pride.

Oren sat on the back porch looking out over the plains. The red grass turned an ominous black as he watched the night sky push the sun over the horizon. The air was still hot and the sky was clear, but a gentle breeze pushed through the thick heavy air. The tall grass began singing of a storm on the horizon, the cattle chimed in with their hollow, bellowing calls. Oren felt it in his bones.

"Nadine, get the children into the basement. Cedric, grab the hands, come here!" Oren called for his eldest son.

Cedric was seventeen and despite being a bit short for a boy his age, he was fit from a life of hard work on the ranch. He and the ranch hands had been playing tiles in the barn. Once he heard the tone in his father's voice, he became aware the same heaviness in the air and knew exactly what was about to come. Cedric and the five other ranch hands grabbed their rifles, meeting Oren on the back porch.

"You think its razor wolves?" Cedric asked his father.

"I don't know... either that or this is a pretty nasty storm. Cattle are spooked to all nine hells."

Razor wolves were vicious creatures, native to Kyrant. They were large, with coarse black hair and have been known to hunt in packs of fifty or more. A single attack could devastate a rancher's herd. They learned to attack right before a storm, when the cattle were spooked. To a green rancher, the signs of a pending attack went unnoticed until it was too late.

If unimpeded, they killed every last creature in the herd, eating their fill and leaving the rest to rot. For this reason, they only needed to eat once every six or seven weeks. If hungry enough they went into towns, hunting people. Kyre legends spoke of them as immortal spirits of a cursed people, others believed they were the forerunners of the Navat.

Feller had dealt with them before. Dangerous and vicious creatures but flesh and blood, mortal just like him. They were creatures of opportunity, once a bullet was put into six or seven of them, they would stop.

The hands and Cedric and Oren split up, getting into three off road transports. They took off to the field where the herd was grazing.

The sky was getting darker. The air was still dense and the electricity in the air caused the hair on Oren's neck to stand up. He stood up on a perch he'd constructed on the old transport. It gave him enough height to man the powerful spotlight. Razor wolves hated light. It was too expensive to rig up lights in the field, even in the barns so they had to rely on the generators in the transports whenever an attack was imminent.

If they could get the herd into the corrals by the barn calmly, they would be safe. A stampede was more than likely, with a storm and the smell of razor wolves in the air. Unlike most hunters, they liked to alert their prey to their presence then they would attack in the chaos. Cedric and a field hand left the safety of the transport to start guiding the cattle closer to the barn. To his relief, the spooked and anxious cattle were moving rather smoothly.

Cedric could hear the sounds of the transport's engines but couldn't see anything above the wall of tall grass that outlined the grazing area. He was confident that his father was just being overly cautious. Cedric could smell a razor wolf from two miles out. This was just a bad storm. He looked forward to getting back to his game with the rest of the hands. He was about to win pretty big.

A loud crack and several pops pulled Cedric away from his thoughts of the game. He tightened his grip on his rifle and decided to step up the pace, alert and ready. The shots and the sounds of the engines were getting closer, something was wrong. There were too many rifles, too many shots.

"Leonard! Back in the bug! We're under attack!" Cedric called out to the other hand.

His father's transport pulled up next to Cedric just as he was getting into his own vehicle. Dante, the driver was shot in the shoulder.

"Who is it father? A tribe?" Cedric asked. He never trusted that the truce between the ranchers and the nomadic tribesmen was not over, despite the treaties.

Oren's face was pale with fear. "Navat, it's a raiding party. Get in the house, bolt the cellar stairs and hide the entrance. Make sure your mother and the children are inside. Tell her what is coming she'll know what to do."

"Navat? Are you sure? They haven't been seen this far back in years."

"Just go!" The urgency in his father's voice sent Cedric flying.

Nadine was on the porch, trying to see what was going on. She heard the shots and wanted to make sure her husband was shooting at razor wolves and not the deck hands again. Her heart dropped when she saw the look on her son's face.

"Oh by the gods! Who did your father shoot now?" Nadine said coming down the steps to meet him.

"Navat, ma, raiders, get everyone inside!" Cedric gasped for breath.

Nadine didn't register her son's words right away. Navat hadn't been in these parts in over a decade. It took her a moment to wrap her head around what was about to happen. Cedric grabbed his mother by the arm and pulled her inside the house.

"Pauline, grab your sisters and your brother we need to get to the cellar now!"

Twelve-year-old Pauline was tending to the baby. She hadn't heard fear in her mother's voice like that before and it scared her. She helped her mother get the rest of the children down the makeshift stairway of the root cellar located under a door in the kitchen floor. She started down herself and called for Cedric.

"Well, ain't you coming too?" She waved him down.

Cedric didn't say a word and guided her down the stairs, holding her hand until the very last moment he closed the door. She saw his sad smile as he looked at her one last time through the cracks in the floor. Pauline closed her eyes for a moment, attempting to burn that image of her brother deep into memory.

Cedric pulled the rug over the cellar door and then dragged the kitchen table over it, hoping it would be enough to keep the Navat from discovering the hiding place.

Pauline and her mother huddled against the dirt wall of the root cellar, clinging tightly to the rest of the children. Outside they could hear the gunshots and the panicked screams of the horses and cattle. Nadine gave the youngest ones blackroot water to sedate them. If they were discovered it was best they were not awake for it. She had an old single shot pistol nestled in her dress. Long before this night, she had resolved to shoot Pauline if the Navat made it to them, to spare her the horror. Nadine had the pistol half-cocked when the dust from their boots started falling on her head from the cracks in the floor. For twenty agonizing minutes, the Navat tore through the small ranch house. The Mother's knuckles were white from gripping the pistol so tightly. She said a silent prayer.

It was still cool and dark in the cellar despite it being mid-morning.

"Nadine Feller? Any of the Feller family alive?" A man's voice called through the house waking up the sleeping family. "Please answer. If you need medical attention let us know!"

Pauline's eyes widened. She cautiously walked over to see if she could spot anyone through the boards.

"Down here!" She called out. "In the cellar!"

In a panic Nadine grabbed her daughter, trying to quiet her. It could be a trap. Nadine wasn't about to answer to anyone except her husband.

The fear paralyzed her as the table was dragged off of the rug. With little option, she grabbed her pistol and put it to her daughter's head. Her mother's hands muffled Pauline's screams and although she tried, she couldn't get away.

Nadine waited, eyes fixed on the cellar door while it opened, ready to do the unthinkable if the Navat came too close. She took several breaths watching several sets of boots walk down the stairs. The old wooden steps creaking loudly under the weight and Nadine's grip around the trigger became a little tighter as she pulled back on the hammer.

Officer Wilder, of Atura Chemical Security Force, froze when he saw the frightened woman holding a gun to her child.

"Ma'am, it's okay. Don't move. We are from Atura Chemical. We are a part of a recovery unit. The Navat raided your town last night, but the raid is over. Please don't panic."

With a surge of relief washing over her, Nadine Feller collapsed in a heap on the floor.

The Feller Ranch was one of the few not burned to the ground. In a town of three hundred and fifty there were twenty-seven survivors. It was the worst Navat attack since the treaties were signed. Oren, Cedric and the ranch hands were all among the dead. Atura Chemical took over the town, pledging to work with the families and the community to rebuild.

CHAPTER 19

The sun was well below the horizon, but the sky was bright with the flames of the burning settlement in Askryne Province. The screams of the people inside cut through the young Shadow as he looked on.

"Come on, they're panicked. This is where it gets fun." Valmer laughed and fired a few shots in the air before he ran to join his brothers among the chaos.

"Sir, I-I know it isn't my place but, do you think Colonel Mason would approve of this?" Hill gulped looking up at Sgt. Channing.

"Well Colonel Mason isn't fucking here and what he don't know won't hurt him." His demeanor softened for a moment. "The Navat are waiting for Opree to forget about them so they can fuck us when the Empire's got their back turned. Keeping the Navat on the defensive is the best way to stop them. Sometimes we need to remind those shitheads in the Senate of what the Navat are capable of so we can continue to protect the Empire."

Although the Sergeant's words made sense to Hill, he was still hesitant to attack civilians. Channing put a hand on Hills shoulder.

"Feel that, son? It's boiling inside of you right now, scratching just below the surface. Feed it, boy." He slapped Hill on the back and joined his men.

He did feel it, like his skin shrunk, pulled taught over his bones. The itsy helped at first but each time he took a hit, it worked a little less. He looked down at his reflection in the small puddle, but he didn't look any different. The sound of the carnage excited him in a way he never felt before. Taking a few deep breathes, he watched as the orange halos formed around his irises. They glowed as bright as the flames.

It was almost dawn when the Shadows, black with soot and blood, walked out of the smoldering ruins of the settlement. Valmer carved a Navat symbol just outside the gates and lit a cigarette off the flames of a burning corpse, handing it to Hill after taking a drag for himself.

"Told ya, it was fucking amazing." Valmer said and patted his young brother in arms on the back. "Twenty seven, impressive, I got twelve on my first, but Navat are harder to kill, so we'll just say ten. You owe me fifty coin!"

"Fuck you Valmer, past shit don't count." Bosch called out. "Kid got the most, you owe him fifty!"

"I'll pay him fifty coin when he earns it." Valmer started to pull out what he would call an "impressive display" from his pants. Channing urged him to quit it for all of their sakes.

Hill took a look back at the black line of heavy smoke cutting the sun in half as it rose up from behind the plains and he felt sick to his stomach.

CYRUS

" Ismarlen kneeled at the feet of his siblings, the gods of the sky, the harvest and the sea, begging for forgiveness. They were moved to spare his life, but they slaughtered his children for they were abominations and an offense against the First Father."

- Nez Porez, Creations 16:9 (translation)

CHAPTER 20

Port Moridge used to be a resort city on the Vernai River. Like every other city in Kyrant, it was abandoned and had fallen to pieces. The Shadows loved to camp at Port Moridge's beautiful beaches and the remnants of luxurious hotels provided comfort rarely afforded to the men.

Cyrus was relieved to be back in Kyrant, even more so to hear that there was nothing but good news to report. In celebration, the men caught two razor wolves and planned to pit them against a ravenous plains bear. These fights were a favored treat for the men. Cyrus had arranged for several cases of beer and fine liquor to be dropped along with ammo and supplies.

A few years back, they'd built a metal cage around an empty swimming pool. It was still sturdy enough to host the grand event. The two hundred Shadows crowded around the pool of the Royal River Hotel, sitting on lounge chairs, broken stools and boxes. The torches and barrel fires contrasted sharply with the beautiful mosaic and stone grounds of the abandoned resort.

The aroma of a wild boar being roasted on an open spit filled the hot air and excited the caged beasts into a greater frenzy. Valmer poked the bear with an iron rod. It released an angry bellowing roar, sending the Shadow into a fit of hysterical laughter.

Channing watched with his cigar in his mouth and drink in his hands as the razor wolves tore into a plains calf. Her shrill cries for help were lost among the merciless spectators cheering for her death. He laughed so deep it turned into a hacking cough.

"This is fuckin' amazing." He turned to Hill, who was less enthused, turning a sallow green as the calf was being mauled, her cries piercing and pained. Colonel Mason gave Hill a hard pat on the back.

"Don't lose your lunch on us, Hill. This isn't even the main event." Cyrus drank his beer, the dew forming on the bottle wetting his beard.

Having seen enough, Hill jumped up to catch some air, leaving Channing and Cyrus to themselves.

"I'm sorry about Lilly. Did you get to pay your respects?" Channing asked.

"Regina won't tell me where she rests until I sign over Lilly's trust. The vapid bitch probably killed her herself. I'll die before Regina sees the coin."

"Fuck it, we can get a team out there in less than a week. We can throw her to the wolves." Channing was serious.

Cyrus laughed. "It would be fitting but too merciful."

"Say the word and the whore will be dog food. Anyway, some stuffed jacket from the Senate came down last week looking around a wormy little shit, round glasses. I could break him in half with my little finger, just thought you should know."

"Hobert Waller? He is a little shit. He was at the Senate hearing. What in the nine hells did he want?"

"Fucked if I know, he mentioned something about auditing some bullshit. I didn't tell him shit, just threatened to use his skin to patch my tent if I caught him poking around here again."

"Ever the diplomat Channing, honestly though, we need to be careful. The last thing we need is to get shut down because we pissed off a little worm like Waller. The rumors back in Opree are turning from mutterings to a low roar. We can't risk another Haven."

"Stop giving a shit about what happens in Opree! Your ass belongs out here with us. Lilly's gone, you got no loyalties back there. Stop trying to kill the monster inside of you. It's time you embrace it. The men need their leader back with his head on straight."

"My men need a decent war. This nonsense is only going to appease them for so long. It seems-" Cyrus cut himself off as the bear was released into the pit with the two razor wolves. The Shadows' howls were deafening as the fight began. Feeding off the carnage, Cyrus watched, silently soaking in the calming violence.

Having seen enough blood for one night, Hill walked over to the beach, away from the madness. Valmer was in the corner taking a piss. "The sight of that boar getting you all hot and bothered, hog fucker?" He laughed.

"Go fuck yourself Valmer," Hill retorted.

"And deny the ladies the pleasure? Never."

Hill sat in the sand watching the river flow under the moon. Valmer stumbled over, too drunk to take a hint.

"Valmer, do you think it's wrong not telling the Colonel about the raids on the settlements?"

"Channing told us to keep our damn mouths shut. Not our place."

"But, don't you think-"

"No Hill, I don't fucking think," Valmer interrupted. "It's not our jobs to think, they point us and we kill. End of fucking story." He laid his head on the sand to stop it from spinning and passed out.

Hill, basking in the silence looked over across the river. Across the river another settlement was being built in the distance. He saw the light shine out from the darkness. It seemed quiet and peaceful, but very far away, too. Thoughts of Askryne Province filled his head and when the peaceful silence became too much to bear, he left Valmer passed out in the sand to get another beer and watch the rest of the fight.

CHAPTER 21

Dawn pierced through the tent, burning Cyrus's eyes. The weight of a stranger in his bed sent him into a brief panic. After noticing the sheets, as well as his arms, were covered in blood, he felt the pit form in his stomach, a feeling that was becoming all too familiar. Cyrus remembered every savage act he committed against her, but it still didn't seem real. Hesitantly, he peeled off the sheets from the unfamiliar form sharing a bed with him. She was bruised and bloody and her hands bound to his bed with leather straps. Six long cuts etched into her back marked each time he had violated her that night. His stomach churned, as the disgust built up in the back of his throat and he vomited. It seemed to always happen after the rage kicked in. Not entirely sure he should be hoping this latest victim of his demons was alive after enduring such an ordeal, Cyrus turned her over. He blinked, or must have

*because the woman was gone. She was replaced
with a small girl of about six, her violet eyes wide
with fear and the curls of her strawberry blonde
hair matted down with blood. She cried out to him
softly, "Daddy?"*

Cyrus had this nightmare many times before, but
there was something in the details that made it seem much
more real. He got up and walked around the room a bit,
the thoughts burned his mind as the images returned to
him, refusing to glass over the worst of his transgressions.

He felt hot and violent but fought against it. *Not tonight,* he thought. He was so tired and it tore at his soul to
replay those images again and again, but it was the only
way to regain control.

He gripped the end of the table as he stared at himself
in the mirror. Tracing his finger across the long scar on
his right cheek, he unintentionally invited the memories
to flood his mind washing away the lies he painted over
his past. His scar stared back at him demanding he pay
notice and evaded any attempts Cyrus made to shove the
intrusive thoughts back into his subconscious. The halos in his eyes were starting to form. It had been too long
since the last time and Cyrus was afraid he wouldn't be
able to satiate it tonight.

He allowed himself to remember the screams and the
sobs, each moment cutting into him like a thousand tiny

blades. It was working though, the rage was subsiding. He remembered the passion and desire, the thoughts he was thinking throughout the brutal attack. He made a game of her that night and the blackest most part of him was relishing in his brutality. It both excited him and made him sick to his stomach, but the halos stared to fade as the rage sunk back down deep within him, leaving him still stuck in his mind reliving that event.

Since that night, Cyrus had gotten better at controlling the rage inside of him, letting go only against the enemy, save a few 'incidents' that occurred from time to time. Still, there were nights like that night, when the rage that dwelled within had gone too long without being fed or was provoked. It would take over and every time it did, he was left to deal with the devastating fall out.

It took all he had to retain his precious humanity. Part of him always believed he could be stronger than the demon, that he could defeat it somehow and get back everything he lost. For years he has been able to keep himself separate from the beast, but he was getting older and clashes with the Navat were becoming few and far between. Placating the demon with itsy, booze, violent memories and disturbing fantasies wouldn't be able to keep it at bay for ever. He was running out of time.

The wind howled outside the tent like a chorus of hungry razor wolves. The thick canvas was beating furiously against the metal frame. Windstorms were common this time of year, but this particular one was the worst Cyrus had seen in almost a decade.

The flames of the hearth engulfed in a passionate dance, casting shadows of the past on the restless walls, painting the room in dark memories. The drink and the itsy running its course in his blood made it difficult for Cyrus to stay focused.

Despite being one foot in the grave drunk and the storm raging outside, Cyrus heard the soft sound of another pair of boots in his tent and within half a breath, had his sidearm pointed at the uninvited guest.

"Ismarlen, I don't recall summoning you here tonight." Knowing his bullets would be useless, Cyrus kept the barrel on his target anyway.

The tall dark figure laughed as he stepped out of the shadows. It had been sixteen years and Ismarlen hadn't aged a day. *But again, the immortal rarely do*, Cyrus thought.

"I've always appreciated your gall, Cyrus, but don't be foolish enough to think that you control the terms of this arrangement. I've come to collect on our deal."

"Bullshit, the Navat have not been destroyed, our time isn't up." Cyrus walked over to his desk, making very sure not to turn his back on the dark god.

"The threat to your empire is over. Peace will soon be achieved. My brother has been pacified and the promise you made in exchange for my help must be honored."

"Peace? Malrus doesn't know the word. He has never been known to honor any treaties. Tell me what happens when he gets bored of this 'peace,'" Cyrus sneered.

Ismarlen rolled his eyes. "That's none of my concern. To be fair, you humans will probably kill yourselves before that happens. Our deal was clear. You fought under your banners and in your own skins with my power until the empire was safe from the Navat. It is." He took a step towards Cyrus, who raised a long blade, keeping the god at a comfortable distance. Ismarlen took a seat in the desk chair.

"You don't own me yet."

"I'm patient. You were mine the moment I placed my mark on you. I will one day have you and your Shadows as my loyal servants, under my banner, no longer under the protection of your gods as their children. One day I will drain you of every last drop of their blood and you will remain immortal and unrecognizable to them. It will give me great pleasure." Ismarlen kicked his feet up on the desk, brushing Cyrus's blade aside with his boot. "You are right about one thing, though. There is something I want from you."

"I have given you my life, my love and my soul. There is nothing left I have to give except my skin and my name, but you'll have those soon enough."

"You're right, I will." His teeth glistened under the flicker of the flames as he grinned. In the light they reminded Cyrus of fangs. "But that's not what I'm after. I want you to bring me someone."

"More recruits? Fine, I've already given you seven hundred thirty-six souls, what's one more?"

"Not any man, the Eyes spoke of an Iranti-born, a descendant of the god Nellis called Harker. They said he will defeat Malrus and unite the Empire. He'd be a powerful ally. I want him."

"The Eyes speak of a lot of things that never occur. If he is so powerful on his own, why would he need you?"

"He doesn't know of his power. An angry young man with the bloodline capable to unite the fractured empire, that can be very dangerous without the proper guidance."

"You mean him to rule over Opree in your name?"

"The first Father gave the gods dominion over the men they created. Malrus and I were skipped over, no children to worship us. After killing off the Old Ones, the Ancients wouldn't bow down, so we made children of our own with our own blood. We were merely defending our children from our father when we killed him." His cold black eyes became soft and sad when he spoke of the great war of the gods. "I didn't want for it to go that way, despite Malrus. Your gods fearing our war was destroying humanity abandoned you, imprisoning us back beneath the ground. Malrus wishes to destroy you, like he wiped out the ancients here in Kyrant. I merely want to save you, adopt the humans as my own children. Give them the opportunity to serve in peace under me. I am your savior."

"I won't help you destroy the empire I've sworn my soul to protect." Cyrus snarled defiantly.

"Fair enough," he cracked his knuckles and stretched. "I wouldn't want to be accused of being rigid. Get him to serve me and I will remove my mark from your skin. Your gods are the most forgiving, as long as you are unmarked, you can have your redemption. Even if you don't help me, I still have my ways. I like you, Cyrus. I want to help you save yourself."

Cyrus stood mute with disbelief, but kept stone-faced and stalwart so as not to betray his true feelings. The heel of an Ismarlen who was bored of humoring the integrity of an already damned man slammed onto the desk, knocking a framed worn picture of a little girl with bright violet eyes and strawberry blonde curls onto the ground.

The Colonel's eyes darted to the photo. He restrained the rest of himself from reacting further, but it was telling enough for Ismarlen.

"Of course, sometimes we are too late to right our wrongs." He paused to scratch his chin. "What if I told you that you could have her back?"

"I will not let you rip her from the gods. It would be an abomination," Cyrus growled and picked up the broken frame.

Ismarlen chuckled. "I'm flattered you think me that powerful, but alas, I could not bring her back from the dead even if I wanted to. Your daughter is alive and I promise that you will have your chance to make things right with her."

"You lie!" Cyrus yelled, the tip of the Navat blade stopping just short of his antagonist's neck. "I can't kill you, but I promise this will hurt."

"I'm not lying. Lilly is alive, at least she is for now. She is running with a dangerous crowd. The Eyes have sung of her death. Bring me what I ask and I will tell you how to help her. Of course you can exact your little revenge here, we can call everything off and I can take you right now. At least you'll just be an idiot, not a traitor, but would you really betray your own daughter for a bunch of sniveling corrupt bureaucrats who would just as easily see you hanged? You don't have to answer now." He side-stepped the Navat blade. "I will hear your decision before the feast of Ma'Arana. Think about it. I'm usually not this generous."

Ismarlen was swallowed by the shadows leaving Cyrus alone, yet again. He could feel the demon squirm just under his skin, making it feel foreign and ill fitting. His fingers brushed the neck of the bottle of fermented peace, but his hand went to the broken frame instead.

Sitting on his cot, he tried to remember her face not twisted in pain. He doubted Ferrin could ever love him, not after what he'd done, but it was enough to see how much she loved their daughter, even the part that was him. Those last few moments she held Lilly at her breast while he watched from the shadows. It was true peace, a peace that eluded him to this day. A hope inside him grew though, Lilly was alive. She was the one piece of him untouched by the remarkable evil that dwelled inside of him. His heart and his humanity lived in her. A lifetime of regrets washed away in her promising young life. He could forgive himself for everything, if he could just save her. He slept soundly that night, a deep, dreamless sleep unplagued by the nightmares that usually haunted him

CHAPTER 22

The sparring pits in the fields of Penderghast were little more than round pits of sand surrounded by stones. All manner of hand-to-hand combat was taught. Iranti, Oprian and Kyre methods needed to be learned. Captain Normandy prided himself on making sure his officers could handle themselves in open combat.

"Very impressive Captain," Colonel Cyrus said, flipping through the manuals given to students.

"It's an honor, sir." Captain Normandy was surprised to hear that Colonel Mason would be visiting Penderghast looking for new recruits. The headmaster had, on more than one occasion, accused the leader of the elite Ni Razeem Shadows of witchcraft and thought the unit was nothing more than a wicked perversion. All of this was said behind closed doors of course and never to a Shadow's face.

While Normandy greatly respected Colonel Mason for his skill as a soldier and his leadership ability, he didn't trust him. He shuddered at the thought of any of his cadets falling into the man's clutches. Most would never return from Kyrant. The handful that did make it back to Opree alive were hollow, the best parts of them still lingering in that rotting wasteland.

"These are children of earls and dukes. We even have King Jonathan's son Prince Arryn graduating from the Academy in a few weeks. I doubt these are the kind of men you would need for Kyrant." Normandy broke the awkward silence.

"I'm only interested in one cadet, a Nathanial Harker." Cyrus spoke in a low, dark tone that gave away nothing. "I was told I could find him here."

Ismarlen had only given Cyrus a name and a place where he could find 'the one descended directly from the gods'. He had not decided yet if he was going to make the bargain with the dark god, but curiosity drew him to at least search this young man out. Ismarlen wouldn't have offered Cyrus that deal unless he was powerless to get Nathanial Harker on his own. Cyrus needed to know what he wanted Harker for. If Ismarlen decides to rule over the humanity, Harker could be the key to mankind's destruction or the key to its salvation. At the very least, he was a weakness of Ismarlen's that the Colonel could exploit in order to get his daughter and his soul back without sacrificing the Empire.

"Harker?" Normandy laughed nervously. "Don't know what you'd want with him. He's got a lot of spirit, I'll give him that but that's all," he lied.

"Nevertheless, I would still like to see him in action."

The class came out to the fields and gathered around the sparring pits. Rumor had spread that Colonel Mason was at Penderghast and everyone was interested in getting a glimpse of a legend.

"All right Cadets, we have a special guest. Colonel Cyrus Mason has decided to grace us with his presence. He will be watching you today, so make me proud." Normandy spoke with an unsettling lack of conviction.

Nathanial tried to catch a glimpse of one of his heroes, but he couldn't see past Arryn's stupid fat head.

Normandy went down the list of names on his clipboard, trying to find someone who could make Nathanial look bad in the pits. He knew Nathanial idolized the Shadows and would often talk about them like noble warriors from the days of the old ones and the ancients. A man like Cyrus took good men like Nathanial and dragged them to their deaths fighting for a cause long dead in a forsaken land.

"Harker...uh, Garitel you're first," Captain Normandy addressed his cadets. Arryn was the only cadet better at hand–to-hand than Nathanial.

The two stood up and faced each other, exchanging cold glances. Neither had spoken to each other since that morning in the Ivory Palace a few weeks before. They bowed.

The whistle blew and the two began to spar. There were very little rules in hand-to-hand sparring; the goal was to make the other opponent tap out or, otherwise, become incapacitated. Arryn had the clear advantage over Nathanial, having two inches and about fifteen pounds on him. They knew each other's strengths and weaknesses intimately.

Nathanial hit the ground with a hard thud but despite being thrown around like a rag doll by Arryn, the young man's resolve never wavered. He recovered and went into a defensive stance. He was an expert marksman, intelligent and a natural leader but in sparring, as good as Nathanial was, Arryn was better.

Cyrus and Normandy watched the two young men from the sidelines. Cyrus was impressed with the skill and tenacity of the young Iranti-born cadet. He was quick, resourceful and cunning. He could also take a hit, bouncing back after taking a swing from Arryn.

"The Iranti boy is tenacious." Cyrus said to Normandy.

"Harker. That is certainly an understatement." He muttered.

"So that's Nathanial Harker. Why do I feel like I know that name?"

"His father was General Alexi Harker."

Cyrus knew of General Harker and respected the man greatly. He had done a lot for Iranti-borns serving in the military. He continued to watch the son of a legend fight the Prince. Arryn fought with technique, skill and pure strength. Nathanial, on the other hand, had a sense of scrappy pluck to his style, raw, emotional and improvised.

"Where is he going after he is commissioned?"

"Rumor has it, he was offered a position as Captain of the Ivory Guard."

"An Iranti-born Captain of the Ivory Guard? I bet the press will have a field day with that one. King Jonathan must have really gone over the cliff."

During the war, Cyrus had fought beside the King in the Navat Wars. The two had been friends ever since, although Cyrus hadn't been to Ivory Castle in years. Cyrus respected a King who risks his own life for his people. It was more than the slime in the Senate ever did.

"He is close with the Prince. Apparently the King has taken quite a liking to Harker over the years."

By this time in the sparring match Arryn had Nathanial completely pinned and was twisting his opponents arm back in the wrong direction. Nathanial let out a scream.

"Do you yield?" Arryn asked.

"No," Nathanial grunted, struggling to get out of Arryn's grip.

Arryn twisted the arm further. Nathanial let out another cry.

"Do you yield?"

"No!" He said again with more conviction.

Arryn felt a twinge of guilt about hurting his friend but not enough to let up on him. He twisted the arm and gave it a hard pull. Nathanial screamed.

"For the Gods Harker, yield! He's going to break your arm!" Halloway interjected.

Nathanial did not yield. He took a moment, breathing heavy through the excruciating pain. Once his head was clear, he pushed himself hard against Arryn and deeper into the pain, letting out a loud agonizing scream. The move threw his opponent off balance. In two lightning-quick moves Nathanial had Arryn caught in a headlock. Arryn felt the pressure in his head build up. He was about to pass out.

"Do you yield?" Nate said between heavy breaths.

Arryn took a minute before finally tapping out, defeated.

The class was in an uproar over the amazing upset. Colonel Mason lifted an eyebrow at Captain Normandy, who had a look of disappointment painted across his face. He blew his whistle and dismissed the class. Arryn and Nathanial glared at each other, not saying a word as the two broke off into separate groups.

"That was impressive. You were trying to hide him from me?" Cyrus smiled, poking Normandy in the shoulder.

Normandy turned around and looked Colonel Mason directly in the eye, something few men had the guts to do without the aid of copious amounts of alcohol.

"Listen Colonel, Harker has the potential for greatness. He is a brilliant leader and a cunning warrior, but he has this idea in his head that what you and your Shadows do is part of some noble sacred duty. I will not let you waste his talents in that shithole of a colony and let a good man rot under the filth you and your monsters create." His voice didn't shake. He growled those words like a marsh lion protecting its young.

Colonel Mason respected Normandy for his candor. A brave man stands up for his men. It was the only reason Normandy was standing there with all of his teeth in place.

"I see you care about your cadets. That is admirable, but I think it's important we let the boy decide. I'll be back for the war games. I'm eager to see him perform as a leader in the field."

CHAPTER 23

Nathanial stood on the balcony of the aging temple watching the early summer sunset. He anxiously drummed his fingers along the iron railing, looking down to the city below as the impending darkness triggered the lights to climb from the undercity up to the multilayered streets. The empty time in between training was the worst for him. War games were in two weeks and graduation in three. He took the trip to the heart of the city to get away from the hostility at Penderghast.

Before the sun dipped completely below the menagerie of towering buildings, Nathanial went inside to do his evening prayers. He lit the candles at the altar one at a time, blue, green, orange, red, gold. It didn't matter to the gods what order the candles on an alter must be lit, but Nathanial would light them that way every night without fail, as his father had taught him. He tried to calm his mind enough to properly honor the Gods, but he was too distracted. The King's proposal remained unanswered and he was still unsure what he was going to do. He blew through the prayers without much thought or reflection. There was one moment though, when his mind allowed him a few seconds of serenity as he watched the orange flame, mesmerized by its hypnotic dance.

His peace was abruptly cut short by Colonel Mason entering the small private prayer room. "Sorry, I didn't know you were still praying." Cyrus quietly crept over to the altar and knelt down next to Nathanial and honored his gods, silently rushing through the prayers much quicker than even Nate had done. He was impressed with the young man's performance in the field. Although not entirely convinced of his divine destiny, Ismarlen wanted him badly for some reason and Cyrus thought Nathanial could at least hold the key to his undoing.

"It's good you still honor the harvest gods properly. These days they have fallen out of favor with many of the young Irant-borns." Cyrus said as he put out the last candle.

"It's the only link to my heritage. Aside from my hair and eyes, it is the only Iranti thing about me. Growing up at Penderghast, I dress, sound and act more like a High Born. The gods serve to ground me as someone who lives between two worlds most of the time."

Cyrus took a moment in the silence, hanging on to the last of his words as they sank in. "It's important for a soldier to keep himself grounded, even more so for a Shadow. Many of my men have their gods and the others have their vices. More often than not it's a strange combination of both. It's a balancing act."

Cyrus took a moment to look at Nathanial's altar. Images and statues of the gods neatly piled among images of dead relatives, offering bowls of fruit, grain and wine. To a non-Iranti all altars looked the same, but an altar was the representation of the self to the gods. One item in particular stood out to Cyrus. A metal figure, dressed in armor carrying a sword and a shield, with its stomach painted red.

"Why do you have an idol of Nellis?" Cyrus asked handing it to Nathanial. It wasn't typical for a Vistany Iranti-born to have idols of the deity associated with outcastes.

Nathanial ran his fingers over the intricately sculpted figurine, scanning it's surface for memories.

"I don't know, I guess I just always loved his story. My father used to read from the Itara when I was young. It's one of the few memories I have of him. The story of Nellis battling the Ismarlen and Malrus was what stuck out to me."

"Cast me out after sacrificing myself to save the world from all that is evil?, curse my name and my children? I'd have put Malrus right back." Cyrus was referring to Nellis's fate to roam outside the Great Fields after he trapped Malrus by swallowing the fallen god, preventing him from destroying all of humanity. His unholy burden made him and his followers outcastes.

"I think it's noble, it's the ultimate self-sacrifice, caring more about your people than your own well-being."

"What about his children? He made that decision that kept them outcasts, all to keep his honor? I call that pride and vanity." Cyrus enjoyed philosophical discussion and wanted to egg Nathanial into an intellectual debate, not something he could do with most of his Shadows.

"I never thought about it that way. I guess his people should be proud and honored they are decedents of a hero, even though it doesn't pay in glory. Do what's right no matter what the personal consequences."

Cyrus could tell the morally rigid Nathanial was going to be no fun at his game of playing advocate for the dark ones. "I think the indigestion would bother me the most." Cyrus said changing his tone.

"Huh?"

"A belly full of flaming god for all of eternity. I have trouble digesting Kyre food." The Colonel laughed softly at his own joke.

"Well I guess that was another thing Nellis didn't factor in." Nathanial said. "I –um, I really must be going though, the last rail out to Penderghast leaves soon and Captain Normandy will string me up if I'm late tomorrow." He quickly but carefully placed the idols, holograms and trinkets in his bag before leaving Cyrus alone with the gods.

He is so serious, Cyrus noted. There was something profoundly special about him though, and it intrigued the aging Colonel. The young man had a bright future ahead of him no matter what he did. No wonder the King wanted him as Captain of the Ivory Guard. He was still too rigid for Cyrus, who was all too aware of how a man can snap if he couldn't bend a little. Still, part of him was compelled to test his fortitude against Ismarlen, especially since it was obvious that Harker was so important to him. For now, Harker was his Ace up his sleeve, a weapon he planned to wield at the right time that would be able to save himself without serving up all of humanity to Ismarlen on a silver platter.

LILLY

*"And the gods breathed and their shackles fell to pieces,
their chains turned to sand. The children of the harvest were
slaves no more, in the glory of the gods, they were free."*

–The Itara, Gospel of Vail, 914:2

CHAPTER 24

It was only noon and Lilly was already dodging the authorities. It was a difficult undertaking while wearing the dress of a lady but she managed. Running across the crowded rail platform keeping a tight grip on the wallet she'd "pro-quired" from her last mark, she ducked behind the dilapidated cart of a fruit vendor to catch her breath. An arm reached around her from behind and spun her around.

"I'm guessing your beginners luck is running out, huh?" Grant released her with a crooked smirk. She shoved him.

"I almost had a fit! Don't do that!" She laughed, adjusting her blouse. "Honestly, I think we've bled this place dry. The authorities know our faces."

Grant cradled her cheeks in his hands. "What this face? Who could forget this face?" He leaned in close for a kiss, but Lilly pushed him away.

She remembered their first night back from Londallin. It was the first night she shared a bed with Grant, or any man for that matter. They kept their tryst a secret from the rest of the group, knowing Caleb would not approve. Not wanting to interfere with the cause, she broke it off when it became too distracting. Still, it was impossible to ignore that crooked smile and what harm would one kiss do?

Their lips hovering just millimeters apart, the shrill whistle of the officer who'd been chasing Lilly broke the magic of the moment. "Shit," Lilly said and ran off with Grant following close behind.

Lilly and Grant took the tunnels to get back home. Lilly hated the tunnels. They were cramped and dark and smelled terrible. The labyrinth of criss crossing mine shafts was home to outcasts, criminals and addicts. There was no light or clean water. The Empire gave up trying to assimilate them and just ignored their existence.

The light from Grant's lantern illuminated only what was right in front of them. In the shadows she could feel others there as they sloshed through the ankle deep water, but she couldn't see them except the occasional reflection from cloudy little eyes. Her nails dug into Grant and she buried her head into his back.

"After six months, you still can't handle the tunnels?" Grant laughed.

"No," she squeaked, her voice muffled by his shirt.

Something cold, wet and hairy brushed against her ankle. The sloppy sensation caused Lilly to scream and climb Grant like a tree. Shaking, she refused his attempts to cajole her feet back to the ground.

"Are you seriously not gonna come down?"

Lilly just shook her head, still buried in his neck.

"Very well, Princess." He adjusted himself to better carry her. "But you owe me for the ride."

Lilly's grip relaxed a bit once she realized she wouldn't have to put her feet down, keeping her head nestled in his back with her eyes tightly shut. He smelled nice, well nicer than the tunnels at least. She felt his heat on her cheek as he carried her through the darkness.

"You're not going to tell anyone about this are you?" she asked.

"Of course I am, everyone is gonna know about how the fearless Lilly Rae Maroody is afraid of the tunnels." Grant smirked.

"Please don't. I won't hear the end of it."

"Well then, you should just walk then." He slid his arms out from under her legs and let her drop a few inches.

She screamed and clawed at his shirt with frantic fingers. Grant just laughed and continued on his way, ignoring the punch to the kidney she gave him for the fright.

Grant was whistling as they sloshed their way down the tunnels. His leg caught on something and the pair tumbled down an old service shaft. In the dark, Lilly struggled to make out anything in the pitch black.

Something about the putrid smell she was choking on made her think that maybe she didn't want to see what was around her.

"Don't move!" A panicked Grant shouted. "Don't move. I'm comin' to get you." His lantern bobbed through the dark as he made his way to her. "Don't look!" He commanded.

Lilly instantly looked around, allowing her eyes to adjust to the dim light. "I looked." She squeaked in fright.

They had landed in a mass pile of bodies. Lilly couldn't ascertain how many there were, as she had no reference point to compare, but she was certain that it was an overwhelming amount. Trying to ignore the bloated corpses as she stepped over them, her foot went through the gooey remnants of what used to be a man's abdomen and the dead demanded she pay them mind. The sensation and the stench was so foul, her stomach lost all ability to retain its contents.

Grant helped a shaking Lilly back on to her feet.

"What is this?" Lilly asked and lowered the lantern to better illuminate the atrocity she was witnessing. Her grandfather used to say that the imagination always painted worse pictures than the dark was able to hide. Lilly would never have been able to imagine something this horrific.

"Looks like well plague. Don't touch nothin'." He whispered, as if the dead could hear him.

Well plague was common in mining towns and near chemical plants. The water and food borne illness was spread through infected wells, food supply and livestock killing roughly half of its victims. What made the disease so devastating was that an infected well would be used for weeks before symptoms started to occur and by then it could infect a whole county.

"It's in the food." A young girl reached out to Lilly startling her.

Her skin was a pale and clammy green-gray, blotched with scars, open lesions and growths, her eyes a milky white, typical of an outcaste living in the tunnels. Lilly tried unsuccessfully to hide her repulsion.

"They ate it and got sick." The girl added, handing a crumpled paper wrapper to Grant.

"Venolin." Grant read off the packet. "They don't even try to hide it. Who gave this to you?"

"They came with the doctors. Some of us got the shots, everyone got the food." She trailed off matter of factly, unsure if she was supposed to be talking to outsiders.

"Venolin musta been testin' the new well plague vaccines." Grant turned to Lilly.

He knew all about the rumors surrounding the large pharmaceutical manufacturer. He always believed the stories about how they restricted access to lifesaving medicine in colonies, but never wanted to think that anyone who carried the one bloodline inside of them could do something like this. "They're usin' these people as lab rats." He said with disbelief.

Lilly was confused. "What do you mean lab rats?"

"How else do they figure out if the vaccine worse or not?" Grant snapped.

"I don't know...why would they do that?"

"Because it's cheaper to do it this way. Nobody cares about these people. Even other Irantis would prefer to ignore the outcasts in the tunnels."

Lilly noticed the girl had ran off. "Well, what do we do now?" People needed to know about this.

"Nothin'!" Grant grabbed on to Lilly's hand and began dragging her with him, she resisted. He couldn't find the words Caleb would use to explain things like this, so he improvised. "Lilly, look, this is just one of the many crimes the Empire has committed against our people. The murder of a few hundred mutant outcastes is not going to get the middys' angry enough to stand up against the Empire. We need to focus on a singular message that-"

"That message is a unified Lo Irant! How are we supposed to be unified if we make it clear that some Irantis are worth more than others? If we tell them how many people died here-" Lilly protested.

"They won't care Lil! The Empire sat on its ass while an entire race of people were bein' exterminated, yet they had no objections to going to war when the idiot son of an Earl gets assassinated. How long will it take you to understand that it is not the quantity of people, but the quality of people who have to die before the middle castes in Lo Irant stand up?" Frustrated that Caleb's words were failing him, Grant took a few breaths to compose himself. "I'm sorry, but it's true unless someone important dies, this war ain't gonna happen."

Lilly's hand landed hard across Grant's face. "Listen to yourself! You don't sound like the Grant I know. The Grant I know cares about the cause. The Grant I know cares about every Iranti regardless of caste!" She screamed.

Usually Grant appreciated Lilly's innocence, but today it was unsettling."Don't talk to me about the cause! I am the only one willin' to sacrifice everythin' for it. I want a free Lo Irant, at any cost. We ain't gonna change nothin' vandalisin' Empire property and stealin' from the Vist. It's gonna take blood and sacrifice and you need to decide if you can handle that."

Lilly threw her hands up in the air, stopping short of slapping Grant again. For the life of her, she had no idea what had gotten in to him.

"Whose blood is it gonna take, Grant? Iranti blood? We're supposed to ignore what happened to these people so we can focus on the cause? Why fight for these principles you so desperately cling to if you're just going to undermine them?" Lilly fumed, waiting for a response from Grant that never came. "Do you even want a free Lo Irant or do you just want to destroy the Empire? Maybe it's you who needs to make a decision." She grabbed the lantern and stormed off into the tunnels on her own.

CHAPTER 25

It was late afternoon when Grant and Lilly returned to the temple. Neither had spoken a civil word to each other the rest of the way home. Lilly was relieved to be back at the temple though. Everyone there was busy working on something. The Children of Azel had added many more to their ranks in the months since Londallin. They were also becoming more organized. The pantries were stocked with food and they had enough money to buy some decent supplies for the people.

Lilly sat in the printing room with Nev, running prints of a new newsletter off the old iron printing press. It called for action against the crimes Venolin committed against the outcastes in the tunnels. She was still so mad at Grant, working was the best way to keep her mind off of him.

The music playing from the illegal radio made the work easier. All radios in Lo Irant had to be registered and licensed. Radio was one of the many technologies restricted in the colonies. The pirate station played songs inspired by the revolution. The Tunnel Rats, an underground news program delivered important coded messages on the hour. Caleb didn't trust any technology created by the Empire. He believed it was a tool of enslavement. "If you distract the people, they will be compliant," Caleb often warned.

Grant however, saw technology as an invaluable tool of revolution, a way to reach out to the people. Lilly was glad Grant had won the argument about having a radio. "Ni Araja Nom" (A unified people), one of her favorite songs, began to play. Nev turned the volume up a bit and the two started singing along, bobbing their heads to the music.

Since the protests at Londallin, Nev and Lilly had become close. Lilly appreciated that Nev was really a devoted and loving member of the Children of Azel. Nobody cared more about Caleb's flock than Nev. They looked to her as a mother figure. When they were sick, she cared for them. When they were scared, she'd stay up all night to comfort them. In the days after the protests, when things were a little tight, Nev often went without food to ensure everyone else ate first.

The two worked hard on the home front, as Caleb called it. Their job was organizing food and medicine drops, distributing the literature to the messengers in each district. Their reach had grown exponentially and the Children of Azel had boots on the ground in almost every undercity district of Core. The people were mobilizing.

"Heard you almost got pinched today," Nev said, tying a knot on the last stack of newsletters ready to be distributed.

"Yeah, it was close...I would have for sure, if it wasn't for Grant." Lilly helped her stack the large bundle in the corner.

"Well, Grant is pretty sweet on you. Not surprised he was hovering over you like a garbage hawk in summer."

Lilly smashed a jar of ink on the floor, the glass shattered, and the black liquid bubbled as it seeped into the old wood floors. "Grant doesn't look at me. He NEVER looked at me! I mean, um...Well what about you and Caleb? Did you see how he was looking at you." She cleverly changed the subject.

Nev dropped a heavy box of tools on the table. The sound startled Lilly. "No," she said curtly. "Caleb is dedicated to the cause."

"Sorry, I didn't know you were so touchy on the subject. What? Were you and Caleb...ever a thing or something?"

Nev stood blankly for a moment, her cheeks flushed with shame. Part of her wanted to tell Lilly. It had been a long time since she spoke about it. She could go months without remembering the truth, living this lie worked so well for them.

"It's a really long story." Nev dropped another bundle of the newsletters into the pile and buried the past under a patriotic tune she whistled as she walked out of the room.

CHAPTER 26

Enraged, Grant punched a hole into the plaster walls still unsure if he was mad at Lilly, at Venolin or himself. The wall offered little insight on the matter so he hit it again for good measure.

"You're late for our meeting, Grant." Caleb met the Grant on the stairs, blocking his path.

"We ran into some trouble with the authorities, had to take the tunnels back. There is somethin' you need -" Grant pushed Caleb's arm aside and continued up the stairs.

"I know what I need, Grant. I need you to be on time for meeting." His voice was deep and cold.

"Caleb, listen to me Venolin is-"

"Are they trying to run this place without their right hand man? Because that's what I'm trying to do!"

"Fucks sake Caleb! Listen to me! Venolin is testin' some drug on the outcastes in the tunnels, a vaccine or somethin. Lilly and I found a whole pit of bodies. We need to do somethin about it."

"I thought we agreed to focus our attentions to the cause?" Caleb said with a twinge of irony.

"Venolin murderin' Irantis doesn't fall into that I suppose?"

"I understand you're upset. I am too, but there are more pressing issues at hand that we must be dealing with now. The word is what is going to save our people." Caleb patted the copy of the Itara he always kept in his pocket. "We focus on the word, and the gods will save us."

The War Room, as Caleb called it, was only accessible to Caleb, Grant and the Six. A large table was covered in maps, newspaper articles and diagrams. Mug shots of both Caleb and Grant were tacked to one of the walls, a reminder of what carelessness can bring. Samrael went to the back corner and came out with a large canvas bag of filled with five, ten, and twenty-coin notes.

"We have more than five hundred thousand coin for the deal," Samrael exclaimed.

"What time is the meeting?" Grant asked and poked at the paper bills bound in large stacks.

It was more money than he had ever seen before. It was enough to fund the cause. They would finally have what they needed to be an actual army, a real force in the revolution. He was anxious to get his hands on the weapons before Caleb decided to do something else with the coin. The last few weeks he had been acting more erratic and reclusive, talking about prophecy and destiny. His focus was becoming less about starting a revolution and more about religion.

"Tonight, at midnight, in the tunnels under the rails," Caleb threw a crumpled piece of paper on the table in front of Grant. "All of the information is there."

"Are you not coming?" Grant asked.

"I have other plans to make," Caleb said. "I can't be bothered with these things at the moment."

Grant was less than surprised at his leader's response, but it didn't make it any less irritating. "Do you plan to enlighten us, Caleb?"

"Now that you ask, Grant, I've gotten a calling from the gods, a vision. Children of Azel will be making a statement."

"What kind of statement?" Grant asked through clenched teeth, trying to maintain his calm.

"It's not important for you to know that right now. Patience, Grant, and you will soon learn your part, dismissed."

Feeling the rage bubble inside, Grant waited until the others left before he lost his temper.

"Caleb, I don't know what has been going on with you, but you're hiding something from me. You've been acting loony since Londallin and I'll figure it out. I swear it. If you jeopardize the cause, by the gods I will end you." Grant warned, slamming the door behind him.

Caleb sighed heavily, it seemed like he only could breathe when he found himself alone. In the dim flickering light of the dying bulb, Caleb stood over the money. He picked up a large stack. It was enough for him to start over. If he took off, he could disappear forever and be out of this shithole. The prospect was more than tempting. His copy of the Itara sitting in his pocket felt heavier, his gods were calling on him to be strong. Out of the darkened corner of the room, a shadow stretched across the floor and the figure lurking in the darkness stepped into the light.

"What I am offering you is greater than just five hundred thousand coin." His voice was threatening as he held the young prophet in place.

"Ismarlen." Caleb clammed up. "I-I- wasn't going to- I was just remembering."

"Remember your promise and I will remember mine. You performed wonderfully at Londallin, but there is still more to do. Finish what you've started and you will have your life back. Your lands, your money, your name will all be given back, but not a moment before. It's still so early, I need to make sure everything goes right. Grant has outlived his usefulness. He has become a threat. I need you to dispose of him." Ismarlen smiled at the thought.

"Grant is loyal to me. I have control over him. There is nothing you have to worry about." Caleb reassured.

"I delivered you the girl, she's the most important part of this. Grant is going to strain her loyalty to you. Your revolution needs a martyr, who better than he?"

"This isn't my revolution, it's yours!" Caleb yelled, his fingers crushing the paper bills. He debated whether all of this was worth it. It had been four years since he killed his father and fled his family's estate. The first year returning home was all he could think about, it's what kept him going. Back then he would have given anything to get his old life back, even start a war. What did it matter to him anyway? It did matter though, as much as he didn't want it to. He didn't mean for it to play out this way. Never was he particularly fond of religion and he found himself yearning for a connection with his gods. The Children of Azel were supposed to just be a means to an end, now they were a family and Grant was his best friend. He looked at the money again and thought of who he was doing this for. *She needs you. Make it right, whatever it takes.* He prayed for guidance, but the gods didn't answer. "When this is over though we get it all back, you will undo it?" Caleb asked, hoping for a way out that didn't involve betraying Grant.

"It will be like nothing ever happened. You have my word," Ismarlen snarled.

"Okay. Consider it done. I will... *get rid* of Grant." Caleb's usually confident voice was hollow and defeated.

"Good." Ismarlen was gone as quickly and as silently as he appeared.

It was a quarter to midnight. Caleb stood on the corner of the rail platform. It was wet outside and the putrid smell of chemicals and garbage hung thick in the air. His hands shook as he lit a cigarette. The northern parts of the city were cold this time of night. *Just leave, don't do it, he has no real power until you let him. No deal was made, not yet. It's not too late to turn back.* His mind drowned in doubt. He prayed again, with everything he had for a sign from the gods telling him it was the right choice to walk away now. The gods gave him nothing.

The rail transport pulled up, the lights from inside spilling out as the doors opened, two officers, one comically tall and lanky and the other a short and stocky, walked by with dogs who growled at Caleb. The false prophet removed his hat, pretending to be a beggar.

"No miscreants allowed on the tracks. Either you are here to travel or to start trouble, which is it?" The officer pulled on the leash of his dog, which obeyed the command to sit.

Do it for her. He thought and shoved his doubt out of his mind.

Caleb raised his hands. "Officers I mean you no trouble this evening. I am simply here to alert you of some suspicious activity going on in the tunnels. Word is LIRA and IRG will be smuggling in some weapons down in the tunnels. As a concerned citizen of the Empire I felt it was my duty to report it." He pointed to a poster instructing passengers to:

Speak Out Against ~~Suspicious~~ ~~Activity.~~ The Empire!!!!

Grant had vandalized the poster a week before.

"It's supposed to happen at midnight." He said.

"Who are you?" The shorter, fatter officer asked. "Why should we believe you?"

The transport's whistle cut off the officer's words. With his hands still in the air, Caleb backed up and leaped into the entrance of the railcar just before the doors closed and the transport moved away from the station.

"What a nut job." The tall officer remarked to his partner.

"Do you think he was telling the truth?"

"Probably was just a dust head, but we should send some men down there tonight just to be sure."

"I fuckin hate this shit hole colony." The short one muttered as they continued their patrol.

CHAPTER 27

The sun rose, poking rays of dusty light through the crumbling walls of the temple. Lilly turned over to avoid the morning, the seductive call of sleep was just too much for her to resist. She lost so much sleep over her Venolin and her fight with Grant. She wanted to apologize for slapping him, but figured it could wait until after breakfast. Buried under her blankets patched together from bits of fabric, she successfully hid from the day for an entire hour.

The kitchen was abuzz with Caleb, Samrael, the rest of the six and Nev, when the well-rested Lilly finally made it downstairs. Nev was tending to Samrael, who had a large gash over his right eye and what looked like a broken nose.

"What's going on?" Lilly yawned. It wasn't unusual for the Six to return from a mission beat up to all nine hells, it was more unsettling to her that the kitchen was this crowded so long after breakfast.

"The authorities raided a weapons buy that Grant and the Six were making with LIRA and IRG." Nev was distracted, trying to keep Samrael still.

"By the gods, is everyone alright?"

"Grant got shot. The authorities picked him up just outside the tunnel. If it weren't for him, we'd have all been pinched." Samrael took off the cold compress and shooed Nev away.

Lilly felt her heart tumble into her shoes. "Is, is he going to be okay?"

"They won't kill him. They probably will fix him up so he can stand trial." His temper took over and Caleb kicked the small wooden stool in front of him. "This is exactly what the Empire needs, a circus to distract the people!" He screamed.

"Well, we're going to save him, right?" Lilly still couldn't grasp what was going on. She flashed Caleb a desperate look. He wrapped his arms around her. "There's no way we could get to him. Plus, Grant was dedicated to the mission." He addressed the room, Lilly still in his arms. "He wouldn't want us to risk everything we have built to save him from prison. He understood that what we are doing is bigger than any one man. We will continue fighting for the cause, even harder now that we lost Grant. We must turn to the gods now more than ever, it's the only thing that will keep us united." Caleb knew his gods were the only path to forgiveness, for the sins he had committed. He clung to the word, hoping to dig out an ounce of hope. "For a Free Lo Irant!" He shouted to the sullen group.

"A Free Lo Irant," They replied with heartbroken, but determined voices.

"Now is the time we make our move. We will answer the Empire's call to war. I will need you all to be your most careful, stay in pairs and hit the streets spreading the good word. Samrael, you are now my best soldier. Get yourself sewed up. It's time we start planning."

"Yes sir." Samrael lowered his head, going over every second from the night before. If he had only taken a different route in the tunnels they might have all escaped. If he had just been able to carry Grant a little bit farther, none of this would have happened.

It was half past midnight and Lilly was still up in the printing room, working on "Free Grant Ardlow" posters. The lantern was almost completely out and her eyes burned trying to focus in the darkness. The smell of the chemicals in the ink gave her a headache. She feared if she stopped all she could think about was Grant, alone and suffering in a prison cell.

Caleb was right, though, they needed to move forward and continue their work if they were going to honor Grant.

The cause was more important to him than life itself. She let the thoughts of his passion motivate her through the pain and fatigue.

"It's not gonna do any good if you work yourself into a sickbed." Nev came up with some dinner, boiled cabbage mostly, there was a slice of cold toast, and an amorphous blob of something that might have once been meat, but Lilly wasn't very hungry.

"Too much to do, getting ready for the vigil tomorrow. You heard Caleb, all our funds is gone. How can you have a revolution with no funds?"

She mumbled not looking away from her work. She had a good pace going, the rhythmic sounds of the giant press was drowning out her sadness.

"I know you were close. I saw you leaving his room that night after Londallin." Nev, put her hands on Lilly's arm, breaking the momentum she had going.

"Great! So I guess you're gonna tell me, I brought this on us. Isn't that what Caleb would say?" She blurted and wiped her tears away with her sleeves. She was so used to seeing blood when she felt pain this bad, the unfamiliar sight of tears staining her jacket was unsettling. She was angry, at the Empire, at this war, but mostly at herself. There was so much the cause needed and all she cared about was her fight with Grant. It was like she was still that selfish little plantation brat from the Southlands. Lilly hated that girl more than anything.

"Of course not. Sometimes our business ain't nothing for Caleb to be concerning himself with." Nev thought she sounded like her mother, she smiled at that thought.

"They won't hang him. I don't know if that helps, but it's somethin." She fished through the pockets of her jacket, pulled out a bracelet, the three starfire stones glistened even in the dim light. "Grant said he lifted off some Imperial pig headin over to Camden's. Told me he was gonna give it to you when he got back, said somethin about an apology and then gave it to me to hold on to. It's beautiful." Nev placed it gently into Lilly's hands.

Holding it reminded her of the necklace her father gave her, that was probably still in Elana's jewelry box. It felt heavier than it looked. "It's too fine a thing, for a girl like me. This could feed us all for over a month." Giving Nev back the bracelet was easy, like it never should have belonged to her in the first place.

CHAPTER 28

The Spring air was warm as the sun dipped below the horizon letting a sea of dark purple spill into a night sky blanketed with stars. Lilly stood against the rusty chain-link fence, drawing lines in the dirt with her foot. The Spring Market Festival was tomorrow and the transport station was packed full of people coming into Core for the occasion.

The Market Festival was a "gift" to the Iranti people from the corporations, a huge carnival with rides and shows, the latest goods from the Empire available duty-free. For many in the Riverlands it was one of the few days off they got all year. Caleb got word of a shipment of tainted food being brought in by Venolin. Their goal was to stop the shipment.

A Vist couple walked by Lilly paying no attention to the girl or her sign asking for coin to feed her family. Lilly spit as they passed. Over the last few years Market Festival had turned into a tourist attraction for the wealthy to get a rare glimpse to see how the other part lives. This was their home, not a zoo with their lives on display. Lilly's cold stare followed them as they turned the corner, her life in the Southlands feeling more like a distant dream than ever before.

The wooden box she was sitting on, creaked under her shifting weight as she slipped her jacket underneath her to use as a cushion. It was so boring sitting out begging for spare change. Caleb told her to act as lookout for the authorities, but it seemed they were too busy helping the Vist tourists off the rail cars to cause trouble for them. The minute hand of her watch lurched forward and she groaned. Time was moving impossibly slow. She carelessly shoved the small, silver timepiece she'd pilfered from a Vist businessman into her pocket. If she only knew what Caleb and Samrael were doing.

Caleb told her little other than they were sabotaging the tainted food supply that was coming in by rail that night. She banged her head against the fence out of boredom and frustration. This was taking forever.

He'd promised them all a proper holiday after this. Lilly needed the break. Things had been getting tense since Grant was arrested. The group had split and only a handful were still left in the church.

Samrael stood over Caleb as he set another device under the iron tracks. He shifted his weight on the balls of his toes getting a look at the people pouring out of the railcars.

"These are all passenger cars, Caleb, are you sure we have our information correct?" he whispered.

Caleb gently connected the red wire with the yellow, and then waved the pocket com over it, the device beeped. The sound made Samrael jump.

"Of course the information is correct. These won't go off until well after midnight. No passenger trains will be there."

Samrael kicked some pebbles and muttered quietly to himself. Caleb's hand touched his shoulder and he signaled to quiet. The sloshing of boots on gravel: someone was coming. The pair stood frozen, waiting to see where the noise was coming from. A railcar blocked the view, but they could see the light from flashlights shining from behind them.

"Over there! There are two by rail seven!" A man's voice yelled and a chorus of dogs began barking loudly.

Samrael grabbed the collar of Caleb's jacket and pulled him under a railcar. The bottom of the railcar hovered less than an inch from Caleb's nose, and considerably less than an inch from Samrael's. They waited until the men passed, then rolled over to the other side. There were now at least a dozen men on the tracks with dogs looking for Samrael and Caleb as the two ducked between moving rail cars.

The sounds of the dogs shocked Lilly out of a daydream. Her panicked eyes scanned for signs of Caleb and

Samrael on the rails, but she could only see armed men with dogs. Her slender fingers were wrapped around the fence, ready to pull open the hole they had precut to access the rails. Jagged, rusted metal dug into her fingers. The sensation helped her stay focused.

The force of the explosion knocked Lilly off her feet just as she heard the deafening boom. Gravel and bits of hot metal rained down on top of her as she tumbled down the rocky hill. Through the smoke she saw figures running past her, their skin ashen gray spotted with a red so dark it was almost black. She had to blink twice before she recognized the ghastly, misshapen figures as people. Two more explosions shook the ground, the bright flash penetrating the thick gray smoke, and then a third. A pair of hands jerked her arm and dragged her off the ground.

She was stuck among a swarm of people screaming, running, some of them unaware they were in pieces. Bodies, and parts of bodies littered the ground, left to their own in the chaos. There was nothing familiar about the place, although she could have drawn it from memory if she was asked just an hour earlier. Still, everything moved so quickly that at one point she no longer saw the dead or mangled people fleeing past her. *Go!* was the only thought she could process and she held on to the arm that was pulling her along the wave of panic.

Only after they stopped did she notice the jacket, even covered in dust, the dark olive sleeve with the gold stars and the red armband let her know it was Caleb. His eyes, blue as polar ice, looked wild as they pierced through the dust and blood. She was loaded into the back of the large cargo transport, with Caleb and the rest of the Six. Caleb slapped the rusted metal, signaling the driver to move it and they drove off just before a fleet of Imperial forces pulled up to the scene.

Cold water fell on her face, washing away the thick gray ash. Samrael offered her his sleeve to dry off and smiled at her. Lilly blinked and gave weak smile, but it was all she could muster.

"She's okay, just a little shaken up," he called to nobody in particular.

It felt like she was being thrown around in the back of the busted up cargo transport. Everything hurt. Caleb sat at the edge, his feet hanging over the side looking at the carnage fading off into the distance. He was silent. His expression made Lilly feel that his was still on the rail platform and needed some time to catch up. She was unable to say anything, the words falling apart in her throat before she got a chance to speak.

Samrael was fidgeting, running his hands over his head, frantically attempting to gain understanding. It felt like if he sat still, his skin would peel off his bones and run off. The truth was chasing him. They had set off the bombs. They had just committed a terrible act. He was responsible for all of the death that occurred today. Samrael rejected that reality with every ounce of his being, yet it branded itself on his mind, burning the soul crushing mark of a murderer that would stay with him forever.

He paused and took a breath. The road they were taking hadn't been used in years. The sky was littered with starlight as the transport drove along the bumpy abandoned highway. It was a beautiful night, the kind that had once brought him peace, but the stars would never shine that way again. His world would never be the same.

Nobody said a word the entire ride, although Samrael uttered a brief "whoa" as the transport crossed over a rickety rusted bridge and it buckled under the weight. The transport slowed to a stop and the loud hum of the engine reminded Lilly of the night she hitchhiked. *I would kill for some breakfast right now*, she thought. Her cheeks flushed, ashamed for thinking such a thing at such a time.

Everyone piled out of the transport. Lilly knew they were somewhere in the northern forests, but not much beyond that. The wood and brick building looked like it had seen better days, there are garbage dumps that look like they've seen better days than this place, she muttered silently to herself. It had once been the headquarters of a coalmine, back when the Empire used coal. Caleb ripped off the rotted wooden board nailed over the doorway and ushered everyone inside.

Nev, the twins and what was left of Caleb's flock, about a dozen boys and girls, were waiting for them.

Candles lit the place. Tents fashioned out of bits of wood and old blankets lined one corner. Lilly smelled the food cooking. It smelled delicious, but her appetite had vanished.

"By the Gods, what happened?" Nev jumped up to check out Samrael's wounds.

"The Empire had bombs. It was a trap. They knew we'd be there. It was a set-up." Caleb said, leaning on the table for support. The blast had broken some ribs and the adrenaline was wearing off as the pain settled in.

Samrael shot Caleb a glare so sharp, if it were a knife, would have cut through the liar like he was made of rice paper. He swallowed his venom.

"It's true." He forced those words over his tongue not breaking his gaze with Caleb. "We were set up."

"I'm glad we decided to head for the mountains. No doubt the Empire will run with their lies. It's best we stay here, until it's safe." Caleb addressed the small group.

"When will that be?" Nev asked, concerned. "We got your message and just ran. We didn't have time to stock up on much supplies."

"I'm not sure, but the Six and I will get you anything you need. It's late and we've been through a lot. This is a test of our dedication to the cause. For Grant's sake, for the sake of the patriots who were killed today, we must remember why we are here." Caleb had a way of speaking that could calm a raging plains bull.

Samrael slunk away with Nev under his arm to a little space she had set up to sleep. He spent the night awake, listening to the soft breathing of Nev, and the occasional muffled coughs of the others. It seemed like a lifetime, but the sun rose, its rays leaking through the holes in the dusty and boarded up windows. The hideout was not familiar, but he couldn't for the life of him think of a place that would be at that moment. Watching Nev's chest rise and fall with each breath, he let her fingers curl around his. He took comfort in her peace and kissed her forehead.

CHAPTER 29

Lilly inspected the weapons laying on the table, rifles, explosives, knives, they had a heaviness to them she didn't expect when she held them. The Empire's response to the train bombing was swift and hard. That night dozens of separatists were arrested in the middle of the night, and the arrests continued. The unity and pride Lilly saw at Londallin had faded to fear and panic. Businesses and homes who once proudly displayed "Free Lo Irant" signs, flags and banners had taken them down, many shuttered their doors completely to avoid the Empire's scrutiny.

It still somehow seemed unreal, everything was happening too fast. Her mind kept returning to the day at Londallin when she saved Grant's life. She killed someone that day. Something inside of her told her she should be devastated by that, but she wasn't. Grant would have died if she didn't. This was a war, as much as she didn't want it to be it was. For the first time since her first night in the temple, she missed the plantation. Everything was so simple back then. The only people who died were old people and once in awhile sick people and even though it was sad, it didn't feel wrong. The last month had brought so much devastation. Two days ago she heard stories of fathers being dragged out of their houses, by Imperial forces and shot on their front yard while their families watched. Yesterday she heard about a temple honoring the sky gods being burned to the ground while the loyalists were inside worshiping. She prayed for both sides and felt like a traitor for it, like she was betraying her own people. Every bone in her body was believed in a Free Lo Irant. She wanted to believe only soldiers died in war, but that wasn't true and it was a fact that was getting harder and harder to ignore. The weakest part of her questioned if she even truly believed in this war, the cause yes, it was the cost of it all that fueled her doubts.

She scoured the grounds to find a spot to be alone with her thoughts, but the little mining office was stuffed to the brim and buzzing with activity. LIRA and IRG had moved their headquarters to the abandoned mine. Lilly over heard them talking about the minerals messed with imperial surveillance equipment. Caleb and Samrael signed an accord, joining The Children of Azel, officially to the separatist movement. Several clans from the Northlands agreed to offer support for the war, with men and supplies. The Empire thought that fear would quiet the raging storm brewing in Lo Irant, but it strengthened the resolve of the separatists and inspired many more to get involved and she was in the middle of all of it.

Caleb was reading out loud from the Itara on the stair case, his followers sitting around him. A few of the IRG and LIRA had joined in the small prayer service. He had lost his harshness, since the rail bombings. He was quieter, less quick to anger. He was always able to get people to believe the words that came out of his mouth, now he was starting to believe them too. For three weeks, he was able to be a part of something greater than himself. These weren't just the musings of an angry working class, there was something to fight for.

"The harvest gods are the most forgiving." He preached, his voice was both strong and soft, filled with conviction and hope. "They understand man is weaker, prone to stray. You don't cut the weak vines, you tend to them, support and nurture them. We repay their mercy with obedience and prayer. Pray for our weaker brothers, so they may grow strong in the light of the Gods."

Lilly leaned on the banister, smiling. After the bombings everyone was in such despair, Caleb brought them back. He spoke of the world after this conflict was over. They would buy a farm, live off the land. She hoped all of this would be over quickly. The Empire was a democracy. She knew Oprian colonists from back home. All of them were kind and decent people. Once the people in Opree saw what was happening, once they could not ignore it any longer, they would support a free Lo Irant and there would be peace. How could they not?

Moonlight bathed the forest in its brilliant silver glow. Everyone else was asleep, except the patrols guarding the perimeter, and Caleb. He nestled himself in the shadow of a boulder at a quiet spot alongside of the entrance to the old mine. It was his thinking place. He dug his fingers into the cold dirt and felt rooted, connected to the land. *I'm home*, he thought looking at the crumbling soil in his hands the way he did when he was a child learning how to work the farm.

The gods work in strange ways. He recited the proverb in his mind. He began to find peace in the Itara's teachings and thought about that after all of this time pretending to be a man of the gods, it was truly his path to redemption. For so long redemption meant getting his lands, his name and his money back. He heard them though; the gods spoke to him the night before Londallin and again after the train bombing. He was going to be a shepherd of a devoted flock and earn his place with his gods. His mind went to the bombings and Grant and he cringed.

An iron cart, rusted through in some spots and vines wrapped around it, as if it was being pulled into the ground, gave him comfort. The world seemed to have a way of reclaiming itself, although it may take time, the gods had an amazing way of bringing everyone back home.

"It's funny, isn't it?" Ismarlen crept out from the shadows, wearing an IRG uniform. "Watching Iron crumble to dust?" His gaze drifted to the mining cart.

Startled Caleb jumped up. "Ismarlen, I wasn't expecting you tonight." He said, choking on his fear.

"Congratulations, you've started a war." His tone was so flat it was difficult to gauge his sincerity. "And quite a good one, I might add." He squeezed the young man's shoulders. To Caleb, they felt like the tendrils of a sea beast ready to drag him into the abyss. "Honestly, I am impressed. I couldn't have done it better myself. But there is still that last part of the deal." He dragged his finger across his neck, in a grim gesture. "After that you are free to go home. All your sins forgotten...."

The weight of those words sat in Caleb's stomach like a stone as he processed them. He thought of home. Years of clawing up from the pit of shit with a singular goal, but he didn't want that anymore. He didn't want to go back, he was already home. He had made peace with his gods, started a new life, a life that wouldn't be tainted with a cursed soul. In the darkness the god's orange eyes, seemed to glow brighter and look through him, like his soul was a bug trapped in a glass jar. "No." He said, barely audible.

"No?" He made a face giving Caleb the impression he was about to be torn in half. An eerie ghostlike chorus of wolves howled, in the distance. They didn't sound like any wolves native to the area. "You made the promise, you wanted to go home-"

"Well I changed my mind. I'm not going to kill her. I regret ever summoning you. I'm done with this no more deals! I've heard my gods. This war will be won, but it won't be tainted with the likes of you." He pushed Ismarlen's hand off his shoulder and faced the god, looking him in the eye.

"Those voices you heard were your own. Your gods abandoned you. They don't hear your prayers. I'm the only one left who cares about the fate of humanity." Ismarlen softened a bit.

"I don't believe you. I'm saved Ismarlen, by their glory. I am free." Caleb stated with confidence.

"That's not how this works. You don't have a choice." Ismarlen barked. "I am Ismarlen, eleventh son of the first father. There is no turning back. How would everyone feel if they knew it was you who tipped the authorities off to Grant? LIRA and the IRG would hang you as a traitor. Opree will hang you for treason. The only way you get out of this alive, is through me."

Caleb, stood there for a moment, pondering the hypothetical scenario and decided to challenge his bluff. Eternal life in the great plains was reward enough in itself. "I do have a choice! I've made peace with my gods. Strike me down right here if you want, but I won't commit one more evil act in your name."

"Oh, piss! I'm already tired of this." He scoffed.

A rustling of leaves on the trail above interrupted the conversation.

"Caleb?" A soft voice called for him from behind a tree. It was Nev, she approached with a cautious determination. "What are you doing? Who is that?"

Caleb, looked back to Ismarlen, who was wearing an Imperial officer's uniform and holding a large black bag, the gold glistening brilliantly under the moon.

"Just giving Caleb, his reward," Ismarlen grinned, removing his hat politely to greet the confused girl.

"For?" She was trying to hold back her disgust, but didn't do a very good job of it. If this was one of Caleb's tricks, it was a reckless one.

"He alerted the authorities ma'am, stopped a weapons deal that led to the arrests of several terrorists including leaders of the IRG, LIRA and Children of Azel. This man is a hero and now very rich!"

The words trampled her like a wild herd, dragging away her disbelief. "You're the one who sold out Grant?" Hot bile rose in her chest. "Did you really snitch on him and sent him to prison? He saved us and you betrayed him!"

"Nev, it's not true!" Caleb and to explain, but she pushed him away. Afraid.

"Nev, this isn't what it looks like. He isn't...!"

"True?" Ismarlen arched an eyebrow. "Tell her, Caleb, look her in the eye and tell her you didn't sell out your best friend."

Her eyes were eager to accept any explanation. She wanted to believe him so badly, he could have sighed and she would have interpreted at a yes. It was the only time she was thankful Caleb was a good liar. His earnest expression faded as soon as her eyes met his and he looked down, his guilt shining bright as the coin in the big black bag.

Nev, backed up the small hill slowly hand still hovering over her open mouth. She wanted to scream, but nothing came out.

"Nev, let me explain! Nev, I thought we could go home!" He reached out to her and she warded him off with a stick.

"Damn you Caleb!" As soon as she felt the air come back to her lungs she screamed out of pain and frustration. Caleb thought she might wake the whole Province. "What makes you think I wanted to go back home! Do you remember what it was like? The things they said about us?"

"I'm not going to though. I told him no! " Caleb pleaded.

"Grant is in prison because of you! You can't just erase the past Caleb! What you did is unforgiveable!" She yelled, as bits of her crumbling world fell alongside her tears.

"Nothing is unforgiveable Nev. I need to explain." He pleaded on his knees and wrapped his arms around her. "I was wrong. I know that now. I made that deal a long time ago. I did it for you. I wanted to go back to like how it was before I killed Papa. I swear it Nev, I did it for you. I'm sorry and I swear I'm taking it back." He sobbed.

"I'm glad Papa is dead!.You killed him to protect me and the folks back home didn't care, they still wanted to string us up for that. This is our home, this is our family, Grant was our family. You can't just take it back! They are going to hang you! They might hang us because we followed you! Did you even think?!? Damn, Samrael was right." She kicked him aside, and ran her fingers through her hair, wracking her brain for a solution.

"I can't believe I'm doing this...but I won't tell. Not for you, but for us. It would be easier for the IRG to hide a dozen bodies than risk traitors. Leave now, take your ugly money and don't ever come back, or I will kill you myself." Her lipped quivered when she cracked on those last words.

"Nev, no you need to listen." A tearful Caleb grabbed her shoulders, shaking her violently.

"Let me go!" She yelled throwing her head hard right into his nose. The impact made a squishy crunch sound and the blow was delivered with enough force that he dropped her.

Pain and instinct took over and his fist swung at Nev, knocking her off of her feet. She landed with a hard crack on a sharp rock hiding in the soft bed of dead leaves. Caleb's hands shook, as he waited for Nev to get back up. A few breaths passed and she was still on the ground unnaturally still.

"I'm sorry. I didn't want to hurt you." He squeaked and knelt by his beloved sister's side. His hand touched something warm and sticky on the ground. In the dark it looked black, but in the moonlight, the dark red hue was unmistakable. "Nev?" He shook her shoulders, but she was unresponsive, her eyes staring blankly at nothing. The black pool forming beside her head in his shadow, bubbled as it saturated the thirsty ground. Helpless to stop it, he could only watch as a small river of her blood stained the soil.

"I didn't mean to...She was going to...I had no choice." Caleb, white with fear, mumbled to Ismarlen. "It was an accident. Nothing is unforgivable, I can still go back... I had no choice."

Ismarlen said nothing as he placed his boot on the dead girls chest, carving his mark into her cheek with his knife. It smelled like burning hair as her flesh was being branded. Caleb knew it meant that her soul would never find its way to their Gods. She'd serve Ismarlen in the underworld forever.

"You always had a choice." his voice was hollow and devoid of feeling, "but like you said, nothing is unforgivable.... although, you can take it back." He smiled, black teeth glistening like an eel.

"You can save her?" Caleb gulped, hoping the dark deity wasn't pulling his leg.

"Well, her soul at least. Join me, and when this war is over, I will restore her soul to your gods."

"I'll do whatever you want. I'll do anything." Caleb pleaded as the weight of his guilt crushed his chest.

"Good." Ismarlen placed his hand on Caleb's chest.

Caleb felt a numb tingling at first, then his skin started to crawl from within as Ismarlen made his mark on the desperate young man. The pain was astounding as his flesh bubbled and blistered, a light inside of him went out and he felt the best parts of him rip from the fibers of his every being.

Ismarlen's laughter turned to the fading sound of the wolves' chorus as he slipped back into the shadows.

Nestled back into his thinking place, Caleb rocked back and forth whispering psalms to himself, his fingers digging into the ground, dirt caking on the patches of not yet dried blood still on his hands. It was the same soil that welcomed him and called him home just an hour ago, except now the land felt cold and foreign. The Itara always preached redemption for a man who turned his back on his gods, now his gods had turned their backs to him and he knew he would never find home again.

An hour past dawn and the resistance movement's base of operations was already buzzing with activity. Barefoot with her hair unbrushed, Lilly weaved through the maze of boxes and people looking for Caleb, he had not returned from his walk the night before. More than once she had to stop herself, take a breath and slow down. Remembering how he scolded her for making a fuss last time he didn't return on time, she decided to keep quiet about it until she was sure he was actually missing, but it had been a few hours and she was having a difficult time controlling her panic. Lost in thought, she barreled through the tight corner into the kitchen, colliding with a frantic Samrael.

"Sorry, Lil. I didn't see you." He helped Lilly onto her feet and brushed the wild mass of hair from off her face. "Have you seen, Nev? She went out last night, never came in and now I can't find her"

"No, I was looking for Caleb. Should we tell someone?" Lilly asked.

Samrael looked around. "No one will listen." He scoffed. "We're just a bunch of kids." He was still sore that he was turned down to take part in an important mission because of his age.

The front door opened and a flood of early morning sun flooded the hall. Lilly and Sam watched the silhouetted figure stagger inside. It was Caleb, covered in mud and blood. The whole room fell silent, as all eyes were watching him. "We were attacked." He said through heavy breaths, his under caste accent much more pronounced.

"Imperials, killed Nev." He lowered his head, but his gaze remained level with everyone else. "'In the name of the King' they said. Then they did things I don't care to mention. They desecrated her body, so she couldn't be claimed by the gods. I found her by the river." He rattled out the painful details with the cold perfection of a rehearsed speech repeated so many times its words lost all meaning.

"Did anyone follow you?" An IRG Commander inquired. Caleb shook his head. "Are you sure?" He said with an impatient condescending tone.

"Fuck! They know where we are! It's only a matter of time before..." Someone in the back called out and the room erupted with chatter. The subject of Caleb and Nev was swept away in a sea of 'official business.'

Caleb limped over to Lilly who met him at the stairs. Wrapping her arms around him, she could feel his tears on top of her head as he gripped her tightly. Pale and dumbfounded, Sam slowly fell back letting the wall guide his grief heavy body to the floor. "We're going to get them back." He sobbed softly into her ear. "We are going to make them pay."

NATHANIAL

"His children shall bear his shame, cursed for his sacrifice. They walk as outcastes as they honor him in darkness."

- The Itara, Creations 24:19

CHAPTER 30

The forest just north of New Empire was one of the few places in Opree that was still wilderness. Six hundred acres of giant red pines stretched across the mountainous terrain into the polar circle. It was a cold gray day for late spring. The rain fell in thick slow drops and the fog hung close to the ground. Nathanial's boots were already soaked through when they got to the Blue Team's base camp. It was nothing more than tarps pulled over poles to keep the electronic and digital equipment dry and even then the glass screens flickered on and off whenever water leaked through the tarps.

He walked over to the paper maps laid out on the table and ran his fingers over the paper as if he could absorb the information the maps provided through his skin. There was something more reliable in the old way of doing things.

"Newbridge," he addressed the seventh year cadet standing next to him, "I want you to make sure everything that is going on that screen, you track on the map."

Thirteen-year-old Daniel Newbridge twisted his nose at such a tedious task, but dared not speak out against it. "Yes sir."

"Isn't that a little redundant, General? Maybe we could use Newbridge on the field. Everything that is going on will be displayed on the monitors in real time. Why waste the time making sure the boy learns such an outdated skill?" Armand Donovan, Nathanial's second in command, asked.

Nathanial felt it was the respectful thing to have Donovan his second, although he was beginning to worry that may have not been the best idea he ever had.

Nathanial watched the image flicker on the screen again. "Don't rely on your technology," he said, quoting Captain Normandy.

"Leave it to the Iranti-born to fear technology," Donovan muttered.

"Excuse me Donovan, did you say something?" Nathanial said curtly.

"No sir."

"How odd, I could have sworn I heard something that sounded something awfully like piss and hot air. I think you should check on how the rest of the team is doing." He said with a sharp coldness the rest of his peers were used to.

"Yes sir." Donovan turned and walked away.

Nathanial massaged his temples with his fingers. No wonder Blue lost to Silver every year: Donovan was an imbecile.

Nathanial spent the better part of an hour showing Newbridge how to track troop movements and measure distance on the maps. When Nathanial was his age, paper maps were still being taught for land navigation and to track troop movements. He spent hours trying to memorize famous battles. Now everything was done digitally. With a touch of a button your position was recorded and mapped. Understanding the value of such technology, Nathanial always felt there was something about knowledge so vitally important being kept inside a small box inside his pocket, instead of safely locked inside of his mind, that seemed reckless.

The sky turned dark purple as the hidden sun dipped below the mountains. Blue Team was still preparing for tomorrow's games. Nathanial checked his watch against the time displayed on the screen and set it to the proper time. It was a gold pocket watch that had once belonged to his father. It usually sat in a box of family belongings he'd received from his attorney a few years before. Once he turned old enough to manage his affairs, he insisted what was left of the Harker estate be liquidated and what could not be sold, either donated or destroyed. One small box was all that remained of his family memories his attorney insisted the young man should want, as they were the few items recovered from his childhood home after the attacks. The box contained the watch, one of his brother Devon's toy soldiers, a photograph of his mother that was burnt in the upper left corner, and a tattered stuffed dog, torn down the middle and covered in dark brown stains.

He wound the watch until the gears wouldn't turn any more. The fluttering ticks were reassuring in a way that was lost to most in his generation so obsessed with technology.

At midnight a low tone beeping blasted from the speakers set up around the camp, signaling the countdown. Six hours until the War Games commenced. Arryn was already in bed. Silver Team had set up camp in a little under three hours and as reward Arryn had allowed them the time to rest up before the big game.

The sound of the rain on his tent was soothing, but Arryn hoped it wouldn't be too muddy for the Rugged All Terrain Transports. He gasped and sat up in his bed, removing the silk sleep mask from over his eyes. Had he remembered to test them? Usually Nathanial had those little details under control. A few moments passed and he was able to relax once he reassured himself that he must have instructed someone to make sure the RATTs were operational.

In the darkness Arryn felt alone. It would be nice to not have the silently hostile sleeping arrangements he and Nathanial had shared for the last several weeks. Having his former friend in the same room with him made it easy to be angry, angry at Nathanial's betrayal, his hot-headedness and his pride. Alone, however, all he could think about was a stupid joke he'd heard the other day. It was a joke he only snickered at, but knew it was the rare kind of humor that would make Nate go over the cliff in a fit of laughter. It was the kind of joke that in the past, Arryn would tell to get his tightly wound friend to relax at a time like this. Arryn tossed and turned, still mad, but unsure of who or what he was so angry with.

At 0700 hours the siren's moan cut through the crisp morning air. The war games had begun. Nathanial bit his lip as he watched the little blue dots on the screen move further out onto the map. Unable to focus he squirmed in uncomfortably in his chair. Normally he was commander out in the fields and Arryn stayed in command on base. Two minutes into the game, he was already frustrated with the thought of watching everything from afar.

He radioed his second in command. "Donovon, what is your position?"

"Um, about 100 meters out." Donovon didn't hide the attitude in his voice.

"Right, uhh, just make sure you radio back at the next checkpoint." He said stiffly, rolling his eyes at himself.

Silver held the higher ground. Nathanial's plan was to lure Arryn's men down past the second mock village built specifically for the games. Although it was technically against the rules, for decades teams had scouted the field, laid traps, hid supplies and spied on the opposing side, who were doing the same.

A few of the silver dots approached a cluster of twelve blue ones on the screen. Nathanial's men were holding checkpoint eleven just south of the second mock village. The paint rounds being fired were designed to sound like live fire. In the distance, it sounded like a rapid series of cracks and pops crescendoing, then they faded. He watched as each of the twelve blue dots disappear off the screen. "Dammit, come on, fall back to position, fall back to position!" He whispered to himself. "Fuck!" He slammed his fist on the desk. Those in the command tent went silent and stared. Looking back at all the other blue dots still on screen, the loss didn't seem as bad. Maybe he had overreacted.

It was the first altercation in the conflict and it left him feeling dry and empty instead of exhilarated. He should be in the field, facing the opposition head on, not watching twelve little blue dots disappear from the screen.

"Newbridge, you keeping up with that map?" He turned to the boy, who was leaning his head on his hand, pushing the tiny colored cubes across the paper with the other.

"Yes sir." Newbridge sat at attention.

"Good. Keep it up." Nathanial stepped to the edge of the tent and watched the rain fall softly outside. "I'm going to check on the RATTs before we deploy Farrow Squad."

In the tent the team continued with their duties. Newbridge sulked in his chair, and gave a heavy sigh as he waited for the screen in front of him to refresh.

The faculty at Penderghast sat in the Gray Lodge, one of the few structures as old as Penderghast, watching the glass monitors set up in the great hall. The Grays were an old family. Petir Gray had left Penderghast his estate and massive land holdings with the condition that they keep the giant pine forests intact for when the Sky gods returned. Cyrus took a moment to admire the understated beauty of the place. In the wild forest regions of Opree the culture reminded Cyrus of the Iranti Northlands where his ancestors had come from. The gods of thunder, war and winter hailed from this region and their ancient marks were carved into every giant red pine beam in brilliant platinum. Heads of the now extinct Morrow Wolves and Tiber Bears crowned the walls. A giant chandelier made of antlers hung over the massive stone fireplace in the center of the room. He imagined what it would have been like before the cities swallowed the forests.

Among the faculty and their guests was a handful of government officials taking advantage of the free food and photo op. King Jonathan and Colonel Cyrus Mason stood beside a group of Navat War veterans swapping war stories. Cyrus scanned the room as Jonathan told the group about the time he and the infamous Colonel Mason were pinned behind a Kyre Mission against a squad of Navat stalkers. A small group of Senators stirred their drinks with plastic grins plastered on their faces that barely masked their boredom as Captain Normandy spoke about the kind of training that Cadets received. Cyrus silently commended the man for being able to stomach such worms.

"I swear, if it wasn't for this man right here, I wouldn't be standing here today." The King finished his story that Cyrus had heard so many times he could repeat it himself.

The other men laughed deep hearty laughs the way that salty old men do. They'd heard the story many times as well, but they liked the King. He was becoming a popular public figure, grounded in a way that was lost among

the cold, bureaucratic servants of the public that currently governed the Empire.

"You should run for Senate, your grace," one of the
veterans said. "It's perfectly legal if you get the votes and
the people love you so that wouldn't be an issue. Someone
like you would get things done. It's about time we had effective leadership in this empire." He laughed.

"I'm afraid he would never qualify. His head isn't
nearly bloated enough and the man has entirely too much
common sense," Cyrus joked.

They responded with a soft chuckle, uncomfortable
with the concept of a Colonel Cyrus Mason who cracks
jokes. One by one they excused themselves from the circle
until it was comprised of just Jonathan and Cyrus.

"Captain Normandy tells me you were scouting
Nathanial Harker. I'm surprised. Didn't think you would
be interested in High Born Officer Candidates for your
Shadows. Hardly the rugged, rough and tumble type required for life in Kyrant," the King baited.

"Yes, I was just curious. I heard about the Iranti-born
boy attending Penderghast and I decided I needed to
check it out for myself. He's definitely impressive. Do you
know him?"

"Quite well actually, my youngest, Arryn befriended
him as a child. He spent half his life growing up in Ivory
Castle in the palace whenever he wasn't at Penderghast. A
quiet and gentle boy, but I would never make the mistake

of underestimating him. He's the son of General Alexi Harker"

"Yes, so I've heard. Well, maybe I could use the son of a legend on my Shadows. Maybe a gentleman's upbringing would smooth out the rough edges my Shadows are so well known for." He smiled, watching the textbook Riddarker maneuver Nathanial was using against Prince Arryn's troops.

"If anyone could, it would be Nathanial, but unfortunately you are too late. He accepted my offer to be Captain of the Ivory Guard just last week." The King folded his arms, contented.

"That is unfortunate." Cyrus paused, "How about I'll fight you for him? To the death, of course, you can choose venue and weapons." His tone was flat and dismissive, never breaking his gaze on the screen.

Any other man would have been frozen in terror at the suggestion, but the King knew Cyrus enough to know that he was only half-serious. The king picked up a glass of wine off the tray a servant was carrying and took a sip.

For almost twenty years the two had been friends, and yet he couldn't remember a time since the war where they held a conversation for this long. Jonathan dismissed it as the kind of friendship that started in the war when a fool-hardy young Duke decided to risk his life fighting for his Empire. Jonathan was forever in Cyrus's debt for saving his life. Many times since then Cyrus had called in favors when he needed it, but the King was happy to oblige.

In almost twenty years Jonathan expected Cyrus to have aged more than he did, look a little more worn. Maybe he wasn't expecting a large gut like his own, but more lines on his face, more than just a few streaks of gray hair. Something that gave away the toll seventeen years of fighting a forgotten war would have on a man.

"I apologize, but I'm king so I win."

"Very well, have him. Had I known you'd have been such a pain in my ass, I would have thrown you to the Navat." Cyrus sighed, eyes glued to the action happening on the screens.

It was almost sundown. Arryn lounged in the Silver Team's command tent, muddy boots on the table, balancing on the back two legs of the chair. This war was going nowhere very slowly. Obviously the two teams were evenly matched, for the last hour neither had made a move. Part of him wanted to surrender, just to end this nonsense. He rubbed his temples, trying to massage a strategy out of his brain. *This is ridiculous, Nate, when are you planning to pop your fat little head out of your ass and make a move?* He thought. His eyes were fixed on the mock village in the center of the map, the lowest part of the field. He could easily have the place surrounded and have direct access to the east and west. Currently Blue Team held it with just a small group of men.

The front two legs of his chair met the ground as Arryn leaned in closer to the map. The image flickered when his finger traced over the valuable checkpoint. "You stupid mud farming simpleton," he whispered to himself. "I got you now."

He jumped out of his chair and grabbed his field gear. "Marland, get your disfigured barbarian ass and your unit out to checkpoint number twelve. I want everyone out there to surround the place and wait for my orders. Bring your cigars. We are about to crush Blue in a massacre!"

Nate watched as a thick circle of silver surrounded the small mock village in the low ground and snuffed out the blue. *Now I got you,* he thought and kicked Newbridge's chair to wake the sleeping cadet. The kid picked his head up with an involuntary groan only to have it slapped by his Commanding Officer.

"Pay attention, Newbridge. I'm not going to tell you again or I'll stick you in a silk dress and have you flogged out in the rain." Nathanial noticed he was starting to sound like Captain Normandy. One of the other cadets, who also recognized the resemblance, snorted as he tried to hold in a laugh.

Thompson, one of Penderghast's few female cadets approached him. "Sir, we have a live feed coming from checkpoint twelve."

Women had been fighting alongside the men in Oprian military for centuries. Although it wasn't common, it had never been expressly forbidden. There was no gender differentiation once a person joined the military. Everyone trained, lived and served together. That was primarily why High Born women didn't go to Penderghast. They were discouraged from doing anything besides looking pretty and preparing for marriage and a masculine woman did not make a desirable bride. Although there had been no girls in Nathanial's class, the classes below him had a number of Vistany girls joining their ranks.

"Let's see it, Thompson," Nathanial said.

Thompson pressed a button on the controls and a window popped up displaying Arryn's smug face. Nate thought the prince looked ridiculous wearing an antique helmet and goggles that harkened to a time when their grandfathers served. Nathanial rolled his eyes. "You're live on his feed now too," Thompson said.

"What do you want?" Nate was annoyed. He knew this was just war games, but he hoped his former friend would take it at least a little seriously.

"Victory is mine. Do you wish to surrender now?" Arryn toyed.

"You've captured a checkpoint. You don't win until you hold my base and yours, but you know this." Nathanial groaned. "What in nine hells are you doing?"

"Nothing..." Arryn turned the camera to Blue Team. Several of them were at gunpoint, ballroom dancing with each other and wearing women's evening wear by the light of barrel fires. Silver team was doubled over in hysterics. Nathanial recognized one of the finely dressed men as Donovon, who looked like he was about to murder Arryn. The prince was giddy as he turned the camera back on himself, "just livening things up a bit."

Nathanial buried his face in his hands. How was he supposed to handle the situation? There were very important people watching this and the prince was making him look like a fool. This stunt was outrageous, even for Arryn. "Just let them go. I'm sure you're breaking at least a dozen rules. I'd rather not win because you disqualified yourself."

"There are no rules in war, my dear friend, but I'd hate to be accused of being unfair. Come down here in good faith, and my men and I will retreat back to the positions and we can start again."

Nate looked at the map. The majority of Arryn's forces were concentrated on their current spot. He was bored and wanted this to end in one big decisive battle.

Nathanial saw his opportunity in a narrow passage that took them through a pass on a hill, it would require his team going out of bounds, but the rules were gone a long time ago. He picked up his radio.

"Davidson, Marcus, Pildridge, abandon posts, and report to base at once."

Nathanial drove the RATT the three kilometers to where Arryn and Silver Team were. The small particleboard buildings were charred and music was blasting as Silver Team celebrated their victory. Cadets who Nathanial had known to be astute, serious and respectable had succumbed to the madness. Nate had never realized how influential of a leader Arryn was to his men, and thought it a shame he didn't focus that ability properly. Although part of him acknowledged that he was a bit jealous to not be a part of such festivities. Being on the other side of Arryn's hijinx was proving tiresome.

He climbed out of the RATT and was greeted by two Silver Team armed escorts. "His Grace, The High Born Prince Arryn of Ivory Castle, wishes to see you," someone from Silver Team said. Nathanial didn't know his name, but recognized him as being a year or two behind his class.

"His grace?" The only time Arryn had people refer to him as 'His Grace, High Born Prince Arryn...' was when he insisted on being difficult. Nathanial pinched the bridge of his nose, hoping to avoid the headache Arryn was giving him.

He followed the two down the dirt road. Rows of barrel fires lit the path, reminding him of the images of war-torn Kyrant in his books. Arryn was leaning on a heavily armored RATT, smoking a cigar. He slid down to greet Nate by blowing a puff of smoke in his face.

"You came alone? I think you may trust me too much." Arryn grinned with the cigar clenched between his teeth. He looked around, the firelight blackened the hills above him. "Or not at all."

"I've got my men where I need them," Nathanial said, flicking the dirt out from under his nails. "Are we done with this now? I'm not sure what point you are trying to prove."

"My dear Nate, I'm merely trying to win. That's all. Unless you plan to take out all of my men by yourself, I think I'm doing a good job."

"You are trying to make me look like a idiot! This stupid feud needs to stop. Arryn, at this point you might even get expelled for this little stunt. You burned the village down!"

Arryn surveyed the damage with a sense of pride. "I also culled the livestock and locked all of the women and children in that temple, just over there." He pointed to a smoldering pit of ash at the edge of the village. Wooden cutouts of animals were standing with their heads removed, except "I won't lie, despite all of my dastardly deeds I was moved to mercy at one point. I spared your wife." He was referring to a cut out of a pig, on which someone had drawn a sad face and written "MRS. NATHANIAL HARKER" in large block letters on its side.

"Enough, Arryn this isn't funny. Everyone is watching this. Your Father is watching! If you won't take this seriously, I don't know what else to do. I thought I could talk reason into you." Nathanial picked up his radio. "Davidson, take out his graces two escorts, please."

Two paint rounds whizzed through the air and hit their targets, one on his forehead just under the helmet, the other right in the neck. The cadet who was hit in the neck let out a loud cry. The other was curled up on the ground, cursing. Arryn stiffened up.

"Well, that got my attention," the Prince admitted raising his hands in the air.

"Go to your base, let's start this over," Nathanial said. "This is my last warning. I don't want to make a joke of this Academy. I know deep down you don't, either."

"Very well," the Prince pouted. "This party was getting dull anyway. I'll see you when I take over your base later." He patted Nate on the chest and turned around. "Come on boys, let's go back home."

Nathanial watched as the Silver Team walked off in the distance. He untied his men, who were still in the fairly expensive women's eveningwear. "Donovon, how could you let them do this to you?"

Donovan sulked with his head down. "They were going to shoot us."

Nathanial looked at his rifle filled with paint rounds with disbelief and disgust, then shot Donovan point blank in the crotch. The disgraced cadet fell down and howled in pain. Nathanial walked past him, shaking his head. "Fucking imbecile," he muttered.

He made the cadets who had surrendered to Arryn walk the three kilometers back to base, while he took those who had 'died' with honor back in the RATT. The darkness was Nathanial's first hint that something was wrong when he arrived at the base. "You, take the wheel," he said to one of the ninth year cadets he couldn't name. He jumped out of the moving vehicle.

The cadet grabbed the wheel. "But, but I'm dead. I'm not supposed to," he called, but Nathanial ignored him. He jumped into the driver's seat and drove through the broken down gate.

"Shit..." Nathanial tried to take a deep breath, but he couldn't control the hot bile building up in his throat. "Shit!" His voice cracked. The main power line was cut, the power stations destroyed. He ran into the darkened command tent, boots sloshing in the mud. He grabbed his mag-light from his belt. The whole place was tossed. Cadets sat in their chairs riddled with paint rounds, looking at him eyes full of shame. Newbridge was tied up to a pole, calling for help through the gag in his mouth. Nate rushed past him to the paper map on the table. The tiny blue and silver cubes were arranged to spell out "PRIDE." Nate bit down on his lip until he felt the blood well up into his mouth. The word stared at him, mocking him. The cadets on Blue Team watched silently as their commander shook with anger. He let out a scream and flipped the table, sending it flying. It crashed into the surveillance equipment and monitors. Even in the dark, the white letters painted under the table were plainly visible: WRATH. Nate's rage went wild. He showered the tent with a barrage of obscenities as he showered the table with paint rounds.

"...Did....looks like we both had the same idea huh?" Arryn's voice came in shaky on Nathanial's radio. He sounded amused.

"I am going to fucking murder you. I am going to walk over there and ring your prissy little neck." Nate sounded almost manic, but his rage bubbled through as his voice cracked.

Arryn's laughter sounded like static over the radio. "So I guess we are both going to have to do this the old fashioned way. Last man standing gets to rule the graveyard."

Nathanial's eyes narrowed. "How many men do we have left?" he asked Newbridge, who had been untied.

"Seven on base. Nineteen on the field, don't know how many are still....active." The kid stood a few paces away from his commander, lest he get the brunt of his rage.

"Alright." He picked up the table and map, setting it back. The map was ripped in half and covered in mud, but it would suit his purposes. "This is how we are going to do this."

At the Gray Lodge, most of the great hall was empty, except for a half a dozen faculty members, King Jonathan and Cyrus. They were all sitting at the same table watching the monitors. The room was darkened, and the remnants of the excitement from earlier in the day hung low like deflated balloons. The King yawned and stretched.

"It really was a brilliant plan. Prince Arryn is a cunning strategist. Maybe I was scouting the wrong cadet," Cyrus reassured his old friend, "both of them really, something else."

Cyrus seemed to be the only one thoroughly enthralled by the drama unfolding on the screens in front of him. "I like the dresses. The boy has a sense of humor. I like that." He bit into an apple.

"I worry about him." Normandy sounded groggy. "He has so much potential, if he only applied himself."

"Who, the Prince? I wouldn't worry about him. You'll see, he will turn out just fine. It's the Iranti-born one, Harker who I'm concerned about. Too serious for such a young man. I'm weary of any man who acts like he has a grand destiny to fulfill. Those are your troublemakers. Loose cannons, those ones."

"Pay no mind to the Colonel. He is just seeking to snatch Nathanial away from me." The King said, lifting his head off of the table. "Take my boy Arryn. He could use a few years in the desert to knock some humility in him."

"Be careful your Grace, I just might take you up on that offer."

The hazy blue glows of the screens slowly became the only light as the fire died in the great stone hearth. A servant went to relight the flames, but one of the instructors stopped him. King Jonathan took the hint and stood up, legs aching from tired.

"I think it's about time to retire. Hopefully this thing will be settled by morning." Jonathan shook his head.

Cyrus was still focused on the screens enchanted by what was going on. "I'll stay here," he said without looking away. "I was shown my room earlier. I know where it is."

They left him there sitting alone, watching the war between the two young men that was being waged in the forest.

The sky was a pale indigo, signaling that the sun would be rising soon. Nate leaned against a charred tree, arm in a sling, struggling to breathe. He looked down at his side. About three inches of tree branch was sticking out from in between his ribs and may or may not have punctured through his right lung. He used his last shot of painkillers that he smuggled out of sickbay before the games to curb the agony of his injuries. The last seven members of Silver Team had Nate cornered in the Blue Team Base. Silver Team's base had been burnt to cinders a few hours before. A thick smoke hung heavy in the air, everything smelled like burning leaves.

"Come on Nate, you got nobody left. You're seriously hurt, give up so we can take you to sick bay," Arryn called. "Do you really want to die over this?"

A burst of paint rounds hit the tree just above Arryn's head. *That was a stupid question*, he thought. This stand-off could take hours. He contemplated just giving up, letting Nathanial win, but that would just be worse. Nate would insist on a rematch.

"Enough of this. Williams, Gregor, Taylor...umm the ginger tenth year, sorry I forgot your name. Go get him please." He sent them out.

Arryn adjusted his position to attempt to see, but he couldn't get a good view without compromising his position. He heard the rustling of leaves as they descended on Nathanial's position. There were four snaps. Arryn caught the four walking out of bounds with their heads down. "Dammit, Nate!" Arryn yelled.

Nathanial's throaty gargling laugh carried well in the cool air despite the smoke. Even from that distance, Arryn could tell how injured Nate was. *You stubborn son of a whore*, Arryn wanted to call, but stood still listening. Something was moving up ahead of him. He could hear the rustling of the leaves and he couldn't make anything out in the smoke.

Three loud pops cut through the forest. Arryn watched the remaining three members of his team walk sullenly out of bounds out of his peripheral as he focused on the hazy brown blob coming into focus as it moved toward him. Slowly, Arryn stood up as the bear approached him. He gripped his rifle knowing paint rounds would probably just piss it off. "Bear," he squeaked, barely audible. "Bear!" he finally shouted, much louder than he should have.

"What?!" Nathanial called from behind his tree.

"Bear, there is a bear." He pushed against the tree, creeping backwards. It stopped and stared at him. On all fours its head was at about Arryn's shoulders.

"Where?"

"Right, riiiighht in front of me, Nate." He was desperately trying to recall whether or not looking the creature in the eye was the best or worst thing to do.

"Well, what's it doing? It might not be dangerous. Is it doing anything threatening?"

Arryn rolled his eyes.

"It's not running away in fear, nor is it fashioning it-self into a rug. I consider all other bear activities to be threatening. So yes, I think it's behaving threateningly..." Looking the bear directly in the eye was definitely the worst idea. It growled and stood on its hind legs, towering over the cowering Prince. "I feel threatened! I'm threatened now!" he yelled.

He felt bear's hot foul breath on his face and Arryn braced for impact as it gave a loud roar. For such a large, clumsy-looking creature, it sure moved fast as it turned to Nathanial, who was firing paint rounds at it. All the Prince could do was shrug when Nate gave him a look that said, 'well, now what do I do?' Nate stumbled out of the way of the bear's first swing, but at the second bat of its enormous clawed paws, Nathanial hit the ground hard and rolled down the hill. The bear followed.

Arryn scrambled back to his feet, rushing over to his friend. A loud howl rose up from below his feet just before he reached the hill. He was almost afraid to look. Peering over the rocky ledge, he spotted a mass of brown fur gored on several large wooden spikes jutting upward. Nate was lean-ing on the spikes, supporting himself. He grinned, mouth full of blood and he coughed. "I knew these would come in handy." He said admiring his late night handy work.

"You built those? For my team?" Arryn asked in disbe-lief. "You know you could have killed someone?"

"In hindsight, I might have gotten a little too intense with this war." He looked at the tree branch still lodged in his side.

"Well, it's over now. Let's get you to sick bay." Arryn started down the hill.

"Wait! Don't move."

Arryn froze, hoping another ferocious woodland creature wasn't behind him. Instead, two paint rounds hit him in the chest. Nathanial coughed, too injured to actually laugh about how smitten he was with his victory. "Now it's over. I win," he said, then collapsed.

The medics landed an air transport in a clearing a few hundred meters away. Arryn followed the stretcher as they moved Nathanial. "You dropped this." Arryn handed Nate a gold pocket watch. "I think it broke though, it doesn't tick." Nathanial wound it up with his free hand and it began to tick again. He held it close to his chest, taking comfort in the rhythmic movements of the gears.

The prince looked at his friend, with his punctured lung, broken arm, concussion. He had fought a bear with sticks and paint rounds. Together, they had nearly burned down six square miles of forest, and destroyed millions of dollars of military equipment. "I think it's a bad idea to be adversaries, my friend." Arryn took advantage of Nate not being able to speak. "I'm glad the Ivory Guard is going to be in the hands of someone who will protect it with his every last breath. And after you fought that bear, I don't want to hear any excuses when I need your help defending myself against Elliot." He patted Nate's hand as they stepped into the air transport.

Cyrus stood on the rocky hill overlooking the charred field of the war games. It reminded him too much of home. He thought it astonishing how all of this destruction had been caused by the vanity and pride of two young men suffering a petty feud.

"I told you he is promising." Ismarlen's dark voice cut through the colonel, sending a shiver down his spine.

"I never took you for a liar, Ismarlen," Cyrus said curtly.

"So you'll get me the boy? We have a deal then?" He outstretched his bony, parchment-white fingers. Cyrus half expected the forsaken god to burst into flames when the sunlight touched him, but it never happened.

"No. I won't Ismarlen. The boy has promise and a great future ahead of him, but it will be serving alongside the Prince, not with you and me." He stated with confidence.

"That's truly a shame." He spoke as if Cyrus had just turned down an invitation to go fishing. "Your daughter, such light snuffed out, but it's your choice. He will serve me eventually."

"It won't be me who hands him to you. As for my daughter, I've already had my people track her to a little mining town called Parlow in the Riverlands. I'm close, I know it. I promise you this, I will get to her before you do." He walked off onto the path, leaving Ismarlen to bask among the destruction.

"I'm counting on that, Cyrus." His voice carried into the air after he slipped away in the shadow of a boulder.

OPREE

"The gods left for the heavens to protect their children from their constant wars, the world became colder and the sky became darker and as the children of gods, man's destiny was now his own."

- The Verinat, Roteramis, 9:32

CHAPTER 31

Never did Prince Arryn Garritel feel more at home at a party than when it was at a party in his honor. It was still hours before his birthday extravaganza, but the grand ballroom was magnificently preserved and restored to its original decadence, marble and gold, giant carved ivory railings made from creatures not seen in over four hundred years. On the floor, brilliant blue, silver and gold marble design of the night sky. On the ceiling, the summer sky was painted in intricate detail, the bronze and stained glass chandelier hung like a giant star right in the center. Tonight, however, the floor was covered in a layer of thick fog, lights hung from scaffolding and the music blared from speakers crudely rigged around stone statues of the gods.

The large double iron and glass doors pushed open into the ball room, Arryn wandered into the room, arms outstretched as a gentle rain of glitter fell from the ceiling. The room was all ready for the guests, tables dripping in florals, jewels and candelabras, mountains of food artistically displayed, a fountain featuring living statues of painted women. Nathanial's mouth gaped open at the spectacle in front of him.

"What do you think, Nate? This is an event. This is what being royalty is all about!" He vanished into a covered archway of exotic flowers and plants.

"This is.....something." Nate muttered to himself, leaning against the doorway. He wondered how Arryn still manage to surprise him with how far he was willing to go to make a spectacle. It was an impressive spectacle, he noted as he spotted a scantily clad woman swinging from the ceiling. She smiled at him and waved coyly. Her hair was braided with flowers, and her skin ornately decorated with blue paint and crystals. With the grace of a swan she lowered herself down. Nathanial offered his one good hand to help her off the swing. His other arm, was still in a sling from the war games. He had gotten out of the hospital a few days before, just in time for graduation. His lung healed nicely, and he had some fancy new scars.

"What happened to you?" She asked crinkling her nose, her voice sounded the way strawberries and champagne tasted like.

"I saved the Prince from a bear." He said dryly.

She giggled at first, but her curiosity piqued as her fingers ran over his cast. "Wow, you must be brave. Are you coming to the party tonight?"

"It should be entertaining at the very least. Sometimes this place can be an incredible bore." He checked his watch against the large ornate clock on the wall, it stopped again. He shook it gently and wound it up. The stupid thing hadn't worked right since the war games.

"Wow, must be terribly dull, having a jungle paradise in your castle." The girl dragged him back into the conversation. "I live in a tin box over a rail station in the University District of New Empire, the roaches throw these wild balls that go on for days. I just came here for the quiet and to remind myself what life was like living at a missionary." Her sarcasm was delivered playfully, her eyes sparkling under the lace mask she was wearing.

"Week-long Cockroach Balls? I'm afraid there is no way I'll be able to compete with that." He took second moment to consider her, but not a third. "There is a beautiful stained glass observatory, doesn't have a view of the rail station, not sure an exciting, worldly lady such as yourself would be interested."

"And I'm guessing you like to show beautiful women to this serene, out of the way place often? Doesn't seem very gentlemanly to me, should I be wary of my virtue? Because I am first and foremost a lady." She curtsied holding the three inches of lacey fabric barely covering her. Although this wasn't the most noble of professions for a middle caste girl, there was nothing illegal about it and it paid for her schooling. She promised herself she wouldn't buckle under the pretty smile of the first Vistany socialite, but this was the one hundred and seventy sixth pretty smile and she was struggling to not find him charming.

"I'm offended, by the thought." He stated flatly, eyes looking at everything except her. "While I admit you are not hideous, it would take quite a woman to distract from this kind of beauty. I swear, you'll be indistinguishable from a one eyed scullery maid and your pristine virtue will remain untarnished." His eyes fell to meet hers, and extended his arm, flashing an almost too perfect smile that hinted to mischievous intentions. "My name is Nathanial Harker, future captain of the Ivory Guard. Would you mind accompanying me to the stained glass observatory so I may look up on you as a one eyed scullery maid and uphold your reputation as a gentlewoman?"

She paused a moment, and rolled her eyes. *Why not? You might get to meet the Prince after all of this.* She thought, and allowed herself to be led down the hallway.

Malcolm and Elliot, home from a long day of observing Senate budgetary meetings, wandered into the ballroom. The day had been tedious and frustrating, for Malcolm especially.

"This is obscene." Malcolm said with amazement, taking his first awestruck steps into the Grand Ballroom.

"Did father see this? Did mother see this?" His hand was still over his mouth as he took everything in. Their parents were furious at Arryn after his antics at the war games, his father blamed Arryn for the entire debacle. Both were lucky to not have been expelled for destroying hundreds of acres of ancient forest. The King made a rather large endowment to the school in good faith. This party would only strain their already worn patience.

Elliot followed, admiring his brother's handiwork. "Would we really expect anything less from Arryn? I think it's magnificent."

"Magnificent? Elliot, this is a circus."

"It is going to be on the cover of every social paper, newspaper, talked about and broadcasted for weeks. It's brilliant." Elliot dug out his pocket com from his breast pocket.

"I fail to see the brilliance of this. I'm going to get father to shut this down, before anyone else sees this." Malcolm turned to leave, but Elliot grabbed onto his jacket, motioning to wait until he was done with his conversation on the pocket com.

"Hello, James? It's me....yes, thank you....no, this is about something else....yes, I know......listen, I need a favor....because you owe me....my brother is hosting an event, some birthday party....It's tonight...I don't know.... ten, ten thirty? I want to give access to the press...it's at the palace.....everyone....well High Borns of course, but I think we should invite some Vistany, well the ones that matter anyway....well that's why I need you....get me everyone who is *actually* important. Thank you."

Malcolm's eyes narrowed and his mouth tightened. "Elliot, what was that?"

"Remember that conversation we had today, about legitimizing the aristocracy, revitalizing our role in society by actively engaging the people?"

"I hardly think throwing extravagant parties is the way to get the people to see us as relevant and our presence vital to the Empire. It's shallow and an obscene display considering the state of things in the colonies. I know you are generally amused by Arryn's antics, but I'm putting a stop to this before he embarrasses the whole family." Malcolm was working hard to recreate the image of the aristocracy focusing on philanthropy, scientific pursuits, humanitarian and educational efforts.

Recently he spent two weeks in Lo Irant strengthening ties with Iranti community leaders convincing them to promote the vaccine program in their counties as a voluntary program, effectively halting a senate order authorizing the military to forcibly inoculate Iranti children. That was the work they all needed to be doing to improve things, not throwing parties.

"Listen brother, I know you think you're making a difference massaging the egos of peasant colonists to avoid a political hiccup, but believe it or not I'm on your side. We both want the aristocracy to be respected. Press is power, Malcolm. Your efforts made it to page twelve in the papers, right next to an article about some artistic cat who has a gallery opening in the Potters District next week. This even will turn heads, and once everyone is listening, then we will have the ability to change the conversation. Arryn has the ability to turn heads and it's time we learned to harness that ability." Elliot, took a crisp green apple off of the display and took a bite.

Malcolm hated to admit his brother was right. "Fine," he sighed, defeated, "but this is now a charity event, for the Vaccine Program."

"That's hardly sensational enough, how about widowed orphans of diseased puppies? Is that a thing?" Elliot poked away at his pocket com, pulling his influence from across the empire.

"Vaccines are fine, but let's get on it. The party is scheduled for what, six hours from now?"

"Five to be exact, don't you worry. I'll be on it."

Arryn, walked out of the mist, carrying a small monkey on his shoulder. He handed it a piece of orange fruit and both monkey and Arryn stared down the two princes with a disdainful mistrust. "Don't worry, you'll be on what?" He questioned. It was always cause for alarm whenever his brothers weren't arguing. It meant they were agreeing and any notion the two of them were concurrence on was almost always bad for Arryn.

"This spectacle of yours, it is now a benefit for the effort to vaccinate children in Lo Irant." Malcolm said in a tone that left very little room for argument

"This spectacle of mine is my birthday, benefiting the effort to celebrate me!" Arryn always had room for argument.

"Think of it this way, Arryn," Elliot persuaded. "You have a chance to do something good, help people."

"Fine, but I'm not changing anything. You'll need to work around it. Spay and neuter all the children you want, I'm going upstairs to get ready." He handed the monkey off to a nervous servant.

A half dazed Nathanial backed out of another door leading to the ball room adjusting the belt on his pants with his one good hand. A blue girl with a mat of crumpled flowers in her hair climbed back onto her swing and raised herself back into the rafters, a handprint smeared down her back. Nate straightened himself out, looking like typical serious Nathanial as he approached the Princes who were looking at him with amusement.

"I uhh, she wanted to....I showed her the stained glass observatory, she is interested in...art." He stammered, trying to save face. "I need to go check on security for tonight. Garmin in his infinite wisdom gave half the guard summer holiday and brought in Imperial Guard and a private contractor for tonight's event. This should be a nightmare."

Half his face was covered, his shirt, his pants, his hair all streaked with glittery azure colored paint. The princes were speechless as Nate stiffly walked passed them. They all noticed the two perfect handprints on the seat of his pants. The sight sent Elliot into a fit of laughter.

"The boy has all the social graces of a rabid badger, how is he able to always do that?" Malcolm wondered out loud.

"The scullery maid line, gets them every time." Arryn sighed.

CHAPTER 32

....IVORY PALACE TO HOST BENEFIT FOR VACCINES IN HONOR OF PRINCE ARRYN'S BIRTHDAY....the hazy blue letters floated across the screen in the dirty Ivory Castle under city hotel. It was dark, humid and the plaster walls were stained as if there had been about six feet of water in the room at one point. Something about it reminded Lilly of her motel room in Parlow. She assembled the rifle on the bed while peering at the singular ray of sunlight poking out from the blackened windows. As a child she always wanted to visit historic Ivory Castle. To her dismay, Caleb made sure they sat out of sight. There was supposed to be a demonstration outside of the palace tonight. The sight of the weapons made her nervous, since Nev was killed, it seemed violence in the colonies had only gotten worse. Caleb assured her that it was going to be a peaceful demonstration, but they had to be prepared for another Londallin. Still holding the rifle, her mind wandered to Grant. She racked a round into the chamber before setting it beside the others and moving on to the next one. It seemed there were more guns than people in the cramped hotel room and she was unsure if that made her feel more, or less safe.

"I'm bored." Nara signed after stuffing a brick of plastic explosives, masked as food rations into a black duffle bag. "When are we leaving?" She loved it when Caleb needed her and her sister to build what he would call 'diversions'. For over a week they got out of their regular duties of catering to the IRG and LIRA soldiers so they could work on their latest pyrotechnic masterpiece.

Since they had been old enough to walk, they worked in the mines. Their nimble fingers and small frames made them perfect for setting explosives into the tiny spaces larger men couldn't fit. The two of them knew how much explosives was needed take down a side of a mountain or blow the thread off of a button, without damaging the fabric.

"When Caleb, Samrael and the rest of the Six get back." Lilly signed back and looked at the time.

They had been gone for hours, leaving Lilly with Ariel, Nara and a few others to prepare. She hoped they would be back in time. No sooner had she started worrying, she heard Samrael's signature knock on the door.

"Who is it?" Lilly asked, pressed against the wall beside the door.

"It's me." Samrael said.

Just you? Lilly thought as she opened the door. Samrael walked in the door, holding a bunch of passes and uniforms. He was wearing the bright colored street clothes of a middle caste Oprian. She wasn't sure if the clothes were two sizes too large or that was just the style.

"IRG has contacts with the caterers. Caleb is with the rest of the Six talking with them right now. We are to go meet them at the palace and wait for instructions there." He said doling out the uniforms. He sounded unusually rushed, Lilly attributed it to nerves. Sam hadn't been the same since the night of the train bombing, then again none of them had.

Ariel was having difficulty figuring out where the sleeves were. Lilly held the oversized black tunic as Ariel twisted and turned until she escaped. A blond tuft of hair protruded out of the left sleeve and the twelve year old had to start over again. Nara rolled her eyes, embarrassed about the genetic resemblance between them.

"How are we going to carry all of this gear unnoticed?" Lilly pointed to the half dozen partially dismantled firearms and four giant duffle bags already stuffed to capacity.

"Caleb said to not bring anything. IRG has everything taken care of." He said, checking to see if the hallway was clear. "But we have to go now."

"Ugh, all that work for nothing? Is he serious?" Lilly complained to Nara, who just shrugged, her hands covered by the long sleeves of the catering uniform. Lilly rolled them up so the girl would at least almost look like she was old enough to be working.

"If we are going to be by the food, do you think we'll be able to eat when we're there?" Arial asked half aloud, half signing.

"I'm hungry." Nara replied emphatically.

Lilly didn't say anything just hurried them out the door.

CHAPTER 32

Nathanial nibbled on some hors d'oeuvres in the corner, he was already bored. A parade of High Born and Vistany women decked out in fashions that weighed twice as much as they did and not one of them the slightest bit entertaining. Silk dresses and stiff corsets aside, it always seemed to be the same girls at these events. Proper ladies bred for one sole purpose, marriage. A few of them held high positions in companies their families owned, Nate could at least hold a conversation with them, unfortunately they were all too plain to hold his interest for longer than a glass of wine.

"Sir...we have an alarm going up.... In zone twelve. Should we send a team up there?" A static voice came through the small earpiece. Nate adjusted the frequency, but it just sent painful waves of high pitch feedback. *First thing we change are these terrible radio links.* He thought as he played with the small silicone coated receiver in his hand.

"We need our guys alert the third floor staff to check on it. A new maid probably tripped the alarm." The agitated voice was the soon to be retired Captain of the Ivory Guard, Captain Garmin.

He is nearly seventy, too old to have such an important job. He put the bud back in his ear.

"You should probably send a team, up sir, just to make sure." Nathanial interjected.

"Seriously? Lieutenant, why are you on link with us? You aren't Captain yet." Garmin scoffed. "You should be enjoying your last few weeks off. Last holiday you'll see until you're my age" He chuckled.

"Just a precaution sir, but I think we should send up a team to check it out." Nathanial scanned the floor. Arryn was posing for the press. "The only threat I spot to the royal family down here, is Arryn." He mumbled to himself.

"What?" Garmin asked. Nathanial forgot he was still broadcasting we spoke. He needed to learn to be less familiar with the royal family.

"Um...nothing. I don't foresee any threats down here. Take a few guys off of the door, we should be fine."

"Fine...send them up." He sighed, defeated.

Hazy green light and smoke poured from the cracks in the large glass and iron doors. It was a last minute invitation by the King, but since Senate hearings seemed to be dragging on, he wasn't leaving for Kyrant for at least another week. He left the check made out for one million coin blank because he forgot what charity they were raising money for and wasn't up to facing the awkwardness of having to ask. Whenever he was in Opree these events always seemed to run together in his mind and over the last few years he became accustomed to just having Barlow send a check and apologies.

Even after all of his travels, Cyrus was impressed with the room. It had been transformed into a jungle paradise, women and wildlife in cages that hung from the ceiling. The Royal family watched on from a small balcony. Queen Andrea looked mortified, her hair pulled back so tight her face looked like it was in a state of constant surprise and King Jonathan was holding a stiff drink in his hands. Cyrus knew this because every drink the King had was a stiff one. The King's expression amused him. There was a time when both were young men, when Jonathan would have appreciated such a spectacle.

"As Captain of the Ivory Guard shouldn't you be in the control room for an event like this?" The Colonel said, tapping the newly commissioned Lieutenant Harker on the shoulder.

"Good impression Arryn, honestly it's getting better, but Colonel Mason doesn't sound like a drunken oaf." Nathanial turned around.

"Colonel Mason." Nathanial stiffened up. "It's an honor to see you again." He desperately wanted to slink behind the curtains to hide.

"It's okay. I've gotten much worse from much more powerful people and in your defense I am a little drunk." Cyrus grinned.

Nathanial swallowed hard, not sure whether to laugh or cry. "I'm not the Captain for a few weeks yet. I'm on holiday until the feast of Ma' Arana."

"Have I been away so long that I missed the fashion of radio link buds with formal dress?"

"Oh what the hell is it now?" Nathanial looked back up at Colonel in horror. "Sorry sir, not you- -" It looked like he was speaking to the cuffs of his jacket sleeve. "It's just— What do you mean not answering? No! No! Don't send— Fine...don't touch anything...put them on the doors, use our guys to check out the situation, we can't have strange contractors roaming the palace. I apologize Colonel, something requires my attention." He darted awkwardly behind a portable wall.

"Descendant of the gods? This one?" Cyrus whispered to his glass of scotch before taking a sip.

Nathanial brought up the security data on the pocket com, little blue dots flickered on and off before the whole thing shorted out. Damn technology was useless. He could have the whole palace on lockdown in under five minutes, although it would be a disaster. There was plenty of reasons for the alarm to have gone off, especially since the equipment barely worked anyway. Captain Garmin was known to ignore radio link calls. Nate would be the laughing stock of Ivory Castle if he blew this out of proportion. He took a breath to silence his inner voice telling him to be worried. He was on holiday. There was no reason for him to be even dealing with this. *What if it is something?* He thought. *It would be foolish to act if nothing was happening.* He needed to get the royal family secure and the Ivory Guard back downstairs. A breech is a breech and it would be impossible to get this place secure with the party still going on. His finger hovered over the panic button that would bring the whole event to screeching halt.

"We got them sir...just a couple of vandals. There is a few more running around." The voice in his ear said. Nathanial could breathe again. Thank the gods he didn't hit that button.

"Use our men to round them up quickly and quietly. Then tell them to get back down to the ballroom as soon as they've finished their sweep." The security, he was told, was comprised of top rated, Empire trained veterans, they could manage guarding a birthday party for ten minutes.

The eastern wing of the palace was one of the oldest structures in the Empire. All the heavy drapery, rich carpet and artwork couldn't completely remove the dark cavernous feel to it. Lilly shuddered as her and Samrael sprayed the bright orange paint over the priceless artwork. "Just one of these paintin's could feed a whole district for a month. It's disgustin'." He said through the red scarf he was using as a mask covering the bottom part of his face.

She ran her fingers over the ornate gold frame, it seemed a shame to be destroying such beautiful things, but it was an even greater shame that the Empire seemed to value pieces of wood and fabric over people's lives. Lost in the image of an unfamiliar face staring blankly back at her, she didn't notice Samrael wander down the labyrinth of corridors and halls. The blade of her knife cut smooth through the canvas, the face disfigured and unrecognizable as she carved "SWINE" into the old painting. It made her giddy to be a part of this mission.

Nara tugged on the back of Lilly's tunic, the startle almost led to the small girl getting slashed with the sharp blade.

"Nine hells, don't do that." Lilly said under her breath, allowing her nerves to settle down. Nara stood there, with Ariel. The twins were covered in splotches soot and electric blue paint, their server's tunics overflowing with bits of cake, tarts and other food from the ballroom. Nara held out a hand offering Lilly a several fudgy clumps of what looked like chocolate cake, speckled with electric blue. She politely refused the sweets and Nara shoved the entire thing into her mouth, wiping off the excess fudge with her sleeve as she savored the treat. She pulled down the mask back over her face, still chewing.

"Where were you guys? Have any of you seen Caleb? Where is everyone else?" Lilly asked.

"Caleb wanted us to get you. He said we need to leave. We're down in the cellars underneath the kitchen."

"What are they doing down there, you're supposed to be trashing the South Wing." This was chaos, it had already been almost ten minutes, the Ivory Guard should have been all over this place by now.

"Special mission, top secret, IRG needed us to wire up the place. Make a big exit, but we gotta go now." Ariel, pulled on Lilly's hand.

"They had you set up a bomb?" Lilly jerked the girls hand back, throwing her off balance.

"Good thing we did it too, they gave us way too much." She pulled some small bricks of plastic explosives, smeared with frosting and sprinkles from one of her pockets. "This woulda sent the whole place up. We remembered that you said we was just supposed to mess up their pretty palace, so we fixed it."

"Little boom, big mess," Nara signed proudly.

Panic coursed through her veins as she surveyed the damage she had caused, mouthing a silent prayer begging the Gods to get her out of this. IRG didn't want to just send the Empire a message, they wanted to kill innocent people while doing it.

"We need to leave right now! Try to sneak back in with the staff and run. Don't speak to anyone, not even the IRG or Caleb. Meet me back at the hotel. I need to find Samrael."

"Rrruuunnn!" Samrael screamed as he turned the corner, barreling down the hallway. Lilly didn't wait to see who was chasing him before she started a dozen paces ahead of him.

Her chest burned at each frantic breath she drew in, but she kept running. She had no idea where she was running to, somewhere with a window she could escape from. These halls were impossible to navigate, but if she didn't stop soon, she was sure to collapse. She ducked into a room and stood behind the door, pressing herself firmly against the wall, holding her hand to her mouth to quiet her gasps for breath. Her heart beat loudly in her chest, her ears throbbed with each rapid hard pump.

"We got four...do a quick sweep for others. Looks like just vandals...angry little mudrat brats. Don't use deadly force. I repeat, keep it clean." Lilly heard the radio go off in the hallway outside.

"How the hell did they get in here?" A different voice chimed in.

"I don't know but someone is losing their job over this. They messed this place up pretty bad." A Guard spoke into her radio as she pushed the door open, the heavy wood squished Lilly against the wall, but she remained silently hidden. Standing on her tip toes, she closed her eyes as she listened to the Guard search the darkened room, hoping she wouldn't find her. Fingers wrapped around the door, Lilly could feel the wood slowly peel away from her face and she braced for what was about to come.

Several loud pops blasted through the guard's radio. It was followed by static and screams. "We're under attack! We're under attack!"

The first blast blew out all of the glass in the north side of the ballroom. The second, knocked Nathanial off of his feet. He stared out through the rubble pinning him to the floor, he heard the screams and gunfire, but couldn't see. Letting the chaos and pain feed him, he pushed the heavy debris off of him. Still covered in bits of plaster, wood and glass, Nathanial made his way to the balcony where the King and Queen were. He watched helpless as the panicked crowd scattered. His duty was to protect the royal family above all others, turning his back on the rest of the people was necessary. Andrea dug her heels into the carpet, as Nathanial attempted to drag her down the corridor, with his one good arm. "I will not leave my sons to be slaughtered." She protested.

Despite her size and her age, the Queen had always been a strong, determined woman. There was a piece of Nathanial still hesitant to disobey her. "My Queen, I need to get you to the safe room before I can help them."

Andrea saw an impatient, fearful look in his eyes, a look of concern for her welfare greater than duty required. Although she never warmed up to Nathanial, keeping the boy at a distance while she coddled her own, natural born children, she had been the closest thing to a mother he had. "Very well my boy. Now go find your brothers. They will need your strength." She said, ignoring the sentiment of her first reference to Nathanial being a part of their family and she followed her husband down the steps to the safe room.

The flood of panicked guests made it difficult to tell what exactly was happening. Nathanial's radio link was dead and he was unarmed. A heavy hand slapped him hard on the back and handed him a rifle, sticky with the blood of its former owner. Colonel Mason grinned, his eyes wild with excitement.

"Now this is a party!" He laughed, clenching his cigar between his teeth and he ran back into the fray, shooting at their attackers.

Nate stayed close to the wall. The literal jungle Arryn had built would be dangerous to navigate. He spotted the back of Elliot's jacket leaning against a pillar. There were three or four guests cowering behind a potted tree and the pillar. Elliot was holding a tablecloth to the stomach of a Senator, applying pressure to his wound. The Prince's own face was draped in blood-soaked rags, covering his left eye. He was also grazed in the leg, however, at first glance it didn't seem like a very serious injury.

"By the Gods, Elliot are you alright?" Nate kneeled down to tend to the prince, who shooed him away.

"I'm fine, I'm fine." He said still focusing on the gravely injured Senator. In all of the years he had known the prince Nathanial never once saw him voluntarily get his hands dirty for any reason, and here he was, expensive shirt soaked up to the elbow with the blood of another man, holding him together.

"Where's Arryn and Malcolm?" Nate asked, ducking a shot that only just narrowly missed him.

"I don't know, security rushed them out of the room right after the blasts. Where are my mother and father?"

Elliot looked up at Nate with a face that begged for good news.

"Safe. What do you mean rushed out? Elliot, they are the ones who are attacking! Where did they take them?"

"I don't know!" Elliot yelled over the chaos.

Nate picked up the rifle of a fallen contractor, and slid it over to Elliot. "Give me your Jacket. It's got the royal seal on it. That's probably how they targeted Arryn and Malcolm."

Elliot complied.

The palace was riddled with secret passages, tunnels and crawlspaces. As a child, Nate had explored all of them. The one behind the Regal Steed, an old painting of a King's favorite horse seemed so much bigger last time he had been it, although he had been twelve at the time. He crouched as low as he could, but it still took some degree of effort to worm through the narrow passageway to the great hall. He backed out into the great hall, Elliot's jacket draped around his shoulders, and was greeted with the clicks of a dozen rifles pointed right at him. He put his good hand up in the air and stretched his other as far as it would go.

"Please, don't shoot!" He called out as he turned around slowly.

Although it would have been impossible for her to tell anyone how she got there, she made it down to the main corridor amidst the explosions and gunfire. Bodies of guards and servants lined the halls. She hurdled over several fallen IRG members. The deep blue carpet looked almost black with blood. She got a clear view of the main doors leading out to the courtyard. It was a beautiful night, aside from the bloodcurdling screams and sound of the battle raging within the castle, it was eerily quiet outside. She wanted to make a run for it. She studied the layout at Caleb's briefing, it was just over the far hedge, an iron fence and then she'd be clear.

"Don't. The place will be swarming with Empire dregs in a minute. You'll be pinched within a mile." Caleb dragged her into the dark corridor into a large room. Bathed in the lights of the candles refract in the stained glass, the conservatory was peaceful. Lilly looked at the brilliant yellows, blues portraying a night sky crafted by the gods. Two men, well dressed High Borns, knelt on the floor underneath the chandelier made up of thousands of pieces of silver and yellow glass, forming two perfect halves of the sun and the great moon. They were surrounded by Samrael and the Six, both of them wore the royal crest on their jackets. They were members of the royal family, Lilly recognized them as two of the princes.

"I just got this from IRG. He was trying to escape." Caleb said to his captives, tossing a jacket with the royal seal in front of them, it's blue fabric torn, and stained with blood. "Just another dead imperial pig," He lifted his mask just high enough to spit on the jacket. One of the princes stared off expressionless, the other hung his head mournfully, face grimaced with pain.

"What are you doing?" Lilly asked, careful not to use names.

"Fighting a war, pet. What did you think this was?" Caleb said grabbing the hair of one of the princes.

"They've surrendered. We don't kill people who surrender! That's what they do. We're supposed to be better than this!" She furiously scolded.

"They're the Empire!" He jerked his hand back, pulling the Prince backward. His brother moved to help, but he froze at the sound of rifles primed to fire. "He is the Empire. Everything he stands for, every fiber of his being is an offense to our gods. He eats the food stolen out of the hands of starving children. He enjoys the warmth of fuel dug from the ground by the bloody, broken hands of our people! Look at him and tell me he isn't guilty of apathy. A fraction of his vast wealth could stave off hunger and disease for years. He is guilty and will be the first to be punished." Caleb shook with rage. Even with his mask on, Lilly could tell he was red faced with passion and hate. It was a face she was used to since Nev was killed.

He removed his pistol from its holster, and looked at Lilly, who shook her head, quietly pleading with him to not-

CRACK!

Caleb blasted a round into the skull of the brother of the Prince he still held in his grip. A thick pool of red black formed on the floor and bubbles of hot blood popped on the cool marble. The surviving Prince cried out. His alabaster skin speckled with bits of his brother. He cradled his brother's head in his lap futility attempting to stop the river flowing from his fatal wound, sniveling prayers through heavy sobs.

Lilly wanted to throw up, but she was empty. Her hands grabbed at her hair and she attempted to pull herself out of this reality by it. She screamed in pain and frustration, looking at Samrael for guidance. Sam had been the voice of reason. Sam was gentle, intelligent and fair, but his eyes offered only the same hate Caleb had. In every face of every Oprian all he saw was the soldier who murdered Nev.

"They already have four of us! Nara and Ariel are somewhere! If we are caught we will all be killed! What do you think they are going to do to Irantis after this? How is this supposed to make their lives better?"Her voice cracked as she broke under the tremendous weight of guilt. "This-it wasn't supposed to be like this."

"What do you think war is princess? It's death, and fire, it's sacrifice and pain." A voice came from out of the Shadows. A sallow looking man in an IRG uniform, only he had a black wolf, with orange eyes as his emblem patch. Lilly had never seen him at the compound before.

"I'm no princess." Lilly sneered pulling out from under his cold bony hands that he laid on her shoulder.

"Aren't you though?" He smiled and stepped over the body of the dead prince like it was nothing more than a piece of ill placed furniture. "The Irantis want freedom, to not be slaves, mere cattle able to be slaughtered as the Empire sees fit. This is the cost. Well worth it, dontchya think? Good job my boys, now let's get out of here before the dregs have this place swarmed."

He seemed to disappear into the shadows, Lilly watched as Caleb, Samrael and the Six follow out a door.

"Come with us." Caleb called out for her. She stared at him, but fear kept her still. Her eyes fixed themselves on the Prince mourning his brother too lost in grief to notice anything else. She thought of her grief when Grant was arrested, when Nev was killed, and realized that there was only going to be more.

"No." She said proudly.

"What about the cause?" Caleb asked anxious to leave.

"Fuck the cause, Caleb! You keep talking about the cause. 'Do this for the cause, support the cause.' It's very convenient that the cause seems to always be changin' to fit your needs. I wanted to help ease the suffering in Lo Irant, that was my cause. How is war going to stop their suffering, Caleb? Is it worth it to win at any cost, if it means losing everything you are fighting for?" She didn't wait for Caleb's answer, she just turned her back on them.

If the halls and corridors in the Palace were difficult to navigate, the narrow hallways of the service wing was downright impossible. Lilly could barely see in the dark. She could hear the commotion over her and wondered if she was going to die down there. *I just want to see the moon one more time. Please let me see the moon. Then I will be okay.* She thought while trying to discern if she had passed this room before.

The slam of a heavy body throwing her against the wall disoriented her, but it was the cold steel penetrating her abdomen took the air out of her lungs. What she felt wasn't necessarily pain. It was pressure, cold, the way her insides felt when exposed to open air. She forced herself to look down, a large hand still holding the blade inside of her, twitched a hair, but it sent a pain she never knew through her.

"Not yet bitch, I'm not done with you, yet." Her assailant whispered in her ears. The acid hatred burned her soul as he spoke. "I'm going to make sure you suffer before I kill you. You will leave this world unrecognized by your gods."

Tears flowed from her eyes, soaking the scarf still covering her nose and mouth. She was afraid to look up. The last year had been a whirlwind of strange faces; she doubted she could handle another one. She closed her eyes. *I don't care about the moon. All I want to see is a familiar face, anyone, even Regina. I don't want to do this alone. I don't want to die alone.* Against her best effort, her eyes dragged themselves upwards and she felt relief. The god's had granted her last wish. It had to be a hallucination, but it didn't matter. She smiled, happy and ready to go. She pulled her mask down...and with a weak voice she cried out, "Daddy?"

It had been almost ten years and Cyrus thought he would be able to recognize those eyes in pure darkness, but he didn't until now. His hand was gripping the blade still inside of her, frozen in terror at the realization of what he had just done. He killed hundreds, if not thousands of times. He knew a fatal wound even before he inflicted it. Not a surgeon in the Empire could seal this wound, not in time. He only had a handful of minutes. There was a time, right after he received the letter from Regina telling him Lilly died, that he would have given everything for just a handful of minutes, but now it seemed so unfair.

"What have you done my little spitfire? What have you done?" He cradled her in his arms like he did when she was an infant, tears rolling down his cheeks. He sung her the song Ferrin used to sing to her back in Kyrant, one he would sing to her every night he was able to. It was a mournful song of loss and struggle.

"I'm sorry, I'm sorry." He whispered as her breaths became too shallow. He shook her trying to wake her, but she was fading fast. He was losing the best part of himself and he was helpless to stop it. "FIX HER PLEASE!" He screamed in the darkness. "I'LL GIVE YOU WHATEVER YOU WANT! Just fix her, let her live...." He gently rocked his beloved daughter in the darkness as the battle raged on above him.

"Whatever I want?" Ismarlen asked in a voice as smooth as the darkness he appeared out of. "Done. I'll be back after the feast of Ma'Arana." He said and was gone.

The color in Lilly's cheeks came back. She took a deep hard breath and screamed in pain. It was music to Cyrus's ears and he whispered a prayer of thanks. She was still seriously injured, but his daughter would live.

AFTERWARD

*"With all of the blood that was shed in his name,
it could not polish the tarnish from the crown of
the first father and the gods fell silent."*

- The Verinat, Histories 30:12

`For weeks the streets of Ivory Castle were cloaked in black, as was custom for a Royal funeral, but the grief lingered in the city even after the symbols of mourning were taken down. Nathanial had already packed up the last of his few belongings, it was sad for him to see the room devoid of his presence. It was sadder yet that the room did not seem that much different without it. Uncomfortable with the idea that after seventeen years, his existence could be erased entirely, he plucked the tin soldier that once belonged to his brother Devon, and put it on the shelf.

When the news about the attacks being perpetrated by a radical Iranti separatist group came out, the King never explicitly asked Nathanial to rescind his acceptance to be Captain of the Ivory Guard, but he didn't fight Nathanial's decision either. The papers were not kind to Nathanial Harker in the weeks since the attacks. Some went so far as to insinuate that he was complicit in the terrible act. Nobody who knew Nathanial would have ever believed the slander, but he felt that he would be forever under a cloud of suspicion. Part of him wished the tension would just culminate in an act of violence, he could handle that. It was their looks and whispers he could not bear.

"Don't shoot." He whispered to himself replaying his failure in his mind.

He proved himself a cowered that night and it was killing him. A week before Colonel Mason gave him an offer to serve with his Ni'Razeem Shadow Guard. Nathanial felt a lifetime of exile in a barren wasteland was more than he deserved. However, it would give himself a chance to get away from the controversy that engulfed him in Opree.

"Nate?" Prince Arryn knocked on the door and entered before hearing an invitation to come in. "Sorry, I was just making sure-"

"I'm fine." Nate interrupted. "I'm just fine."

"I was going to say, I wanted to make sure you didn't take my good shirt I let you borrow for the funeral." Arryn delivered the sharp quip with an uncharacteristically flat affect.

Everyone in the Palace became something less when Malcolm died and although it seemed that, on the outside, Arryn was handling his brother's death the best out of everyone, Nathanial couldn't help but notice the spark of vigor his friend normally carried inside of him was gone. He was a dry shell of himself, perfectly preserved, rigid and hollow.

"Arryn, really with the sarcasm? Now?"

"Being polite isn't going to bring Malcolm back. He is dead. We are not. There is no point in shutting ourselves in his tomb. Mother won't leave her chambers. Father is pleading with the Senate, trying to desperately trying to avoid a war. Elliot is ready to go to war with the entire colony of Lo Irant by himself and you run off with Colonel Psycho to fight in his grand crusade against the boogey men. This is exactly what they wanted, to break us. People die every day, we can't fall to pieces every time they do." Arryn scanned the room, his eyes falling on the newspaper sitting on Nate's bed. On the cover, the Iranti flag dripped a blood hued crimson over a picture of Nathanial. In thick block letters the headline read. THE RED THREAT, CAN IRANTI-BORN'S BE TRUSTED IN OUR GOVERNMENT? "Is this why you're leaving? This garbage?" Arryn waved it in Nathanial's face.

Nate snatched it out of Arryn's hands. "I don't belong here Arryn. I'm tired of constantly feeling like an outsider. I'd never go to Lo Irant, the Shadows are the only ones who will accept me."

Arryn fumed. "You self-righteous ass! We accepted you here, but it wasn't enough was it? How many people will it take for you to feel accepted? Ten? One hundred? A thousand? Will ten thousand people with banners cheering your name be enough for you to realize your place is here? Why can't you see th-"

"I said I was one of them!" Nathanial shouted. He paused and calmed himself. He was unsure if he was willing to divulge the truth, but it clawed at his insides like a rabid animal desperate to escape. "They caught me coming out of one of the passages and I panicked. I pretended to be one of them and said that I killed Elliot so they wouldn't shoot me. I deserve to be hung for that. I was supposed to protect everyone, it was my job to save him and I hid like a coward Arryn! I don't deserve a place here."

Arryn grabbed the tin soldier off the shelf and closed his fingers around it. He never understood what it must have been like for Nathanial to lose his brothers, now he did.

"Nate, your priority was to protect my father and mother and you did. You were quick enough to take Elliot's jacket and convinced the assailants that he was dead, so they didn't hunt him down too. You survived. I don't care how you did it. I'd forgive Malcolm for stepping on grandmothers and babies, if it meant I could have him back. You are my brother and I am thankful to the gods for sparing you and believe it or not, Elliot too."

"Well I'm not going to tell Colonel Mason I changed my mind about becoming a Shadow." Nathanial thought the mood was getting too heavy.

"I'm not afraid of him, but maybe some time in Kyrant will be good for you. Maybe you'll come back a little less full of yourself." Arryn sounded more like himself again. "No, I'm not that lucky. Knowing you, you'll vanquish the entire Navat army within a fortnight and be back on my doorstep and spend the rest of your days being a pain in my ass. When do you leave anyway?"

"Not for a few weeks, just after the feast of Ma'Arana. I just wanted to get the packing out of the way."

"We've been cooped up in this place for far too long. You know, we never did make it to Madame Q's to visit Cassandra and her sister. My treat?"

"What will the papers say if they catch us at a brothel?" Nathanial frowned.

"You're going to be a Shadow, you can just stab them or something."

Arryn put the tin soldier back on the shelf and the two men left their grief in the confines of the Palace so they could enjoy themselves for the first time since the attack.

Book Two Coming Soon.....

30086889R00219

Made in the USA
Charleston, SC
04 June 2014